THE OFFICIAL MOVIE NOVELIZATION

NOVELIZATION BY **GREG KEYES**

TITAN BOOKS

GODZILLA X KONG: THE NEW EMPIRE – THE OFFICIAL MOVIE NOVELIZATION
Print edition ISBN: 9781803368108
E-book edition ISBN: 9781803369228

Published by Titan Books
A division of Titan Publishing Group Ltd
144 Southwark Street, London SE1 0UP
www.titanbooks.com

First edition: March 2024
10 9 8 7 6 5 4 3 2 1

A CIP catalogue record for this title is available from
the British Library.

Printed and bound in the United States

For My Eldest,
John Edward Arch

PROLOGUE

PROLOGUE

Some say the world will end in fire,
Some say in ice.
From what I've tasted of desire
I hold with those who favor fire.
But if it had to perish twice,
I think I know enough of hate
To say that for destruction ice
Is also great
And would suffice.

—"Fire and Ice", Robert Frost

2016
The ice sheet
Greenland interior

When the coring drill shut down, Dr. Magezi Maartens heard something strange. At first she thought it was just audio persistence in her ears from the drill, but the sound was quite unlike that of the core sampler. Definitely a machine noise, though. She turned around slowly, searching. Whatever was making the sound, there was nowhere for it to hide.

It was a fine summer day in Greenland. The sky was a turquoise dome, the sun a blindingly bright jewel in the south that *looked* like it should be hot but wasn't. Downstream, on the coast, the temperature was above freezing. Jakobshavn Glacier was calving icebergs into the fjord, and in some places it was warm enough to go in shirtsleeves, so long as you didn't step into the shade for very long. Up here on the thickest part of the ice sheet it was a balmy negative ten degrees Celsius. Nothing met Magezi's gaze but ice, sky, the core sampler, the handful of grad students she'd brought up here with her, and the cluster of prefab huts that made up their camp. Greenland had plenty of wildlife—birds, arctic foxes, polar bears, musk oxen—but those were all on the coastal fringes. Here there was nothing to eat—or drink, for that matter. All the water here had been frozen for hundreds of thousands of years. Central Greenland was a desert, far more lifeless than the arid, hot deserts of her native South Africa.

She'd tracked the sound now to an aircraft of some sort, flying toward them, undoubtedly headed someplace further east.

Except that it wasn't. As she watched, it slowed and then began to descend. It was shaped like a plane but was behaving like a helicopter. She had never quite seen anything like it.

Her students were looking up now too, distracted from their tasks.

"Hold on," one of them—Max—said. "What's that?"

"You've got me," Magezi said. "Wealthy tourists, maybe?" But she didn't think so. She squinted through the glare off the ice as the vessel settled. It had an emblem of some sort painted on its hull. It looked like a stylized hourglass on its side. It wasn't Swedish military, or American, or any other nationality she recognized, for that matter. But it did look… military. And expensive.

"You guys stay back here," she said. "I'll go check it out."

She trudged across the frozen surface toward the aircraft, some hundred meters away.

Well before she got there, four figures emerged. She couldn't tell much about them: like her, they were bundled up in arctic gear. But when she got close enough, one of them pulled down the scarf across his face.

"Doctor Maartens?"

"Yes," she said. This man knew her name. That was a surprise. What was this? All of her permits were in order, she was sure. He was an older fellow, fifties, maybe early sixties. He spoke English with what she judged to be a Japanese accent. Close up, she guessed the other three might be women.

"My name is Ishirō Serizawa," he said. He nodded at his companions. "This is Doctor Graham, Doctor Russell and Doctor Andrews. We were hoping to have a word with you."

"I guess you must have been to come all the way out here," she said. "Am I in trouble?"

"No, not at all," he said. "This concerns your research. If you want to step inside, I can offer you some hot coffee, or tea, and we can talk more comfortably."

That sounded sketchy. Few things had been drilled into her during childhood more persistently than to not get into a vehicle with people she didn't know. Then again, she was a long way from help, and she was able to make out that there were at least two more people in the plane. If these people meant her harm, there wasn't much she could do about it.

"That sounds wonderful," she lied. "Perhaps my crew could be invited in?"

"I'm sorry, Doctor," Serizawa said. "We need to speak to you in private. But we can have coffee brought to your crew."

She sighed. "I don't know who you people are," she said.

"We work for an organization called Monarch," he replied. "You may have heard of us."

That did ring a bell. "The Godzilla chasers?" They had been in the news, lately. A supposedly multinational, government-funded organization that had come to the fore after the startling realization that giant monsters lay sleeping in the earth.

Serizawa smiled. "Yes," he said. "Godzilla chasers."

That was alarming. What could they want with her? Unless…

"Wait," she said. "Do you think something's buried out here? One of your monsters?"

"No," Serizawa said. "As I said, this is about your research."

"I'm a paleontologist," she said. "I look for very tiny fossils, not gargantuan ones."

"I've read your papers," the person Serizawa had identified as Graham said. Her accent was soft, something British. "You're really very brilliant. Please, come have a coffee, and have a look at something. You could really be very helpful."

Magezi glanced back at her students.

"And you'll bring them some?"

"Of course."

The inside of the craft was full of instruments and screens, but there was an area in the back that could only be described as a small meeting room—complete with table and video displays. The coffee was good: far better than the dehydrated stuff they had brought with them to the glacier. A guy in a vaguely military outfit put on a parka with the hourglass insignia on it and took insulated cups out to her people.

She sipped and smiled nervously at her four hosts. Serizawa seemed to be the leader. Graham and Serizawa seemed… close. Not romantically. More like colleagues who had known each other for a long time. Russell was a little intense. Andrews, the youngest, didn't say much. She looked a little out of her element, like maybe she was wondering why she was even here.

"So, what's this about?" Magezi asked.

"You have a theory that Greenland froze very quickly at the beginning of the last glaciation," Russell said.

She nodded. "Seems like you guys are familiar with my paper. I've been taking ice cores, trying to establish a chronology for some fossils I've been collecting. When I got down to the old surface, I found a layer of ice that was… different from the rest. Laid down very quickly. Like instantaneously."

"Because of the size of the ice crystals," Russell said.

"You *have* read my paper," she said. "Yes, the quicker water freezes, the smaller the crystals. That's why you want your frozen shrimp to be flash-frozen, not just iced in a freezer. Bigger crystals turn the shrimp to pulp by exploding their cell membranes from the inside."

"And when did this happen?" Serizawa said.

"Greenland iced over between two point five and three million years ago," she said. "But that was just the beginning, you know. The seed of the Ice Age. Ice Ages come in pulses. Things get cold, ice forms at the poles. Ice reflects sunlight— which means it pushes radiation that might become heat back into space. It gets colder, more ice forms. The last big pulse was a little over a hundred thousand years ago. But this event two and a half million years ago—I think this is what started

11

the pulses of glaciation. But since there's been a more recent thaw, there isn't much left of that first layer."

"What might that event have been, do you think?" Serizawa asked. "What explains the instantaneous freezing?"

"What's this about?" she asked. "Does this have something to do with Godzilla? Or those things he was fighting?"

Serizawa smiled. "Everything is connected," he said. "Just not always in the way we may think." He leaned forward on his elbows. "Do you have any ideas on what could have caused it?"

She shook her head. "Sometimes weather patterns just collapse. But even a polar vortex wouldn't have frozen things *this* quickly. It's like everything was hosed down with liquid nitrogen or something. I have no explanation. But I'm looking for one."

"Was there anything else peculiar about the ice?" he pressed. "Something you didn't put in your paper?"

She took another sip of coffee. "Look," she said. "That paper got me pegged as a fringe scientist by half of my community. They say I'm trying to bring back catastrophism as an explanation for geological data. You know—'Noah's Flood,' 'Maarten's Icebox.'"

"And yet you keep testing," Russell said. "You took a crew to Siberia, didn't you? Tested four more sites. And the Canadian shield. You didn't publish those results."

"Yet," she said. "Not yet."

"Are your claims corroborated?"

She shrugged. "Yes. Same thin layer of weird ice in each location."

"Just how weird was it?" Russell pursued. "Not just tiny crystals."

She looked at each of them, trying to see any sign they were mocking her. But they seemed deadly serious.

"No," she said. "There was something else. In all of the

samples. A sort of pattern in the ice. Frozen compression waves, like some kind of... sound. Like the ice froze so quickly it recorded a sound signature. But there's also... ah... trace signs of a radiation burst. As if a... I don't know. A bomb went off. Not like a nuclear bomb, radiating energy that becomes heat. Like... the opposite of that. A radiation that slows atoms down. Makes them stop in their tracks. Not just something cold, but the... the essence of cold."

Russell looked at Serizawa. "I see it now," she said. "How did I miss it? It's a bioacoustic signature."

"Yes," Serizawa said. "But more than that." He looked back at Magezi. "You haven't published about that."

"Like I said, I've already lost a lot of funding."

Serizawa nodded and tapped a device in his palm. On the screen in front of her, two pictures popped up. An extremely magnified ice sample, and an electron microscope image of presumably the same sample.

"Does this look familiar?" Serizawa asked.

"That's it," she said. "That's my data. How did you get it?"

"We didn't," Graham said. "This didn't come from Greenland, or Siberia, or the Canadian Shield."

"But it's the same," Magezi said. "Right down to the compression waves. Although now that I've been looking at it, the resolution is better than mine. You've got better equipment." She looked up. "Where the hell is this from?"

"We can't tell you that," Serizawa said. "For now. It's a site we're curating. Trying to learn more about."

"That's it? You're just going to walk in here, tease me with this, and walk out? Where is this from? It could go a long way toward vindicating me."

"Is that why you do this?" Graham asked. "Do you want vindication?"

She had thought she did. But the instant the question was asked, she knew the real answer.

"No," Magezi said. "What I really want? Is to know. To know what all this means."

"That," Serizawa said, "is up to you. I can hire you on a contract basis. I can get you funding. And we can show you this data in context. But you can't publish it for an audience outside of Monarch. At least not right now."

Magezi ran her gaze over them. "Is this for real?" she asked.

"It is very real," Serizawa said.

"You," Magezi said, lifting her finger to indicate Andrews, who hadn't said anything during the entire conversation. "What do you do?"

"Me?" Andrews said. She seemed a bit startled. "I'm, well, I'm an anthropologist. And a linguist."

"That's interesting. What does that have to do with ice core samples and rapid glaciation?"

"I…" She glanced at Serizawa, clearly unsure if she was supposed to be talking at all. He nodded at her.

"Well," she said, "I guess there's a feeling that some of my research into belief systems might have a part to play here."

"Belief systems? You mean like religion, folklore, mythology?"

"Yes," Andrews said.

"That has to do with this? Rapid glaciation that happened before our ancestors were even human?"

"Well, but our sample is much more recent," Andrews said. "It—" She cut herself off.

"More recent? How much more recent? Recent enough for humans to have witnessed it happening?" Magezi sat back, thinking. "So within the last hundred thousand years or so."

"I probably shouldn't have said that," Andrews sighed.

"No, it's fine," Serizawa said. "You talked about pulses, Doctor Maartens."

"Yes," she said. "Yeah, of course. There are probably multiple layers of this stuff. I was only looking at the earliest possible horizon, the ice right at the old surface level. But maybe the onset of every glaciation expansion in the last three million years has a layer like this." She looked up sharply at Andrews. "What myths? What legends?"

"I think I'm here more to listen than to talk," Andrews said.

"You guys aren't going to tell me anything unless I join your little club, are you?" she said.

"You said you wanted to know," Serizawa said. "This is how you find out."

"Is there a dental plan?" she asked.

"An excellent one," he said, without a trace of a smile.

She glanced outside at her grad students, standing around their little collection of tents. She had funding for another week, and after that, there was nothing in the pipeline. Then it was back to the classroom. And she liked teaching well enough, but she had never fooled herself that it was ever anything more than a way to get funding for her fieldwork. That was all about to go away, though, wasn't it?

And these guys? They *knew* that.

"Why me?" she asked. "You already have my data. It's clear that you have plenty of money and equipment. Any decent paleontologist could do what you're asking. So why me? Because I'm desperate?"

"No," Serizawa. "We had this ice profile before your paper was published. We had noticed the fine granularity of the ice crystals. Not one of our scientists noticed the compression wave patterns. Nor did we suspect that there was a greater, worldwide pattern. You saw that. That's why we want you."

She finished her coffee and sat silently for a moment.

"That's very flattering," she said. "It explains why *you* want *me*. But what I want is a reason to work for *you*. And not money. I can get funding. It won't be easy, but I can get it."

Serizawa kept his poker face, but she didn't miss the flicker of eye contact between him and Graham.

Then Serizawa went to his device again.

"You didn't see this," Graham whispered.

A new image came on the monitor. More ice, not magnified this time. Just a regular image, like a part of a glacier. Something in it... She noticed the scale. It was huge.

"Shit!" she swore. "What the hell is that?"

Serizawa smiled, put his device down. The screen went black. They all watched her. No one said a thing.

"You got me," she said. "I'm in."

ONE

For most of human civilization, we believed that we were Earth's most dominant species. We believed that life could only exist on the surface of the planet. Well, after a certain point you have to wonder—what else were we wrong about?

Today's new frontier is not outer space. It's right beneath our feet. We have mapped less than five percent of Hollow Earth, but our ecosystems are linked in ways that we never could have imagined. We are not two separate worlds. We're one. The answers to some of life's fundamental questions are waiting for us down there. But only if Hollow Earth is protected.

—TED Talk, Dr. Ilene Andrews

2027
Godzilla's lair
The South Pacific

He sleeps, but he feels the world on his skin and in his bones, in the rivulets and rivers of his nerves. He tastes the atmosphere and the water, the iron, the salt, the life, the death. He feels the pulse of the planet's magnetic field, the sleet of solar radiation it turns away from the delicate life beneath.

The surface and shallows of a world are dangerous. The life-giving sun could become scorching death. The very winds could carry poison around the globe. Masses of metal and ice might be hurled down at speeds lethal to the thin film of the biosphere, disrupting it for millions of years. Longer.

But all was relatively well, now. His sleep has been peaceful, for a time. Because the others were in their places, also resting. The ones above, the ones below. His territory is unchallenged, and it is thriving. But lately, things have begun to change.

Now something stirs on his skin. Something amiss, a distant call, the pulse of energy where it should not be. This happened before, not long ago. He stopped it, and there had been no greater threat. So he had returned to rest. But now this had to be dealt with.

And now he knows another has felt it, too.

He feels the pricks of her six legs as she begins to walk. He rouses to the next level of wakefulness. Maybe she is just moving from one resting spot to another. Maybe she will settle back down. She understands her place. She will not challenge him again.

And yet she continues to move, striding across the ocean floor. She feeds at the hot places where the rocks grind together, where sustenance seeps up from beneath. She is not only healed from their last fight, she is growing stronger. But she is not moving toward his resting place. She does not seek to challenge him yet.

But she will. The threat he feels—to her it is sustenance. She will feed and grow stronger. He is not pleased. He made an example of her once, but he let her live. He saw her purpose in his territory. But she has not learned. She will not learn.

And so he uncurls himself. He leaves his resting place and begins to swim in the deep waters with long, powerful sweeps of his tail. He stretches his senses. He experiences the rise and swell of tides, the crawling ice at either pole of the world, the subterranean vibrations of the other place, beneath the waters, beneath the stone. He feels the other, whom he did battle with. Whom he fought *with* against something far worse. That one is where he should be.

The others, too, are still obedient to his command, still in their places.

And yet, there is something else besides the source she now seeks, the faintest tickle of something wrong. The sound of something coming in the distance, perhaps not very far away.

But this is in front of him. This must be done first.

2027
Hollow Earth Access Point
Monarch Base
Barbados

Monarch director Hampton switched the monitor to the television, found the channel, made herself a cup of tea, and settled down to watch. She got through the nonsense at the start of the show, mostly by ignoring it. Then they started rolling clips of Titans.

A moment later, Dr. Andrews appeared on-screen. Much as she really did dislike doing these appearances, she was quite adept at it. She made a good impression. Today she had on a black suit and white shirt. Simple. Professional without being stuffy. And as always, she sounded credible. And she had a new haircut, short. It looked good.

The interviewer, a youngish fellow also in a black suit, had a pleasant enough demeanor. He started easy, as they had discussed.

"My guest today is Doctor Ilene Andrews, a Monarch scientist and director in charge of the Kong Research Division. She's the foremost expert on Kong and Titans in general. Welcome to the show, Doctor Andrews."

"Thanks so much for having me on today," she said.

"For those of us who have been sleeping under a rock for the past few years, would you mind bringing us up to speed on Kong? We all know he's a Titan, we all know he had a bit of a tussle with Godzilla a while back, but what else can you tell us about the big guy?"

"Sure," she said. "Well, our exploratory team discovered Kong living on an isolated island in the South Pacific—"

"Skull Island," the host put in.

"Yes," she said. "We discovered that he was the protector of a group of people called the Iwi. His kind and their kind had been living in harmony for generations. When they were menaced by the monsters of the island, Kong stepped in. We decided it was best not to try and fix what wasn't broken. We set up an observation post and tried to intrude as little as possible."

"You said Kong's kind? There was more than one?"

"He had a family. There are skeletons of other Great Apes on the island. But when we got there, Kong was the only one. The last of his species."

"And then there was another tragedy."

"Yes," she agreed. "The Island was surrounded by a constant storm that protected it from the outside. It's one reason it took us so long to even learn of its existence. During the cataclysmic event surrounding Monster Zero's attacks, and the global disruption of weather patterns he created, the storm around the island became unbalanced. It moved ashore, the tides rose: despite our efforts, the Iwi were wiped out."

"Except for one."

She nodded. "My daughter, Jia," she said.

"And Kong survived all of this, of course."

"He did. We built an artificial environment for him, sheltered from the worst of the elements. That could only last for so long. Eventually, we had to find him a new home. When we discovered Hollow Earth and how to reach it, we knew we had our answer. To keep this short, after his fight with Godzilla in Hong Kong, we took Kong to Hollow Earth, where we believe his species originated."

"And he's there now?"

"Yes. He's still settling into Hollow Earth."

"So the big guy likes his new home?"

"We think so. His species was a very social one. It's not natural for Kong to be so alone. He's the last of his kind. Every day he searches for a family he'll never find."

"You've said that only a small part of Hollow Earth has been mapped. Could it be possible that he just hasn't found them yet?"

"We can hope," she conceded. "Everyone needs family. Even Kong. But so far... well, it's been a little disappointing. But Kong keeps looking. It's not impossible."

If Godzilla and his mob didn't finish them all off ages ago, Hampton thought. The fight Kong and Godzilla had had a few years back hadn't been a first-time event. The evidence was clear that at one point there had been a full-on war between Godzilla, the Titans he controlled, and the Great Apes. There were a couple of reasons a war might end: one of them was if one side were all dead. Kong and his handful of ancestors on Skull Island might well have been all that remained of that species, and then only because they were stuck on an island Godzilla didn't care about.

"Well, we all wish the big guy the best of luck. Wouldn't it be great if in a few years you had a little Kong to show us pictures of."

"I… Well, sure," Andrews said. "But, you know, let's not put the cart before the horse."

"Or the baby before the life mate, I guess," the host grinned. Then his expression changed back to serious as he switched topics.

"What about Godzilla?"

Yes, Hampton thought. *What about him?* The memory came with photographic clarity—the jagged edges of what had, a moment before, been a solid hotel-room wall, hot humid air rushing to fill her lungs, the reptilian outline of the Titan's head eclipsing the sky. His eyes, seeming to stare right through her. And the fear, so primal and powerful she didn't even understand what it was until later…

Snap out of it, she told herself. She tried to narrow her focus back to the interview.

"Godzilla is on the surface," Andrews said. "Kong is below. As long as they don't venture into each other's territories, we've got nothing to worry about."

Yeah. Not a thing, Hampton thought as the show cut to

commercial. Except that he had recently attacked an offshore oil derrick for no reason anyone could discern. At least it had been abandoned, so there had been no casualties. No other Titans involved either. That was what bothered her about it. It seemed random, but Godzilla didn't do random. If you looked hard enough, you could always find a reason.

Well, almost always.

When the program came back, Andrews and the moderator had been joined by another guest, a U.S. Senator, to discuss the Hollow Earth Conservation Bill, which would hopefully be coming up for a vote in the House in a few weeks. If it passed there, this nimrod was saying he would shut it down in the Senate. Andrews was doing well—sounding reasonable, collected, and passionate. She was sticking to her talking points. The other guy... Hampton just prayed she could watch the whole thing without breaking into an epic session of swearing and blaspheming in front of her subordinates.

She made it, but she worried she might have incurred a small stroke in the process.

Monarch Crew Residence
Barbados

Hampton was two hours into what was never going to be more than six hours of sleep when her phone began demanding her attention. She groaned, practiced her Te Reo by swearing a bit, and picked up the phone. It was pounding rain outside, she noticed, wondering if it would let up today at all.

"Yep," she said. "Hampton here."

It was her new assistant, Laurier. She let the young woman talk for a moment.

"Okay," she said, when a break came in the torrent of words. "Calm down. Repurpose a satellite—we don't want to lose her, God knows. I'll be in in ten."

She hadn't counted on the rain. One of the walk-overs was a foot deep in water. She didn't have time to go around so she just went through, soaking her shoes and pants legs. When were they going to get the bloody drainage fixed? This was the Caribbean. Rain happened here. Four years, and this place was still under construction. They were still welding things in the halls.

She reached Control, stripped off her poncho. Everyone was watching her come in, of course. She nodded at them and moved up to the monitors. The central one showed a scattering of islands off the southern tip of South America. One of them was marked with a Monarch symbol.

A red dot, which ought to be on the island, was not. Instead, it was moving out into the Atlantic Ocean.

"Heading?" she asked.

"Northeast," Laurier responded.

"Any discernable destination? Sources of radioactivity? Other Titans?"

"The rest of them are right where Godzilla sent them," Laurier said.

"And Godzilla?"

"We're not sure where he is."

"Ah, great," she said. "We're going to find out soon enough, with Scylla on the loose."

"What do we do?"

"If she continues straight the way she's going, where will she end up?"

"Western Africa. Maybe Sierra Leone."

"Hmm-huh," she said, studying the map. "Then she's not

a danger to anyone yet. A few days, maybe." She frowned. Then she pointed to a dot in the Atlantic. "What's this?"

"Ilha de Trindade," Laurier said. "It's a Brazilian possession. In fact they have a small naval station there."

"Ah, super," she said. "We'd better let 'em know then, and right away. Get us cleared to get in there, too. We need to get her contained before Godzilla finds out."

"On it," Laurier said.

Nodding, she took out her phone and called Andrews, who answered immediately. Did she not sleep either?

"We've got a situation here," she said.

"What?"

"Fricken' Scylla. She's not playing ball anymore."

"What do you mean?"

"I mean she's taking a swim in the Atlantic. Without a hall pass."

"Godzilla?" Andrews asked.

"Not yet. Still in the South Pacific as far as we know."

"Only a matter of time," Andrews said. "Okay, I'm on my way."

"Nah," Hampton said. "Get your kid to school first. Then I'll see you. We need to brainstorm this, though."

Hampton pulled up their profile of Scylla. She was a nasty one: a Destroyer, a Titan that just liked to break things. From a distance she looked like a massive spider-crab, albeit with only six legs. Up closer you noticed her head, which was more squid than arachnid or insect, complete with tentacles. She fed on most sources of energy but had a sweet tooth for nuclear fission.

"Okay," she murmured, moving her mouse. "Let's see where our assets are."

Monarch didn't have any subs near enough to make

a difference, but they had a M.U.L.E prepped, and pair of Osprey Mark III aircraft. It looked like they could get to Ilha de Trindade before Scylla and hopefully set a trap, put her in a containment field to give them time to figure what the next step was.

The ever-so-slight problem with that was that containment fields were tailored to individual Titans, and Scylla had never been in a containment field. The tailor, so to speak, didn't have a pattern. She had first been found sleeping underneath an area near Sedona, Arizona, and showed every sign of staying dormant. In fact, a few of their scientists thought she might even be dead. She wasn't high priority. But when Monster Zero called up the Titans a few years back, Scylla popped right up out of the sand. After that, she didn't want to go back down.

When Godzilla cemented himself as the dominant Titan on the surface, most of the other Titans went along with it. Not Scylla. She headed to the Georgia coast and wreaked havoc, searching for an old atomic bomb that had been lost there in the 1950s. She found it, but Godzilla thrashed her pretty decisively before she could do anything catastrophic. He let her live, though, and she seemed to finally agree to play nice. She settled down in a frozen pool on one of the far South American islands and had stayed there. Her presence there had had a positive effect on the global environment, helping reverse sea-warming.

But now here she was, on the move again. And according to satellite data, she was no longer cooling the global climate, but warming it. Not a lot, but if it continued over time, it would add up.

When Godzilla found out, he was gonna be pissed. So they had to get her back into hibernation, pronto—or at the very least, keep her in the middle of the Atlantic until Godzilla showed up so they could have their little tiff far from playgrounds and skyscrapers.

"She still on course?" Andrews asked, when she showed up. Hampton glanced at her.

"Like the new hairdo," she said. "Very professional."

"Thanks," Andrews replied. "I'm not quite sure about it. But it's done. Scylla?"

"Just making a beeline to… someplace," Hampton said. "She's stopping now and then—probably to feed. But she clearly has some idea where she's going."

Andrews scanned the data from the other stations. "Every place else is quiet, including Hollow Earth."

"Let's hope this is just a one-off," Hampton replied. "I always did think Scylla had scorpions for brains. She's just fricken' nuts."

"Right," Andrews said. "Not an intellectual like Godzilla."

Hampton laughed at that. Probably because she hadn't had any sleep, more likely because the whole subject of Godzilla left her feeling… she didn't know. Vulnerable? Which at least partly accounted for her recent lack of sleep.

The next ten hours were tense. They were still tracking Scylla, and the team arrived at Ilha de Trindade. They set up one of their biggest containment nets. When the Titan arrived, they would either drive her or lure in the right direction. Once contained, Monarch's "veterinarian" would deliver an anesthetic he believed would immobilize her long enough to haul her up with multiple M.U.L.Es, transport her back to her little island, and cage her up there, if that was what was required.

Hampton had her doubts any of that would work. She thought the evidence was pretty clear that you couldn't contain a Titan against its will, at least not indefinitely.

"This part always makes me nervous," Hampton told Andrews as the dot representing Scylla closed in on their trap.

"You've done this before?" Andrews asked.

"Yeah. In my head. About five hundred times since this morning."

"It's going to work," Andrews reassured her.

"It had better."

Together they watched as the dot got closer, closer—then vanished.

"What the—" Hampton sputtered. "Containment team, report."

A young man appeared on-screen "We had visual, Director," he said. "I didn't think she knew we were here. Then she dove. And she didn't come back up."

"That makes no sense," Hampton said. "Even underwater, we should still be able to—oh, dammit. Completely dammit."

"What?" Andrews said.

"Laurier," she called. "The island. What kind of island is it? Please tell me it's a coral atoll or something."

"No, Director." she said. "It's volcanic, pretty recent geologically. It's part of a chain of volcanos, most of them underwater."

"A hot-spot chain?"

"They used to think so. But the islands aren't lined up right with the continental plates."

"It's a vortex," Hampton sighed. "One we didn't know about. Remember during the Monster Zero crisis when Godzilla kept disappearing from our instruments and then just popping back up someplace else? Scylla's doing the same thing. She was never going to Africa. She was always going right there, to charge up and disappear. Dammit!"

"Let's be sure, anyway," Andrews said. "If Scylla's in Hollow Earth with Kong, I pity her."

Five hours later they were sure. The containment team confirmed the existence of what had been dubbed "a lateral vortex," a tunnel that dove down to the space-time distortion membrane separating Hollow Earth from the upper world. Instead of punching through, though, it ran along the membrane and likely popped out somewhere else on the surface. Without entering it themselves, there was no way of knowing where it went. The fastest option was to rig a drone and send it in, but they were only halfway prepped for that before the other shoe dropped. A big one.

Godzilla had been sighted in the Java Sea. His wake had already flipped a ship. An hour later Scylla appeared in the Bay of Bengal. Godzilla's projected path was aimed straight at her. Or... maybe they were both aimed at a third thing? The same thing that had attracted Godzilla to that oil platform?

"He knows she's there," Andrews said.

"Yes," Hampton said. "He certainly does. Now let's just hope Scylla doesn't intend to make landfall."

She didn't hold out much hope for that scenario, though, as Scylla began cutting a wake straight toward the southern tip of the Indian subcontinent. It didn't take long to figure out why.

"She's going to the Kudankulam nuclear power plant," Laurier informed them.

"Yep," Hampton said. "Of course she is. I suppose we should start calling people now. Presidents, senators, prime ministers. Do you think Paul Bunyan might be available?"

"I have it on good authority Godzilla killed him in 1887," Andrews replied. "I can see if Babe is available."

Hampton glared at the screen.

Predictably, the Indian military scrambled fighters. Just as predictably, Scylla knocked them out of the sky, unaffected by their munitions. She tore the coastal plant to ruins. It melted down, of course, but Scylla literally ate radiation, using some sort of polluting cloud she emitted. Although she left a smoking, smoggy ruin behind her, it was at least clean of toxic fallout.

But the average temperature in the region had ticked up four degrees; worse still, the ozone layer high above her path showed signs of weakening.

Godzilla was still playing catch-up. By the time he surfaced off the coast of India, Scylla was long gone, skirting up the western coast of the subcontinent, making landfall in Pakistan and cutting a trail of destruction north and west through Iran, where she stopped to wreck a nuclear enrichment facility. From there she continued through Azerbaijan, across the Black Sea, Ukraine, and Poland. She crashed through Berlin, but didn't slow down enough to properly destroy the city before leaving the continent and taking a swim to the United Kingdom, where she did stop to gobble up a uranium pellet manufacturing plant in Preston. Godzilla missed her by six hours. He was closer when she stopped at the Aviano Airbase in Italy to feast on a portion of the United States' nuclear arsenal.

In Rome, he finally caught up with her—although Scylla reached the Eternal City first.

"And here we go," Andrews said.

Godzilla had also entered Rome.

Scylla stopped her rampage and turned to face him. Hampton reflected that they looked like gunfighters in the weirdest Western ever, squared off at high noon. The basilica of St. Peters was in the background between them. It was dusk, the moon was rising. It was a still moment, almost beautiful.

"Get her," Hampton said under her breath. "That's why you're there, right?"

Scylla shrieked like nothing else on Earth, and Godzilla roared back at her. Then they charged each other.

Scylla's six legs struck through roof tiles and paving stones, filling the whole city with an awful *scritch-tik-tik-tiking*. Godzilla's footfalls were almost subsonic; she could feel them in her bones even through the monitors. She watched in horror as masonry from more than two thousand years of Italian history was shattered, scattered, and trampled to dust.

Then they met with the force of two tsunamis, but one of the waves was bigger than the other. Godzilla heaved Scylla into the air and threw her, sending her smashing through several city blocks. Then he ran forward and leaped into the air, crashing down on top of her. Scylla was on her back; her tentacles writhed up and clamped onto his mouth. He pushed down, steadily, and his mouth opened, even against the pressure of her attack.

A blue beam shot out, point blank, into Scylla's maw. Her legs kicked wildly, but Godzilla bore down with the azure flame.

And Scylla exploded, her green blood drenching an area of ten city blocks.

"Oh." Hampton said. "Wow."

It wasn't the first time Godzilla had killed another Titan, of course. The insectile MUTOs and Monster Zero, to name two. But he'd fought Scylla before, beaten her soundly and chosen not to kill her. The same could be said of other Titans, like Amhuluk. His main goal since his victory over Monster Zero seemed to be *controlling* the other Titans, using them to keep the Earth in proper balance—not eradicating them.

But he had totally just executed Scylla.

Maybe it was because she was starting to have a negative impact on the global climate? Or maybe Godzilla had a "two strikes and you're out" rule.

"Something's going on," Andrews said. "He's acting… different."

"Agreed," Hampton said. "But what do we think that means?"

"Godzilla responds to global pressures," she said. "The MUTOs and Monster Zero were both on track to destroy the world as we know it. But most of the other Titans, whatever you think of their dispositions, had some positive effects on the planet. Godzilla beat them into line but he didn't kill them. But some of them are easier to manage than others, and all of a sudden it looks like Godzilla is willing to make examples of those that don't recognize his dominance. Eliminate them from the equation. Because the equation has changed."

"Like there's a new factor added," Hampton said. "Shit. Like another Monster Zero. Another World Ender."

Andrews nodded. "One we don't know about."

"That's a cheery thought."

"What he does next may tell us something," Andrews said.

"Watch and wait," Hampton agreed. "That'll be fun to sell to the powers that be."

Hampton had a number of things she expected of Godzilla in the aftermath of the fight. He might move straight on to another possible rogue Titan. He might go on patrol. He might vanish into some hidey-hole.

He did none of those things. Instead, he stomped his way to the Roman Colosseum, stepped inside, curled up and took a nap.

The calls started coming in, from everywhere.

TWO

You got this new Hollow Earth Conservation Bill. Like that's gonna stop the corporations from going down there, taking whatever they want. You thought the monsters were scary, just wait for Big Pharma, Big Tech, Big Oil—it's gonna be a field day.

—Titan Truth Podcast #82

Somewhere in Hollow Earth

Kong knew what death was, and he knew it was chasing him.

Death was four-legged. Death was swift. Its jaws bristled with teeth, all sharp, all for puncturing and tearing meat, no flat plant-grinders in its skulls. Death was hairy, hunched at the shoulders, thick-tailed.

Individually, these deaths were small. One—or even a hand of fingers of them—didn't worry him. He had met them before, fought them before. Once he had nearly succumbed to them. Their size had fooled him until he realized they did not hunt alone. They did not hunt in numbers he could count on his hands. They hunted as *many*. And today there were more than he had ever seen at once. This death knew it would take more than two hands of them to kill him, and they had brought more than enough. Far more than last time. So he would not fight them. Not here.

He leaped over a ridge and came down on all fours, his knuckles crushing trees as he ran faster, as fast as he could. It would not go well for him if they caught him here, in the open. The mountains ahead promised better ground for the coming fight. Ground of his choosing, not theirs.

A glance over his shoulder showed they were still gaining.

Above, the skin-winged fliers called as they cut through the air. Still further up, the tops of trees, hills and mountains pointed down at him. There was no sky here, except the one that lay in the middle of the land that arched over—or maybe below—him. Neither was there a great moving light in the sky, like the one he had known in the other place, or the dimmer one that glowed in the night. But there was light, shining from bunches of rock that sprouted up from the lower land or hung from the upper one.

The thing inside of his chest was beating hard, and the air in there was starting to burn. He wasn't tired yet, but he would be soon. Then he would slow down, and those sharp teeth would find him. But not yet. Right now, with the wind inside him and the bright world all around, with the chittering of the fliers and the growling of the pack and the smell of broken trees and bruised leaves, he almost felt like he should turn and fight them, see how many he could kill before they brought him down. If they brought him down. He might kill them all. He was Kong.

He looked back again. No, there were too many of them. He knew that, even if his rage did not. So he kept running.

This place with no sky was still new to him. It was big, far bigger than the place he had lived before, the land surrounded by sea and storm, the land where the skeletons of his parents bleached in the sun, where his little ones, the Iwi, had once lived. He was learning it, though. Each day he wandered further, explored new territory. Searching, always searching. At first he had been eager—hopeful even. But lately he was starting to doubt. To feel like the middle of him was hollowed out. He was tired of his own company. He wanted someone else. Even the little ones seemed distant now. He hadn't seen the one called Jia in a long time. A very long time, it seemed.

Right now, he was at the edge of the territory he knew. But he did know it. He knew where he should go to stop death from finding him, as it had found his parents, as it had found most of the Iwi.

He ran on toward the jagged line of mountains, up a slope between two peaks. Ahead, a crevasse cut the ground in half. He pushed himself to go just a little faster, bunched his massive legs beneath him, and threw himself up and forward. Air rushed through his fur, and he wondered if this was what the skin-wing fliers felt as they sailed through it. But no, he felt the pull of stones below him. High above, in the middle of the sky, there was no pull. He had been there, floating, with no weight drawing his huge frame down. But now he wasn't flying, he was falling—he could feel it in his belly. The crevasse below had no bottom he could see, although he knew it must be many times his own height. It might go on forever, for all he knew. The other side was far away, right around the limit of how far he could jump. For a thump of his chest he thought of falling much further, too far, of smashing into sharp stones far below. Then his feet hit the far edge and he tumbled forward across the hard ground, a savage joy surging through him.

Was it too far for his pursuers? Probably. It had almost been too far for him.

But they sensed a kill. He could see it burning in their eyes. The leaders of the pack didn't hesitate. They jumped after him, and all the others followed without hesitation.

As they landed on his side of the gorge, Kong raced on along the path leading up between the peaks.

But not for long. A final dash brought him to the edge of another cliff, but this wasn't one side of a ravine. The mountains ended here in a precipice dropping down into a valley cut by a long, winding water, and beyond that more mountains, but far too distant for him to jump to. The peaks on either side of him were too steep to climb. He was caught between narrow walls and a fall that even he could not survive.

His pursuers knew it. But they slowed down. Now that they had him trapped, they were suddenly cautious. Maybe it worried them that the way between the pass was so narrow they could only get to him a few at a time. He knew from observation and experience that they preferred to come at their prey from all sides. Here they would have to come straight toward him. Even if one or two managed to slip along his flanks, the drop behind him would keep them from coming at him from his back.

He took deep breaths, waiting. Then he rose up to his full height and shouted his rage, his fists crashing against his chest.

Try me. Come and get me if you think you can.

For an instant longer they hesitated, their bloodlust balanced against their fear until the leader snarled and bolted across the broken ground, right across the spot Kong had carefully avoided a moment before.

The ground broke beneath the predators' feet. Or rather, it had never really been there. Kong had spent a long time placing branches, covering them with rocks and sand, until— if you didn't know—they looked just like the stone of the pass. There were animals that looked like something they weren't, that disguised themselves as plants or grass or harmless creatures, that you didn't notice until they were trying to eat you. He had made such a thing. It looked like solid ground, but it was really a hole.

His hole ate the beast, chewing it with teeth he'd made of sharpened logs and placed in the bottom. You didn't have to hold a weapon in your hands to make it work. The little ones knew that well, and so did Kong.

The pack did not. But the others saw the pit now. They saw their leader dying, but that didn't bother them. They would jump across his hole if he gave them a chance.

But he didn't. He lifted up the thick part of a tree he had dragged up from the lowlands, tied with vines which he had also brought. The log swung forward, smashing into the predators even as the vines pulled at the tree-trunks he had wedged into the high cliff faces and piled heavy with boulders. The braces pulled out, and the rocks fell in an avalanche of his making, burying his enemies. Crushing most of them.

He watched, satisfied with his work. It wasn't perfect. A few had survived and were crawling out from beneath the boulders, but these he could count on one hand. Their blood was so hot that they started back toward him anyway, even though most of their pack was dead or dying. There weren't enough of them now, not enough to kill him. But they could hurt him. Fighting them would still be trouble. And he was hungry, very hungry, and ready for this to be over.

One of the creatures had been thrown clear to his side of the trap, but it was as good as dead. He picked up the broken body, lifting it over his head, shouting rage and challenge. He pulled, feeling the dead muscle and sinew resist until they didn't, and the creature tore in half, drenching him with gore. He thrust the half-a-beast with the head toward them, howling his threat, his promise to do the same to them.

That was finally enough. Shaken from their hunger-rage, the remaining members of the pack yelped in fear and ran back the way they had come.

Panting, triumphant, Kong lowered his prize, then dropped it on the ground. As his own fury cleared, he realized his fur was sticky with blood and guts.

Which did not please him at all. It would not do.

He took the carcass and carried it out of the narrow pass, down to the cave he lived in, where a long water fell off the top of a mountain. He stood in the stream of it. It washed down him like rain but was so much stronger. He had bathed himself this way in his old country. Then later, after the storms came, when he lived in a much smaller territory, there had also been a place like this. A falling-water place. It felt good pressing through his fur, carrying away the stench and gore, beating against his sore muscles. But he couldn't enjoy it completely. He kept thinking about the pack which had hunted him—or that he had lured into hunting him. They had failed to make a meal of him, but they had at least been working together. Their strength was in their family. To kill them, he'd had to make a trap, because he *was* alone. He had no pack, no family to help him.

The Iwi had been a little like family. He had protected them. And later, Jia and her family had been like part of his own. But he knew there had once been more like him. That two of them had brought him to the world, and then died. He had seen their bones, but he couldn't remember them alive. Not really. When he tried, all he could feel was sadness and rage. He had always known something was missing. When he had first come here, to this place with no real sky, he had felt at home. Even though he had never seen a place like it, every sight, sound and smell had seemed familiar. He expected to find more apes like him. His family. He found signs that they had been there. He found a dwelling, a throne, weapons they had left behind. But never another like him.

He thought they must all be dead.

When he felt clean, he dragged his meal back up into the mountains and through the huge hole in them to a place he liked, a ledge that looked out over the world. He settled there, weary. Hungry. He tore a leg from his prey and took a bite.

It bit him back. It felt like that, at least. Something in his mouth cracked, and pain struck through his jaw and into his head. He snarled, and reached to touch where it hurt, and found that one of his sharp teeth no longer came to a point. It felt rough, and it throbbed. It had broken. He didn't know that could happen to teeth, but now he did, and he felt... bad. Everything seemed to have turned against him, even food. Even his own mouth.

Next to him, the carcass moved. It slid away from him. For a moment he was confused because he knew it should be dead and therefore shouldn't move. Then he saw that something was trying to take it from him, a creature just less than half his size. Its head was small compared to its fat body; it was covered in bumps and horns, with no hair or feathers, and it sprawled on four short, thick legs.

It was trying to take his meal. His prize.

He grabbed the carcass and yanked back. However small it was, its jaws were strong. It dug its feet in, trying to back away.

Kong wasn't sure he even wanted to eat anymore. His mouth hurt; his whole head hurt. The big lizard-thing didn't act like it wanted to fight. It wanted to steal. But now that it was caught, it wasn't giving up.

He still wasn't sure it was worth it when he heard a booming call, echoing through the cliffs. A distant, familiar roar.

Sometimes when he bellowed in the mountains, the sound would come back to him. He would hear himself, like he saw himself when he looked in still water. But this wasn't that. He hadn't yelled at the creature stealing his food. He hadn't yelled at all.

Something else had made the sound. It sounded like him, but also not like him.

Was it another? Could it be another? Finally? Family?

The pain in his jaw was forgotten as he leaped from his perch and began swinging and scrambling though the maze of cliffs and canyons, pursuing the source of the sound. Another that was like him. He felt a sort of swelling inside, almost like the feeling right before a fight. Excitement. The thinking-ahead-about-something-good-that-is-about-to-happen.

As he searched, he called back, and was rewarded by an answer. Closer. He was almost there.

He skidded down a slope and came to a stop at the edge of another overlook, turning his gaze to the canyon below. He didn't see the source of the voice, but the view was so vast that even something so large as himself could be lost in it. For a blink of his eyes, everything seemed still, full of possibility.

Then the call came again, and he saw. Across the gulf, on a ledge below him. Not something like him at all. It was small, not even the size of his head. It didn't have fur or arms. It was slick and four-legged, like the things that lived in water, the long-jumpers. As he watched, the skin beneath its mouth suddenly bulged, ballooning out until it was nearly twice the size of the creature itself, lifting it from the ground. Then its mouth yawned wide, and a sound rushed out, a sound far too loud for something of that size.

The call. The sound that had brought him here, to find another of his own kind. Instead, he found this. Yet another thing that survived by pretending to be something it wasn't. Something else.

He stared at the ape-pretender, and although the crystals shone as brightly as ever, everything seemed to have grown darker. He chuffed and turned his back to the source of his disappointment, lowered himself to sit. His tooth hurt again, more than ever. Even if he felt like eating it, his hard-won meal was now surely gone, devoured by the food-stealer.

Weary, in pain, hungry, and still alone, Kong lowered his head.

THREE

Music is like a dream. One that I cannot hear.

—*Conversations*, Ludwig van Beethoven

Monarch Crew Residence
Barbados

Jia had been dreaming of Kong. When she was younger, she believed that he and she sometimes shared their dreams. Like dream was a land they both visited at night, just another place, like Skull Island or Hollow Earth. It had seemed so real and made total sense to her at the time. She had never questioned it.

Now, she wasn't sure. At school they said dreams only happened in your own brain, that the other people in them were just created by your mind. It wasn't just that, either. She wasn't sure of anything anymore. Everything was different.

She felt a pain in her jaw and reached up to touch it, but

when she did, she didn't find anything that actually hurt. She sighed and looked at the clock. It was two in the morning. She needed to get back to sleep.

Instead she worried about school. She had a test today, didn't she? She hadn't studied for it. It hadn't seemed worth doing. Maybe since she couldn't sleep, she should do that now. She climbed out of bed and into her study hut, turned on the string lights, and pulled out her pre-algebra book. She stared at the sample test, and—of course—she was suddenly very tired.

Jia sat up in darkness, not sure what had woken her. But as she sat there, she began to feel as if a wind was moving on her skin and in her hair. Her palms and the soles of her feet tingled, and in those sensations she perceived a rising and falling motion, a pulse of rhythm that was not her heart but something outside of herself.

She knew the word *singing*. Her people sang sometimes, although of course she could not hear them. But sometimes, when they all sang together, she thought she could feel it, like this. Their songs on her skin and vibrating gently in her bones.

She rose and padded gently out into the night. Above, the familiar lights of the nocturnal sky blazed down. The stars, the White Sky River—and through the trees, the moon was rising, nearly full.

And in the light, something danced. Hundreds of small creatures with pearl-colored wings fluttered and drifted, glowing in the light of the moon and stars. And they weren't just dancing. They were singing, too. It was what she'd felt. She stood, stock still, for a long time, afraid that if she did anything, they would leave.

After a while, someone came beside her. She could not see her face, but she knew it was Oa, her Iwi mother's sister, who slept in their house with them.

Oa spoke to her in the ancient way, the way that needed no sound.

They only come every handful of years, Oa told her. *They live as worms, high in the mountains, for all of that time. Then they wrap themselves in silk and become this. You are blessed to see them tonight.*

What are they singing? Jia asked. *It's so beautiful.*

Singing? Oa said. *They do not sing. They do not have voices.*

But I hear them, Jia said.

Jia, you cannot hear. And I hear nothing. I only see them flying in the moonlight.

There was much Jia did not know, but she knew Oa was wrong. Somehow, they were singing. And it was the most beautiful thing she had ever heard.

Jia woke again, this time in her study hut, her face buried in her schoolbook. She snorted, rubbed her eyes, and pushed herself up. For an instant she thought the song had followed her from her dream, and was here with her even now. But as she came ever more awake, she realized she didn't feel anything.

She had forgotten that night, hadn't she? It was so long ago, she had been so young. She could not remember Oa's face at all, and now even the words from her memory-dream began to slip away.

Maybe it had never been real. Memory and dream were much the same, when you were that little. She thought she recalled other things that Ilene told her probably weren't true. Maybe it had all been a wish in the night, that just once she could hear music, know what it really was to listen to a song. Just the longing of a girl to be like everyone else.

But she wasn't, and she never would be. Once she'd been at peace with that. Once it hadn't mattered at all, because it hadn't mattered to Ilene or to Kong, or anyone else she knew.

That was before everything changed. Before school, and more strangers than she could count. Before she understood that she would never fit in.

She went back to her bed and tried to sleep again. She managed to, only an hour before she had to get up.

This, she thought, was likely to be a worse day than usual.

Monarch Outpost One
Kong Observation Unit
Hollow Earth

The air of Hollow Earth never quite smelled right to Jayne.

Her career had taken her many places: the highlands of Peru and Ecuador, the pampas of Argentina, the frozen coasts of Antarctica, the Congo Basin, the tropical forests of Yunnan, the Kaibab Plateau in southwestern North America. They had all smelled a little strange to her. She had mentioned that to her mother once, who just shook her head, smiled, and said something about her over-active olfactory glands and how they had made her a nightmare of a picky eater as a child. The conversation had been a bit of an epiphany for Jayne and helped explain why no one else she knew on her various assignments had ever mentioned the scents of those places.

Scent and taste were the two senses humans had that let them directly analyze the chemical content of the world around them. Of the two, scent was the more powerful, the more directly tied to emotion. It was also the least acute of the senses, at least in most people. Compared to, say, a dog, humans were virtually blind in the chemical senses. Humans were sight animals. Everything was about appearance to them.

And the appearance of Hollow Earth was, to say the least, weird. The plants were strange, the animals stranger. And there were things that were a little—or a lot—of both. The sky was more landscape. There were no stars at night, no moon, no true sunsets. There were clouds sometimes, but the shapes they came in didn't look right, contorted as they were by the opposed gravitation forces of "up" and "down" and by the null-gravity zone between them.

But the scents, they were arguably way stranger. Any other place she had ever been, there were whiffs of the familiar. The smell of cow dung, of diesel fumes, of rotting meat, of wet soil—these were similar everywhere up above. The Congo, the Antarctic, the dry uplands of Arizona: all had a shared biological history that went back more than a billion years, and thus a common chemical history.

That history was shared by the Hollow Earth, as well, but things here had gone their own way for a very long time. This was in every way interesting. The media played up the "monsters" of Hollow Earth—the macrofauna—while saying almost nothing about the microfauna. This was hardly surprising. Even above, much more attention was paid to elephants, whales, pandas, and rhinoceroses than to bacteria. But the true rulers of any ecosystem—by sheer mass, diversity, and ecological importance—were mostly unseen to the naked eye. And here, that invisible world was as different—maybe more different— than the big critters suggested. Both worlds had decay organisms, for instance. But they had evolved independently. Each set did the job, but in somewhat different ways, leading to different chemical outcomes. The same could be said for the dead things they turned back into soil. All vertebrates above ground had red, hemoglobin-based blood. Some in the Hollow Earth did, too, but many had extraordinarily exotic blood and tissue in a wide variety of colors and compositions.

So, of course, things smelled weird. Way stranger than anyplace she had ever been. She didn't mind it, but she couldn't help but notice. And maybe think about it too much, especially when Lewis took a notion to cook some of the local wildlife for their dinner. Which, fortunately, didn't seem to be the plan tonight. She'd seen he had pulled out some shelf-stable tofu and rice, and he hadn't been out "gathering" today.

She looked "up," tracing her gaze along the mountains and valleys of the other side of the world, momentarily overcome by the wonder of it all. Being here was a privilege, one worth any number of funky smells.

It was also dangerous. There were plenty of things down here that thought *she* smelled just fine for dinner. It didn't pay to stray far from the base alone. She hadn't: it was only a few steps behind her, a blocky, utilitarian prefab that had replaced the first base about a year ago. She was turning back toward the entrance when something big moved at the perimeter, just past the screen of trees.

She ran. She jerked the outer door open and slammed it closed, then looked back out through the window while she waited for the lock to cycle. Despite all the toothy predators in Hollow Earth, they had so far not discovered any pathogens that affected humans in a big way. That wasn't surprising, in evolutionary terms; pathogens usually evolved to affect a particular host, and if there were any homo sapiens living down here, they hadn't met them yet—although there was evidence that there had once been at least one population of humans, or a very similar species.

As she watched, the trees shook, and suddenly several of them toppled as a creature came into view. It was big. Not Kong big, but bigger than an elephant. She nevertheless let out her breath, which she realized she had been holding. It had a stout, armored body that was pretty similar to that of an armadillo, but the long snakelike neck that coiled out of that ended in a small, somewhat otter-like head. As she watched, it extended its neck to nibble at the leaves of the forest canopy. When threatened, it could somehow tuck the entire neck and head into the protective shell. It had a scientific name, but they just usually called the beasts "dirraffs". They weren't exactly harmless—they had thick, two-hooved hind limbs that could deliver a crushing blow to anything the diraff perceived as threatening. But they didn't seem bothered by humans, and there hadn't been any incidents involving them.

The inner door cycled. She opened it and stepped in.

The outpost was heavily built and resembled a bunker more than anything. Of course it was also a workplace for... well, science nerds. The marks of human personalities were everywhere, from the portrait of Harris's cat back home to the left-behinds from those who had come before. Her gaze lingered on the plastic figure of a spaceman. It had belonged to one of the first scientists down here, Dr. Nathan Lind. Jayne hadn't known him all that well, but she had always been curious about the spaceman. She meant to ask her boss about it, but she didn't know her boss *that* well, and it had never seemed like the right time. Anyway, the boss didn't come down that often these days.

Human touches aside, the outpost was very much a working lab, busily monitoring seismic activity, electromagnetic and gravitational anomalies, weather patterns, and of course Titans, which the bunker had been built to—well, maybe not withstand, but at least to resist. The only windows were as thick as the walls and were basically just narrow strips near the ceiling. They didn't provide much of a view. That came from the banks of screens monitoring the area around the outpost and more remote locations. Several of them, as usual—and as the name of the outpost suggested—were tasked with keeping track of Kong. A short while ago, they had increased the number of sensors, and were adding more after a recent incident in which Raymond Martin, a billionaire Titan-hunter, had entered Hollow Earth in his own version of a H.E.A.V and tried to bag Kong as a trophy. Monarch had missed the whole fight, but found the wrecked remains of the giant mech Martin had piloted in his attempt to kill the Great Ape. Of Martin himself, they only found blood, but enough to safely assume he was now deceased. Dr. Andrews was enraged, determined no further incidents like this would happen.

At the moment, however, one of the screens was playing a television program from up top.

"...taxpayer dollars going to Hollow Earth and classified technologies like the mysterious Project Powerhouse," the host was saying. "Well, here to discuss, Monarch's own Doctor Ilene Andrews."

It's the boss, Jayne thought.

"Let's start with Godzilla," the interviewer said. "He stopped the attack in Rome, but he's still in the city. Should we be worried?"

"First of all, no, nobody's in danger," Andrews replied. "It's clear to us now that Godzilla is a Titan that protects us from other malicious Titan threats. When he is dormant, there's no threat. It's as simple as that."

The view changed to an aerial shot of the Roman Colosseum. The huge reptilian frame of Godzilla was curled up inside it, apparently in peaceful slumber. The crawl at the bottom of the screen said something about the Titan taking over the ancient landmark, and the tourists being in awe. Of course they were.

She would bet the locals had somewhat... *mixed* feelings.

The host looked skeptical. "He takes out all challengers and then just decides to take a nap? Are we sure he's not hurt? Because this is a real long nap."

"We're... not entirely sure why Godzilla has gone dormant—whether it's part of a natural hibernation cycle or something else. All we know is his vital signs are stable and he doesn't appear to be hurt."

Godzilla was actually known for taking long naps, Jayne mused. Like for decades or centuries. Just not in obvious places where anybody or anything could easily find him. And he preferred places with sources of energy, like deep-sea thermal vents and such. What was unusual wasn't the length of his nap, but that he was doing it in public.

Someone suddenly turned the sound down on the program. Harris, at his station, glanced over at her.

"Kong's heading in for the night," Harris said, nodding at another screen, on which the Great Ape was making his way back to the cave he had been using for a home. "Looks like another rough one."

Jayne came closer, leaned forward with her hands on the back of Harris's swivel chair, looking at the tracking data.

"That's the furthest he's gone yet," she noticed.

"Maybe he's looking for a date," Harris said, dryly.

"Good luck with that," Lewis chimed in, from across the room where he was lining up a putt on the little green he'd brought down with him. His wavy, graying hair stuck out from beneath a red baseball cap. His putter clicked against the ball. "Hope he's up for some interspecies romance."

Jayne nodded. It had become a sort of running joke about Kong's search for his own kind. Early signs had been hopeful enough. It was clear that there had been more Great—great-

great-great?—Apes in Hollow Earth. But so far, all that evidence was centuries old, or older. The current theory was that Kong's species had gotten into some kind of war with Godzilla and maybe other Titans subservient to Godzilla. It was hard to watch footage of the spectacular fight between Godzilla and Kong in Hong Kong without the feeling that there was some long-standing antipathy between the two Titans, although in the end they had parted on what one could anthropomorphize as "amicable" terms.

Whatever was going on with Kong and Godzilla, it seemed as if the only survivors of Kong's kind had been the ones upstairs on Skull Island. If so, that made Kong the last of his species.

But Hollow Earth was a big place. Most of it was still *terra incognita*. There could be a thousand Kongs down here. They just weren't in the area they had surveyed yet.

Tell that to Kong, she thought. She knew she might be reading in her human feelings, but the big guy looked dejected.

Harris frowned, and tracked his gaze across the screens, as one of the indicators started beeping.

"Hey," he said. "The monitor's showing a pretty substantial sinkhole in sector five."

Jayne frowned. "That's Kong's hunting ground."

But it wasn't that surprising, really. Hollow Earth was—to say the least—tectonically active, and sector five was heavily monitored precisely *because* Kong was there. She focused on the monitor, which was now displaying a graphic representation of the sinkhole. It looked like it had opened down into a much larger cave system. The computer had labeled it an "uncharted" area.

Before she could properly absorb that, the frequency sensor also started putting up a squawk. Lewis stopped golfing and glanced over at the screen.

"Whoa," he murmured. Dragging his putter across the floor, he walked over to man the station. Jayne joined him.

"More electrical anomalies?" Harris asked.

"No, I don't think so, man," Lewis said. "I haven't seen anything like this before."

Jayne studied the wave patterns on the screen. She couldn't make head nor tail of them either. But it strained credulity to think a sinkhole and these weird readings happening at exactly the same time was coincidence.

"Maybe we should tell them topside," Harris said.

"I'll type it up," Jayne said. "This whole place is an anomaly."

Almost back to his cave, Kong was startled as dozens of flying things filled the sky. They seemed frantic, as if something was coming after them. But whatever had scared them, he felt it too. Or maybe he heard it. He wasn't sure. But something was happening, something he didn't understand.

Something had changed. Something big.

FOUR

The indigenous people of the island named it Ichirouganaim, The Red Land with White Teeth. It was born at the juncture of two tectonic plates, the South American and the Caribbean. When two immense forces meet, something has to give, and in this case it was the South American plate, forced to slide beneath the Caribbean. Where the two plates scraped together, an accretion formed and was forced upward until it rose above the waves. It still rises at a rate of about an inch per thousand years.

When Europeans arrived, they didn't care for the native name and renamed the island Barbados, the Bearded Ones. It isn't at all clear why. What is clear — or became clear as humanity began to absorb the presence of the Titans and the Hollow Earth—is that the same forces that pushed the island from the depths also created a vortex, a pathway from the surface of the world to the hollow one beneath.

The vortex isn't unlike a mouth. Maybe the indigenous

peoples knew all along what Monarch has recently "discovered".

—Internal Monarch Memo, *Initial Reports of Stable Vertices*, Dr. Nathan Lind

Hollow Earth Access Point
Monarch Base
Barbados

Dr. Ilene Andrews strode through the Access Point facility, feeling harried. Apparently, that's what came of being in charge, and as she often did, she wondered how that had happened. She loved research. She could do that all day, every day. But dealing with contractors who had *yet* to fully finish a facility that was supposed to be completed months ago, with a fickle public, and with politicians who didn't know a vortex from their own... well, from a hole in the ground—that was enough to make for a bad day. And lately she'd had a lot of days like that.

She knew her assistant Wilcox was struggling to keep up with her pace through the facility and still take notes. But she couldn't slow down for him.

"Tell the Italian military Rome would be flattened if it weren't for Godzilla. They can threaten him all they want: just tell them to find another scapegoat."

"Do you..." Wilcox paused, looking stricken, "...actually want me to say that?"

She frowned at him for a second. *Probably not?*

"Just make me sound calm," she told him. "And reasonable."

He nodded, looked relieved, and hurried off while she continued on to Control.

Hampton, overall director of Monarch, met her as she came in.

"Director Hampton, what's up?"

Hampton had been with Monarch for a long time, but the two of them hadn't met until Hampton was promoted to director. She approved of Hampton. Beneath her casual, sometimes comic demeanor the New Zealander was intensely competent. Furthermore, she knew it. She had nothing to prove. She just did her job.

"Well, Outpost One is still a nightmare," Hampton said. "Apparently they've discovered a new type of beetle that eats electrical cables, so that's fun."

"Great."

"And they sent this over." She held out a sheaf of papers.

"This is from the sensory array?" Ilene asked, studying the centerpiece of the data, a frequency graph with three huge peaks.

"Yeah, they've been picking up some weird spikes. Could be regular interference."

"But it keeps happening."

"Um-huh."

She had discovered time and time again that ignoring anything that *might* be "regular" in Hollow Earth was usually a mistake, if not a qualifier for a Darwin Award.

"We should prep a survey team," she said. "Just to be safe."

"Okay," Hampton said.

Ilene glanced up at the monitor, where Godzilla was still lying in the Roman Colosseum.

"What about Godzilla?" she asked.

"Oh," Hampton said. "Still sleeping. Like a big angry baby."

"Well. Let's hope it stays that way."

Something *burr*ed in her pocket. Her cell phone, set to vibrate. She pulled it out to see who it was. When she saw, her heart sank.

"I have to deal with this," she told Hampton.

Monarch Base Academy
Barbados

Jia wanted to like school. At least, her mom wanted her to like school, and she wanted to please her mom.

But she didn't. It was awful. That made her feel bad, because she knew she *should* like it. It was a better school for her than most, she'd been told.

When she was little, she hadn't really understood how different she was. Of course, she was aware there was a sense called hearing, something she didn't have. She saw the people in her village react to things she wasn't aware of. She knew these things were called sounds. Eventually she came to associate some of them—the loudest ones—with the stirrings she felt through her feet or hands, sometimes her skin or eyelashes. Sounds were a sort of vibration, just a kind she wasn't as sensitive to as others. Once she understood that, it didn't matter that much to her that she couldn't hear. The Iwi, after all, didn't talk with sound, at least not very often. They had other ways of communicating—with their bodies, their faces, their hands. As long as she was looking at someone, she usually knew what they were saying. Sometimes she believed she remembered something else, whispery thoughts and words in her head that didn't come from her. But she had been very young, and like a lot of her early life, that might have been just a dream.

Then came the storm, and the floods, and after that her people were gone. Kong saved her from the rising waters, took care of her. Kong also communicated without speech. Oh, he made sounds that she could feel—some of them rattled all the way into her bones. But that wasn't how they talked. And they understood each other well enough.

Then Mom came to take care of her. Mom couldn't talk to her the way her Iwi family had, or like Kong either, but she could talk with her hands. They learned to speak to each other that way, and later Kong learned to as well. And everything was fine.

But that was before she also learned that there was a very, very big world beyond the island of her birth, with many people very different from the Iwi, from Kong, even from her mother. Most of them could hear, and none of them spoke like the Iwi or Kong. Only a few of them could talk with their hands. That world—that big world—was not friendly to her. It was confusing and unforgiving, and she had been so happy when she and Mom and Kong were all together in the world beneath, with its crazy skies and animals and plants that reminded her of home. She had been really content there, and hoped they would all stay there forever.

But Mom had to leave, to come back up into the big world of people Jia couldn't speak to or understand. And Jia had to come with her.

But Mom loved her, and Mom found her this school, where there were teachers who could talk with their hands. There were students who could, too. And at first, it all seemed great. She had been excited.

But over time, it became clear to her that the greatest difference between her and the people in the big world wasn't that she couldn't hear. That, it turned out, was just a bit of an inconvenience.

The largest difference was literally everything else.

How they dressed, how they thought, what they thought about, the games they played, the things they thought were funny, the food they liked—well, some of the food was okay. Weird, but okay. And she could have probably learned to accept all of that if they could accept *her*. But they didn't. At best they thought she was strange, and at worst some sort of monster. Some of them believed *Kong* was a monster and said so. And they all knew who she was before she even met them. Who her mom was. Some avoided her, some made fun of her. She could read their posts and see their pictures.

She knew some of the things they said, and how they saw her. They thought the Iwi circlet she wore on her head was strange. Fair enough, no-one else wore one, but it marked her as Iwi, and she was willing to be thought a little odd to keep it. But they even made fun of her yellow backpack. She had chosen it because she liked the color, but no one else had a brightly colored backpack. Everyone else had either a mud-colored, black, or dark blue backpack. How could it matter that she had picked one out that made her happy? But it did. Somehow it did.

And she knew how to fix all of it. All she had to do was be like them, leave everything about her that was Iwi behind, forget Kong. Pretend. Smile. Nod. She was already forced to wear the same uniform as them. She could look like they wanted on the outside. She could take off her circlet. She just needed to change the inside.

Sometimes she wanted to. Really wished she could. She wanted to cut herself apart and put herself back together in a different way so she could live here and maybe even be happy.

But she was the last. The last Iwi. If she stopped being Iwi, her people really would be extinct. And if she cut herself apart from Kong, he would truly be alone. And there was no way she was going to do either of those things.

She had liked learning things before, with Mom, with the other scientists on Skull Island. Each new discovery had seemed like a jewel to be collected, thought about, cherished. School was different. She had to sit still for hours, watching the teacher (or more usually, a signing assistant) tell her what she was supposed to know. Not what she *wanted* to know, which was a lot, but what *they* wanted her to know, which was not at all the same thing.

She trailed her way through the buildings, trying not to make eye contact. From an Iwi point of view, that was rude; it suggested she didn't want to interact with anyone—which was in fact the case. Of course, none of them understood that. None of them knew anything about her people.

She took her seat in Ms. Cadogan's room, near the back, as she usually did. Samah, one of the other students, tried to catch her attention, but Jia pretended she hadn't seen. She and Samah had been friends, sort of, or at least she thought they had been. She had even confided in the other girl. That was before she realized that Samah was using everything Jia told her to make fun of her behind her back—to amuse her real friends.

She turned her head away from Samah and instead looked over at the projects from last week, shadow boxes they had all made of prehistoric civilizations. Her assignment had been Cahokia, a city in North America built centuries before the arrival of the European colonizers. Her shadow box showed a flat-topped pyramid made from what was supposed to be dirt. She had used cardboard and glued sand to it, then made little human figures of wire and clay. It was okay, but she thought some of the others were way better.

A sheet of paper appeared on her desk. She looked up and realized Ms. Cadogan was passing them out.

Right. They had a test today. Pre-algebra. Math with letters that were supposed to be numbers. Angles, and surface area, and volumes of weird shapes. Not that hard, but not her favorite. She hadn't managed to study for it.

Ms. Cadogan's mouth was moving. Jia glanced to the front of the class, where Ms. Gross, the sign interpreter, was repeating whatever Ms. Cadogan was saying.

...No cheating, she was signing. *Okay? Let's make sure we circle the answers completely. Really, really try and make sure you have enough time...*

Jia realized her eyes had closed. She shook herself and looked back down at the test.

If thirty-five percent of a class are boys, and twenty percent of boys play football, what percentage of the class plays football?

Ugh.

An immense vibration suddenly swept through the room, almost like when Kong roared, but it wasn't that. It was something she had never felt before. She looked around the room, expecting to see everyone reacting, but none of them seemed to notice. That was weird, because in her experience a vibration that strong should have made a sound. A loud one.

But no one even looked up.

They didn't look up when the feathery white stuff started drifting down either, like ashes from a huge fire or fuzzy windborne flower seeds. But where were they falling from? The ceiling? The air was filled with them, and everyone just kept taking their tests. Alarmed, she looked around. Ashes were falling in the shadow boxes, too, and one of them caught her attention, a diorama of the three Egyptian pyramids, right next to a shadow box with the stepped pyramid of Teotihuacan. But it seemed significant, somehow, that the Egyptian pyramids were arranged as three, the one in the middle a little bigger.

And wait—there was something on the pyramid. It looked like a little model of Kong. Was that a leafwing, hanging by a thread from the top? Those hadn't been there before. Was someone making fun of her again?

Her gaze tracked across the digital clock on the wall. As soon as she saw it, the red numerals began to blur and squiggle, re-forming into a sort of graph with three bell-shaped peaks.

Then she felt the vibration again, stronger this time, and it was like she wasn't in the room at all—she was somewhere else. Blurry figures appeared, people, but she couldn't see their faces. She knew they were important, though. That they were trying to tell her something. Something urgent. They needed help. *Her* help.

Someone shook her arm. She looked up and saw Ms. Cadogan staring down at her. At the same time, Jia realized she had her pencil, not held with her fingers for writing, but gripped in her fist, and she was scribbling furiously with it. Everyone in the class was looking at her, as if she had done something wrong.

Ms. Cadogan held up her hands and began to sign.
Jia! What did you do?

Then the teacher reached down for her test paper, and Jia understood. The test was covered with pencil scribbles, three peaks, like she had seen on the clock.

So was the desk. But she didn't remember doing it. When had she done it? She thought she might have fallen asleep, but only for a second or two. It didn't make sense.

But clearly she was in trouble.

Ilene met Ms. Cadogan outside Jia's classroom. She could see Jia inside, with spray bottle and rag, cleaning a desk. The teacher had been brief on the phone, but she'd gathered that Jia had been scribbling on it, which was strange. Jia liked to draw, sure, but drawing on something that wasn't hers? It seemed out of character. Or maybe she just liked to think so. Sometimes she thought she didn't know her daughter anymore.

She pulled her gaze from Jia and focused on Ms. Cadogan.

"Jia's very intelligent," the teacher was saying. "The problem is, she's not engaged. Her grades are slipping, she's not interacting with any of her friends. She's distracted. Moody. Isolated. These problems aren't going away, Miss Andrews. If anything, they're getting worse."

Ms. Cadogan handed her two sheets of paper. They looked like a quiz of some sort, but they were covered in pencil scribbles of dark, narrow chevrons. Spear heads? There was something familiar about them.

"What's this?" she asked.

"Well, it's not pre-algebra," the teacher said. Ilene found the sarcasm irritating, but she tried to keep her cool.

"Okay, I'm sorry, it's just… she's just still adjusting to our world."

"I understand that," Cadogan said, "but we have a number of students who are culturally displaced, and they—"

"Sure, but she's not culturally displaced," Ilene corrected. "She *is* her culture. She's the last living member of the Iwi tribe."

That struck home, and Cadogan's demeanor softened.

"We're just trying to reach her."

Ilene looked back through the window in the classroom door, where Jia was finishing her task. She sighed.

"I know," she said. "Join the club."

Ilene decided not to pull Jia for the day. Her daughter had already missed too much school, and there was less than an hour left, anyway. Instead she took a walk along the shore, thinking.

The problem with being good at your job in an organization like Monarch—like most organizations, actually—was that if you were *too* good at it, you ran the risk of being moved out of it into administration, the logic being that if you were competent at field work you would be good at running things, too. In her case, of course, there had been more at play than that. Her position as the leading authority on Kong had landed her on the national media stage, and unlike some earlier members of Monarch leadership, she didn't seem likely to try and end the world. The public not only wasn't terrified of her, they actually liked her.

So, yes, she was good at what she did, but there was a PR element to her selection that she both understood and accepted. Even with all of that, she could have still said no when she had been tapped for director of the Kong Observation Project. On many levels she'd wanted to. She hadn't been sure she was cut out for it, and she still wasn't. But her personal inclinations hadn't been the only factor to consider. There had also been Jia.

Her daughter's childhood had been, to say the least, highly unstable. Not just emotionally, but physically. She had been in more mortal danger by the time she was eleven than Ilene had faced in her entire life, and her life had been quite adventurous.

Hollow Earth was amazing, and it was ludicrously unsafe even with a Titan like Kong as your bodyguard. There weren't many humans down there to start with, and no other children at all. Still, at first it had seemed to work, or she fooled herself into thinking so.

The first wart-dog attack had changed all of that. She and a team had been following Kong when they ran into the pack, and she'd made the mistake of letting Jia come along. The predators had sized up Kong and decided the little things following him were a better bet for dinner. Monarch lost two people, she lost two friends, and she and Jia were also very nearly killed. If Kong hadn't looked back and seen what was happening, they *would* have died. The thought of her daughter dying was intolerable; the thought of her own death was only slightly better. If she was gone, who would take care of Jia? What would happen to her?

So she took the job as director. She put Jia in a school—a good school. She'd hoped for the best.

This wasn't the best, but it was a damned sight better than being torn to bits by wart-dogs.

When she got back to the school, kids were streaming away from it on their bikes and on foot. Most of them lived in Monarch housing, so they didn't have far to go. Jia would normally walk, too, but Ilene had driven here, and left instructions for Jia to meet her at the car. The girl was there, staring at the pad that streamed—via several relays—the surveillance of Kong from Hollow Earth. Jia spent a lot of time watching the Titan, which was understandable, but Ilene was beginning to fear that it was getting in the way of other things.

Jia didn't look up when she arrived. Ilene took hold of the pad and gently but firmly pulled it from her grasp.

What's up? she signed.

Nothing, the girl replied. *I'm worried about Kong.*

Ilene nodded a little, then unfolded the test papers Ms. Cadogan had given her.

Why did you draw this?

Jia took the papers, glanced at them and looked away. She shrugged in a way that meant *I don't know.*

Can we go? the girl signed. She looked away and started to get in the car. Ilene put her hand on her shoulder to stop her.

Look at me! she demanded.

Jia did look at her then. *I don't belong here!* she said. *I don't belong anywhere.* Jia's pain and confusion was as clear as any sign.

You belong with me, Ilene signed. *And I belong with you.*

Jia was still for a moment, then nodded almost imperceptibly.

"C'mon," Ilene said, and they got in the car.

When they got back to their apartment in the Monarch crew residence, Jia went to her room. Ilene let her have her space. Everybody needed alone time, and Jia more than most. She re-emerged a little later to eat a light supper of leftover take-out. Ilene sat with her, poking at her own food.

Anything else happen today? she attempted.

Jia lifted her shoulders and dropped them.

Probably, she signed back.

How's Wyn? she asked. Wyn was the child of one of the Monarch engineers briefly stationed on Skull Island. Wyn and their father hadn't lived on the island—they had been at the nearby facility in Kiribati. Wyn had been over a few times.

Wyn has a sugar, Jia replied. *I haven't seen them lately.*

Sugar?

Like a best friend. That they kiss.

"Oh," Ilene said. Thirteen. Right. *What about Samah?*

Jia frowned. *I'm finished eating. May I go to my room?*

Ilene nodded and watched her leave.

She had a thousand things that called for her attention, but none of them seemed that important at the moment. She took Jia's drawings out and looked at them again, and once more they seemed somehow familiar. She started pulling out her books and notes. Maybe it was Iwi iconography, or something else Jia's mind had dredged up from her oldest memories. It could be the silhouette of a mountain range, or... she didn't know. But something told her it was important.

While she went through the literature she had handy—a lot of which she had written—she put on a documentary about Skull Island. There was a fair bit of footage of Iwi life, craft, and culture. Toward the end it featured scenes of Jia when she was much younger, when Kong had been watching over her—and later, when she had come into Ilene's care. It was only a few years ago, but it already seemed like decades. Jia was so little, and she realized that when she closed her eyes, that's how she still saw her. But she was growing up, fast, wasn't she? She had a friend her age who already had a "sugar".

A faint sound caught her attention. Jia was there in the shorts and t-shirt she liked to wear to bed. She was staring at the screen, at the moving images of her and Kong.

Are you ready for bed? she signed.

Jia nodded. She switched her regard to the monitor feed, showing Kong asleep in his cave.

He's lonely, she signed.

I know, honey. She stood up and opened her arms. She was afraid Jia would ignore it, but the girl stepped in for a hug.

Good night, Mom.

Good night.

Jia went back to her room. Ilene heard the door close. Then she nodded and went back to work.

66

FIVE

(On the subject of the gods defeating the Titans)
Now the others among the first ranks roused the keen
fight, Kottos, Briareus, and Gyes insatiable in war, who
truly were hurling from sturdy hands three hundred rocks
close upon each other, and they had overshadowed the
Titans with missiles, sent them beneath the broad-
wayed earth, and bound them in painful bonds, having
conquered them with their hands, over-haughty though
they were, as far beneath under earth as the sky is from the
earth, for equal is the space from earth to murky Tartaros.

—Works and Days, Hesiod

Monarch Outpost One
Kong Observation Unit
Hollow Earth

The sunrise crystals were dimming, becoming sunset crystals, and night began to settle on the Hollow Earth. How exactly they worked, and why the crystals mimicked the night and day cycle of the surface world—or why they existed at all—was still one of the big unknowns of the Hollow Earth, although it was generally thought to have something to do with the form of energy that manifested down here. Life would be perfectly capable of existing with no night—or, for that matter, no day.

Harris was glad for it though. To have an evening, to have the light turn slowly down, to see the mountains in the sky shadowed and gradually vanish. There were no stars, of course, and no moon, but sometimes there were lights in the sky, courtesy of at least half a dozen different bioluminescent flying species, some of which —although very pretty—would gobble a person down without the slightest pause. But that was the Hollow Earth. Beautiful and deadly. Natural selection turned up to eleven. He didn't go out at night.

But he liked to watch it on the monitors and through the windows.

A scan of the various screens and instruments showed nothing deadly on their perimeter, which was good. Kong was still sulking, but at least he'd found something to eat. Harris wasn't sure what it was; he hadn't seen the kill, but the big ape was back on his perch, and he had the leg of something in his hand. He bit into it and immediately grimaced, then grunted in pain and threw the joint-of-monster away.

"What's the matter, big boy?" he wondered. "You have a toothache?"

As if in response, Kong brought his hand up to his open mouth and gingerly touched one of his canines. Sure enough, even in the dim light, Harris could see it was broken.

"Yeah, that's no fun," Harris said. "I'll make a note for

the people up top. Maybe the doc can do something for you."

Kong hunched against the cliff, looking miserable.

As he typed up the note about the tooth, Harris put some music on: one of the streaming stations he liked, mostly fifties doo-wop bands. Fittingly, the first song was the Five Satins' "In the Still of the Night."

He finished the note and decided maybe he should isolate a capture from the video showing the injury. The Satins finished, and now it was the Moonglows, singing "Blue Velvet."

He could find the still in a minute. It was night in Barbados, too. Even if they decided Kong's tooth needed attention, it would be days before they prepped a mission and came down. Probably they wouldn't bother. Kong had survived much worse than a cracked canine in his time.

He sat back in his chair. Maybe he would close his eyes, just for a second.

He started awake, not sure where he was or what was happening. The streaming channel was still on, but it was a different song. The frequency monitor was going nuts, and so was the seismograph.

"What the hell?" He sat up, looked at the monitors. Kong's were still on, but most of the others were displaying a *no signal* message. It only took him a second to realize that those were the perimeter monitors. All of them.

"Oh, no," he murmured, standing up.

Something huge moved at the window.

"Jayne!" he shouted. "Lewis!"

Then something slammed into the bunker so hard the whole thing shifted. Harris lost his footing and fell. He was trying to get up when it happened again. This time, half the roof was gone.

* * *

Monarch Crew Residence
Barbados

A shuddering woke Jia; she sat up, her heart pounding. The trembling continued, all around her.

She wasn't in her bed. She was on a spit of rock, surrounded by a red glow, the scent of burning in her nose and throat, ashes like those she had seen in her classroom drifting everywhere. Fire burned in every direction; she couldn't see much more than that. At least at first. But then the fire seemed to come together, solidify, until she was again staring at three pyramids, narrow at the base, tall and very pointed. She had no name for them, but it felt like she had seen them before—not once or twice, but many times.

The stone and air quivered more sharply, like something was making a *big* sound. And then she *heard* it. Or she thought she did. It wasn't in her ears, not on her skin or in her bones—it was in her head, and it wasn't like anything she had ever felt before. It was what she imagined sound might be like. Trembling, she felt her gaze drawn up, where a pair of ice-blue eyes peered from the flaming air, a terrible stare full of unfathomable malice and rage. Around the eyes, a face began to form, a face something like Kong's when Kong was at his worst, his angriest. But there were differences, too. This monster was not her friend. It was someone very, very awful. He opened his fanged mouth, and everything shook harder…

She woke up. Again. Only this time she was in her own bed. Her heart was hammering, the terror clung to her. Was she really awake this time? Was there any waking from this nightmare? She wasn't safe. She felt it to her bones.

No one was safe.

* * *

Ilene turned off the documentary and put down the paper she'd been reading. She didn't have any idea what she was looking for; nothing rang any bells.

Maybe she was wrong. She was fixating on a data-driven solution to a problem that had nothing to do with data. She was looking in the wrong place. She had to face the fact that Jia's problems might not stem from her background or history, but from her current situation. From the person trying to parent her who maybe didn't know what she was doing.

She sighed and went to get a bottle of wine, pulled the cork, and placed it on the table. She picked up the scribbled-on test again, looking at it from different angles.

She was so *sure* she had seen it before.

Wait. She wasn't crazy. She *had*

But not years ago. This morning.

She started frantically digging through the pile of papers, books, and photographs on the coffee table. *Where was it? There!*

She pulled up the printout of the frequency graphs Hampton had handed her earlier, the ones recorded in Hollow Earth. She laid the test next to it.

The sharp peaks clustered together. They were the same.

Whatever the instruments at the Kong Monitoring Station were picking up, Jia was somehow also receiving it. And no, she knew that shouldn't make sense. But it also made no sense that it was a coincidence. That she had no explanation for what was happening made not the slightest difference to the fact that it *was* happening.

Her thoughts were interrupted by a loud clatter from Jia's room.

Her daughter's bed was empty and the lamp knocked over.

For a terrifying beat of the heart, Ilene feared the girl was gone. That she'd been taken or had run away. But then her gaze rested on the tent of white linen she and Jia had rigged, suspended from a wire frame attached to the ceiling. The string lights Jia had put up inside of it were on. She called it her "cave" in ASL, which was a hole formed from both hands, palms and fingertips touching. But she added another sign from her childhood, one that she used to mean a hiding place. Besides the lights, there were a dozen or so throw pillows. Every time they went someplace that sold them, there was always a negotiation about getting another one. Jia used it to study in and when she wanted to be alone. Now she sat at the back, clutching the very old doll she had made of Kong to her chest, wide-eyed and shaking.

Ilene bent down and entered the tent. She sat by Jia. Waiting for her to communicate.

I'm scared there's something wrong with me, Jia finally said.

Ilene shook her head. *There's nothing wrong with you. You're perfect.*

I feel like I'm going crazy.

Ilene nodded and rocked her head. *That's called being a teenager*, she said. But she knew it was more than that.

Jia leaned toward her, and Ilene gathered the girl in, wishing she had something better to say. Something to fix it. Jia began quietly sobbing against her chest.

"We're gonna figure this out," she whispered.

SIX

*"I'm saying, why wait until Godzilla wakes up? Why not
take proactive measures while we can?"*
*"Despite the destruction he may cause, some would say
Godzilla is a hero."*
*"Those people are idiots. We are talking about the most
dangerous creature that ever lived."*

—Parker Lamar, political pundit, in an
interview on *America This Morning*

Titan Truth podcast recording studio
Miami

Bernie settled himself and looked over his notes—suggestions,
really, for the most part. Or a shopping list. Some of the trolls
accused him of rambling. It wasn't rambling. Unless Faulkner
was "rambling" when he wrote *The Sound and the Fury*. No,
it was stream-of-consciousness. Truth was often spontaneous.

It emerged from connections you maybe hadn't even made until you started talking.

Wait, he thought, *I should write that down. That's a good point.*

He scrawled in his notes, then glanced around to see if everything was ready. Recording equipment, check. Sound levels adjusted. Kong action figure, dangling from the swinging desk lamp, check.

He glanced over at his wall of photographs, at the one of Sara and him. Happy. Before.

"For you," he said, softly. "Always for you."

He swallowed the lump in his throat, turned on the microphone, and leaned in a little.

"Where will you be when the next Titan attacks?" he wondered, in his most serious podcast voice, still looking at Sara's smiling face. "How will you protect the things and people that mean the most to you?"

He paused, to let it sink in. To let his listeners think about it for a second.

Then he took it up a few beats. "Today's podcast is brought to you by Gargantua Insurance, the *only* insurance company that offers Titan protection for your home and personal belongings. Because Godzilla may not care about your hopes and dreams, but Gargantua does!" He drummed on the desk with his hands for emphasis. "Okay, you Titan Truthers! All right folks, on today's show—and I tell you, we have a lot to talk about—"

Someone knocked on his door. Probably a neighbor. Who should flippin' well know better.

"Recording in progress!" he shouted. "Go away!" He paused an instant, then turned back to the microphone. "Uh, yes, I just wanna let everyone know that there *is* no—"

The knock came again, louder, more urgent.

He needed a sign, he thought, not for the first time. A *recording-in-progress* sign. He kept thinking that, but when he was done recording, he forgot. But of course, that would tip them off, wouldn't it? They might make the connection, figure out who he was. And really, who just came up and *knocked* on your door like this? It wasn't okay.

He bolted out of his chair. "Unbelievable!" he shouted. He bent over and pushed the mail slot open.

"What?"

He saw a woman stoop and look though the slot. Short hair. She looked kind of familiar.

"Hi, uh, Bernie," she said, "Ilene Andrews. We met in Hong Kong."

Holy... it *was* her.

"Oh," he said. "Oh yeah. Yeah, yeah yeah yeah."

He straightened up and began sliding and unlatching the numerous inside locks on the door. "Hong Kong! That was so long ago, I... uh..." He swung the door open.

"My hair was longer," Andrews said.

"Yeah, cut your hair," he said. "Highlights too. It's nice." Inwardly he winced. Did he really just say that?

Down the hall, through a window, flame flared up from a wok in a neighbor's kitchen. He smelled rapeseed oil, ginger and chili pepper.

It made Andrew flinch. Sure. She probably had Titan PTSD, given everything she had been through.

"I..." Andrews paused. "I was wondering if I could get your help with something."

He blinked, not certain he'd heard her right. He'd figured he was in trouble for something.

"Me?"

She nodded. He recalibrated. If she wanted something from him, there might be an opportunity here. If he didn't blow it.

"Ah… sure. Sure, of course, yeah. Come on in, Doctor… Doctor Andrews. Yeah." He opened the door wide enough for her to enter. "Just go straight down that hall, there, to the left."

Shut up, Bernie, he thought. *You sound like a fanboy.*

Bernie's apartment-workspace in Pensacola had been small: a big closet really. His place here in Miami was much bigger. After all, he had sponsors now. A few. But it was every bit as cluttered as his old place. Books, papers, and magazines were stacked everywhere, up to the ceiling in places. He had several tables, all mostly covered. His studio sprawled into his living space, which itself was mostly a library and curio collection. Some distant part of him—the part raised by a house-proud mother—felt faintly embarrassed by the clutter, but it was just a reflex, nothing he felt very deeply. Everything in his place was a treasure to him, and he didn't much care what other people thought about it. He almost never had anyone over.

But Dr. Andrews was… important. They had met, sure. But if you had asked him yesterday if she remembered him, he wouldn't have been sure that she did.

Obviously she did, though, and she had come to him. And the place was a mess. Probably not what she was used to. Probably wouldn't set her at ease.

She followed his directions while he closed the door, set the chains and drew all of the bolts. He found her in his "war room," studying the big board, the It's All Connected Board, where he'd pinned maps, photographs, newspaper and magazine articles, and sundry items, and networked them with string. He thought she looked a little impressed, which she should. It represented the ongoing thrust of his life's work.

Confidence, man. Be confident. He might have made a bad initial impression. Overeager. Nobody responded well to that.

"I guess I shouldn't be surprised that you're here, right?" he said. "I am the world's foremost Titan expert, after all. Ah, but look, forgive me for how the apartment looks right now, I'm just not used to having visitors cause my address isn't on file for just anybody, so you know…" He grabbed the back of a chair and pushed it up on its front two legs, dumping the books and papers on it onto the floor, simultaneously wondering exactly how she had found him. He wasn't all that surprised, but he was very concerned.

But damned if he was going to ask.

"Have a seat," he said, nodding at the now-empty chair. "What can I help you with? You know, mi casa es su home." He plopped down in another chair and propped his elbows on the table.

Andrews didn't sit. She had a briefcase with her; she pulled out some papers and laid them in front of him. One looked like a printout of some sort of waveforms. The other appeared kind of similar, but had clearly been done by hand, with a pencil.

"Okay," she said. "So, the sequence on the right, this is a signal that's been interfering with our equipment in Hollow Earth."

"Okay." He squinted. Was the pencil drawing over a middle school math test? It sort of looked like it.

"And, uh," Andrews continued, "these are drawings by my daughter, Jia, and—you're going to think that I'm completely insane—"

But he saw it. "No," he said. "The patterns are the same in the middle section."

"Yes," she said. "Exactly."

She was relieved, he could tell. She had shown these to

someone else, and they thought she was seeing things. Making a connection that wasn't there. Like she was crazy.

Welcome to my world, Doctor Andrews.

Andrews let out a long breath and finally sat down in the chair he had cleared for her.

"Look," she said. "Our analysts don't know what to make of this. They're talking in circles. They're saying 'radio interference,' coincidence—but I know that you think outside of the box. I didn't know who else to turn to."

"And they sent you because?"

"No one sent me. I came here—"

But it had been building. For years, really. On one level he knew he should just keep listening to her, but it was actually like she didn't understand what they had done to him. Were still doing to him.

"Well, that's what's ironic, you know," Bernie told her, trying to keep his tone reasonable but aware that he was failing. Screw it. He was angry. "Monarch wouldn't confirm my *crucial* part in taking down Mechagodzilla. It's cost me thousands—" *Okay. Truth.* "—*hundreds* of subscribers on my blog. And the trolls online? They question every single thing that I put up, especially this one troll—this one troll, GhidoraStan64, you ever heard of him?"

Andrews shook her head. "No, I don't think I have."

"Great," Bernie said. "Because he's a trashbag, okay? Point is, I'm more qualified than half the people you have working over there. I have a PhD in physics. I have a Masters in engineering—"

"Do you really?" she asked, looking really skeptical.

Back up. Stay in this.

"Maybe not," he allowed, "um, from what you would consider a traditional university. But still I *have* them, you know.

Never mind the fact that I knew, *I* knew, *me*, what Godzilla was going to do before anyone at Monarch said anything."

"Which is why I am here, Bernie," Andrews snapped, cutting him off. "I am *here*. Okay? Can you help me or not?"

He took a breath. This seemed like the moment. This was it.

"That depends," he said. "Are you the new boss down at the MHES?"

"The what?"

"The Monarch Hollow Earth Station," he said. "The MHES, the Mess."

"Yeah, no one calls it that," she said. "I run the Kong Research Division, but technically Director Hampton is in charge of general operations."

"Huh," mused Bernie. "But Director Hampton doesn't have a kid who can talk to Kong." He sat back and twirled in his chair a few times.

Until she got it.

"You want to go to Hollow Earth," Andrews said.

"I'm so glad I didn't have to say that," he said. "I thought you were never gonna ask me."

"No, I am not asking," she replied, putting her hand up. But he pushed on over her.

"I've been needing proof. It would help me with my bona fides for my blog, and I knew that you would be the person to help me do that."

"Okay, well if this happens, and that is a big if, then Monarch would need, you know, whatever you guys call it, final cut on..."

Of course, she was going there. But she needed him, right?

"No, no, no, no. Final cut? You know that would destroy my journalistic integrity. No really good true documentarian would..."

She had her phone out, staring at it. Then she jumped up and started walking off. What was happening? She was leaving. He had pushed too far.

"I could make you a producer," he said. "Final cut. Wait, wait, wait!"

She spun around to face him. "Something is happening to my daughter, and I have no idea how to fix it. You work out what's going on and I'll give you anything you want, okay? This is a promise."

"Well, *anything* is a lot, but that's very generous, very generous of you—"

"But we have to go right now."

"What?"

"Godzilla is on the move again," she said. "Your call. In or out."

Then she was going.

Is this happening?

Yes. In, not out, okay? It had to be in.

He grabbed his go bag. He always had essential stuff in there in case he had to run. From a Titan, or the CIA, or... whatever.

"Wait, Doctor Andrews. Wait!"

He ran after her.

Monarch Control
Barbados

"Yes, Ambassador Paoletti," Hampton said, staring at the screen. "I'm aware Godzilla is waking up. We make every effort to keep informed here at Monarch. It is sort of our job."

The ambassador's image was inset onto a larger view of the Roman Colosseum, where Godzilla was visibly stirring. A nearby screen showed the Titan's vitals spiking. His nap was done, there could be no doubt of that.

"Are you—are you being sarcastic?" the ambassador asked. His salt-and-pepper eyebrows arched almost comically.

"No," Hampton said. "I am not. I'm sorry if you thought so. I just meant to say that we're on top of the situation."

As she spoke, Godzilla rose to his feet and took a step to clear the walls of the ancient building. She winced as he nicked the top of it, shattering the top of the ancient wall.

The ambassador's face paled. "If you're on top of it, I assume you just saw that."

"Er... Yes," she said. "It... um... doesn't look so bad."

"Well, it looks very bad from where I stand," the ambassador sputtered.

"Uh-huh," she said. Godzilla's clawed foot shattered part of the street, and then he stepped in the River Tiber. He took a step or two, cutting right through a bridge.

"That was the Ponte Cestio," Paoletti wailed. "That, too, is just a scratch, I suppose?"

"What exactly are you asking me to do, Ambassador Paoletti?" Hampton wanted to know.

He straightened his tie, sighed. "My government wants to call in an airstrike," he said.

"An airstrike," she repeated. "On Rome."

"Yes, I know it's a stupid idea," he snapped. "I'm asking you for something better. Something I can tell them. I know you have people here."

"Sure, an observation team. We've been trying to predict which way he would leave when he did, but that's like trying to predict where a hurricane will go before it forms. No, worse, because hurricanes follow rules of physics. What we know is, he's done there. He came there to kill Scylla, he did it, he took a nap, and now he's leaving. We don't know where he's going, but he's usually pretty direct in his way."

Paoletti didn't say anything. Was he okay? Was he in shock?

"Hey, snap out of it," she said. "You're not helpless. Tell your boss Godzilla is leaving Rome. He's just walking, he's not on any sort of rampage. He's not going to turn circles and hunt up the monuments. But he's big. He's going to break a few things. He doesn't mean to. But if you shoot at him, that will be a whole different story. He'll trash the city. And you won't hurt him anyway! We know this from experience. Just tell your guys to clear a path. A *wide* path. We'll send an escort—he usually tolerates those—and we can help minimize collateral damage. It will all be over soon. Okay?"

Paoletti nodded weakly. "Okay," he said.

His image vanished.

"Now," she muttered, watching Godzilla continue to wade through Rome. "Don't make a liar out of me."

SEVEN

There are tales among the indigenous people of Borneo of a great dragon that once lived on the summit of Mount Kinabalu, the tallest mountain of that island, and indeed in Southeast Asia. It was said that the dragon had a bright, glowing pearl that it played with. The people loved to watch it. Inevitably someone chose to steal the pearl, thus earning forever the wrath of the dragon. Who stole the pearl and why changes in each version of the story. Some blame a Chinese prince who took it far away—but this is probably a very recent revision to a very old story.

If you climb Mount Kinabalu, you will find the summit to be bare rock, scraped and gouged by the massive glacier that once weighed upon it. Mount Kinabalu is not in Greenland or Siberia. It sits within a few degrees of the equator. And yet it was glaciated at about 1.4 million years ago and again about a hundred thousand years ago, and remained so until around ten thousand years ago. It's easy to imagine the natives of Borneo looking up at the only ice cap in their experience and imagining it was a giant pearl or some other jewel.

There is another story from halfway around the world about a similar dragon and a similar shiny jewel that belonged to it. It too, was stolen, by an evil god or monster, who used it to inflict pain on the dragon, and make it do his bidding.

—Internal Monarch document, *Speculations on a Hypothetical Titan*, Maartens, Chen, and Omar

Monarch Crew Residence
Barbados

Despite what her mother had told her, Jia still worried she was losing her mind. She might be missing one of the senses that most people took for granted, but she had never really felt that lack, never felt sorry for herself that she couldn't hear. She did well enough without that sense.

Here, in her mother's world, she had encountered any number of well-meaning people who thought that since she had "lost" her hearing, her other senses must be "heightened" to compensate. She didn't know about all of that—it seemed like their fancy way of feeling sorry for her. What she did know was that to survive on Skull Island, you had to pay very close attention to any senses you possessed. Plenty of people who could hear perfectly well had died there because they weren't really listening. You had to let the world in through your eyes, your skin, your nose, your tongue. She had learned that at a very young age. She had always, even in her earliest memories, felt in *control* of her senses. When her sight, smell, or tactile senses told her something, she paid attention. She figured out what it meant. And she survived. When they had been on the ship, with Kong all chained up, she had known Godzilla was coming before anyone else. She had felt the Titan's vibrations through the hull. It wasn't that Mom or any of the others couldn't feel those vibrations the way she could, it was that they didn't pay attention the way she did.

Or so she had always thought. But thinking back, the ship had had machines that could feel vibrations and see things at a great distance—but it hadn't. And maybe... maybe something had told her Godzilla might be coming *before* she thought to put her fingers to the metal hull of the ship.

Maybe. All she knew was that now she didn't feel in control at all, and she didn't like it. Feelings and images were *forcing* themselves into her head without her permission. Her body was changing too, also out of her control. Mom said it was because she was a teenager, and maybe she was right about some of it. But maybe there really were things Mom could not feel, had never felt. Things she couldn't understand.

She thought back to the things she had seen the day before. They hadn't been dreams, or at least not the usual sort of dreams. When she was smaller, she used to think that sometimes she dreamed about Kong—no, the same as Kong. Like she could see his dreams and be in them. And even further back, with her people, there had been something about that, about the dreams we dream together. But now, thinking back to that time, she wasn't sure what was real, what she had imagined, and what she had rationalized. Mom's people did a lot of "rationalizing." Telling themselves and each other that something they felt was true really wasn't. And she had begun doing it, too, hadn't she?

She got a drawing pad and some colored pencils. She had

drawn the weird shapes without even knowing she did it, and Mom thought they meant something. That was why she was gone now, again, to ask someone about it. She had promised she wouldn't be away long, this time, and that she wasn't going to Hollow Earth. She would be back for dinner.

But maybe, Jia thought, she could do something while she waited. Maybe she would draw what she had seen last night, in her room. It had scared her, but sometimes things were less scary when you understood them. When you knew what they were.

Trying not to think too much about it, she started putting color to the paper. She finished one drawing, frowned at it, set it aside, and started another. There was something she wasn't getting right.

She was working on a third drawing when she felt it, pulsing through her, as if she was up to her neck in a pool of water something had jumped into, and the ripples were lapping against her.

And she *knew*. Something was happening. She put her pencil down and looked up to her old Kong totem, the one she'd brought with her from Skull Island. The one she had clutched for comfort last night.

Kong.

She jumped up out of bed, slipped on her shoes, and ran toward where Mom worked.

Hollow Earth Access Point
Monarch Base
Barbados

Ilene arrived back at the Barbados launch site to find everything in a state of chaos. She handed Bernie off to an aide with orders to put him in guest accommodations—where he hopefully couldn't do much harm—while trying to catch up with developments on her phone and ignoring incoming calls.

At a certain point she couldn't ignore them anymore. Or at least not one of them. She took it as she made her way through the facility.

"Okay, listen to me," she told the senator, after enduring his opening tirade. "If Godzilla's on the move he senses a threat coming. We don't know what it is."

"And you're not concerned?"

"Of course I'm concerned, Senator. That's why we're monitoring the situation."

"Well, let me tell you, my constituents—"

Hampton was banging on the glass wall of the office. "We've got a problem!" she shouted, causing Ilene to miss the senator's next few words. It didn't matter. She could guess the gist.

"And I am telling you, Senator, that Kong doesn't leave Hollow Earth. Which is why Godzilla has no reason to retalia—"

Something moved on one of the monitors watching the Hollow Earth launch site. Something big. A hand? An arm?

Kong's arm, reaching out of the bay. Perfect.

"I have to go," she said. She didn't wait for the senator's response.

"What's he doing up here?" Ilene asked Hampton as they ran down the metal stairs toward the launch area.

"No idea," Hampton replied.

"Does Godzilla know?"

"Not that we can tell."

"It's only a matter of time," Ilene said.

"What happens if Godzilla starts heading this way?"

"Then we all run like hell."

But maybe Godzilla already knew. Maybe that was why he'd cut his nap short. The timing didn't quite line up, though, since Kong was just arriving. Could Godzilla tell if Kong entered a vortex? But there was another, probably worse possibility. Maybe Kong and Godzilla were both reacting to an even greater threat.

Ilene reached the platform overlooking the launch area, a semicircular bay circumferenced by electric towers. The actual vortex was below the water. Kong was already fully out, pulling himself onto the land.

Jia was there, watching him, which was... strange. How could she have possibly known this was happening? And even if she did, how was she already here? It was a twenty-minute walk from their apartment.

Maybe Jia had been here all day, waiting for her to get back from Miami. She was a familiar sight around the installation. Most everyone here had a tendency to let her wander at will. Not necessarily a good thing, and totally Ilene's fault.

Kong turned around and reclined against the hillside, groaning, draping one arm across his chest.

Jia saw her.

He's hurt, the girl said.

Ilene could see that, but she didn't see how he was hurt. There were no obvious, recent wounds. If he'd been injured, she should have gotten a report from Jayne. Of course, she'd been in Miami, and then the Godzilla thing had happened, so maybe she'd just missed it.

Kong grimaced and opened his mouth. Something looked odd, but it took a second or two to figure out what.

He'd broken a tooth. Was that what this was all about? Were they all about to die in another dust-up between Kong and Godzilla because the big fellow needed a dentist?

She sighed. They didn't have a Titan dentist around, but they did have… someone. He would have to do.

The Maximum Utility Load Elevator, or more affectionately the M.U.L.E, was part hovercraft, part flying industrial transport, and part crane. It was the same bright yellow as a bulldozer, which Trapper loved, because as a kid he'd been partial to bulldozers. He clung to a ladder on the inside of the cargo bay, with nothing but air between him and quite a long drop. Kong was right where Ilene had said he would be, sprawled belly-up on the shore. He hadn't really expected the big ape to move around, given the amount of tranquilizer he'd prescribed.

Passing over the overlook, he saw Ilene and her daughter, Jia, watching the M.U.L.E arrive.

"The good news is," he said, "it's just an infected tooth." He hoped that was true. It was what his remote drone-assisted examination had turned up. If he was wrong, he had already cost the taxpayers… well, a lot of money. He didn't really keep track of the details. "Luckily," he went on, "you have come to the best doctor in town. Let's have some tunes."

He hit play on his ancient boombox and began mouthing the lyrics into the big hook in his hand as the pilot got them into position.

I gotcha…

"Tranqs at a hundred percent. Vitals are stable. Trapper, you are clear to swap the damaged tooth with the replacement."

Sure. It wouldn't do to be in Kong's mouth when he woke up, would it? So he'd better hurry. He swung over and put both feet on the block-and-tackle rig, held onto the cable, gave the thumbs-up to the pilot and got one back in return. Then he was in free-fall, plummeting toward Kong's gaping maw.

"Yay-hey-hey-hey!" he hollered. God, he loved this job.

The rig slowed up and he landed gently on the ape's head.

"Touchdown Trapper!"

Seriously, he thought. *Best be quick.*

The broken tooth looked a little worse in person, but it confirmed his diagnosis. No wonder the big guy was in pain.

"We'll fix that," he said.

He secured the tooth with a winch clamp, then ratcheted it tight. In his sleep, Kong growled and belched. It smelled like he'd eaten an abattoir.

"Ugh!" he said. "What'd you have for breakfast?"

He stood up, took hold of his lifeline, and flashed a thumbs-up toward Ilene and Jia.

"This sucker's ready to come out."

Which meant he was out, too. The next instant the winch pulled him up toward the M.U.L.E almost as rapidly as he had come down. He got a secure grip on the ladder.

"Right, let's roll!" he told the pilot.

It was the old tooth-and-doorknob trick, except in this case the slamming door was a twenty-ton M.U.L.E accelerating at speed. This was a first, and he hoped it worked.

As it was, the M.U.L.E barely clocked the jerk as the tooth came loose. Kong felt it though, groaning in his sleep.

Now for the really tricky part. Putting in the new one before the big ape woke up.

Ilene and Jia watched from the overlook while the M.U.L.E returned and lowered the new tooth down. It was an odd grey color and would not be mistaken for one of Kong's real teeth, but she doubted the Great Ape would care what it looked like. Trapper directed the new canine to its proper place, but at this distance it was hard to see exactly how he was fitting it. That was fine—there should be a full report later. Well, eventually. Probably. After being reminded a few times. He'd been involved in Project Powerhouse, back before it had been shut down. Her involvement had been somewhat tangential, so she hadn't worked with him directly. But she had read his reports, which apparently usually had to be chased down, and with some difficulty. Trap was good at what he did. He always had been. But paperwork, follow-up, accountability—these were not things she associated with him.

Hampton reported that Godzilla was being escorted by several ships, which fortunately didn't seem to bother him. No one appeared to have any idea where he was headed, but if he was on his way to Barbados, he wasn't taking the most direct route. That seemed like good news, but it might not be. Godzilla had been known to take shortcuts through Hollow Earth—or at least through subterranean passages that riddle the Earth's crust that either connected to vortices or the remnants of ancient vortices. So he might know a shorter way to the Monarch station than following the curvature of the Earth. If he went off radar, they should probably start packing. Or skip the packing and get out.

Maybe Godzilla didn't know Kong was on the surface. But as she'd told Hampton, it was only a matter of time. Then they would have a problem. A big one. Or more accurately, *two* big ones.

It looked like Trapper was done. He was walking away from Kong, anyway, and the M.U.L.E was lifting off. So he was staying, at least for a bit. Maybe she would get that report after all.

Kong still looked like he was asleep, but he was starting to stir a little.

Stay here, she told Jia.

I want to talk to Kong.

You will. But not right now. He may be angry when he wakes up.

He won't be. He'll just be confused.

Stay here, Jia, Okay? I have a lot to worry about right now. I need to know you're safe.

Jia nodded, but she didn't look happy.

Much as she would have loved to watch Kong get his first brush with dentistry, Hampton had concerns that outweighed that simple pleasure. Kong was above ground, and that could be very, very bad.

"Check the time when Kong emerged," she told Vales, the tech on duty. "I want to know if Godzilla so much as blinked an hour each side of the vortex passage."

"Yes, Director," Vales said. There was a bit of a pause.

"No," he said. "Godzilla's changed course a couple of times, but it doesn't appear to be in response to Kong's arrival."

"What do we think it *is* in response to?"

A map appeared on her screen, with tracking data and a bright blue line that marked Kong's passage.

"He went north out of Rome, but then turned back west, and then southwest. He entered the Mediterranean—the Tyrrhenian I guess, technically—and now he's traveling west, trending north. If I had to guess, I'd say he's looking for something."

"Yeah. But what?" she wondered. Apparently not Kong. And that was a good thing, right?

"Check in the with the sub," she said.

"Copy that," the tech said.

She switched to a live aerial feed; Godzilla's spines cutting through blue water, a naval vessel right alongside him, pacing him.

The sub didn't have much more to say, just that they couldn't determine Godzilla's trajectory and they suggested all Monarch sites should stay on high alert.

No kidding, she thought.

What about the other Titans? No reports had come in, but sometimes that was because those who were positioned to report weren't in any condition to do so. She went down the checklist, but everyone was calling in, and none of them were reporting movements of the other Titans—or any unusual activity at all.

What had gotten into Godzilla? This wasn't one of his usual patrols.

"Map a cone in the direction he's going now," she said. "I want to know anything of interest in that area. If there's a kid wearing a watch with a radium dial, I want to know about it."

Ilene went back into the facility and followed the stairs down to the beach. By the time she got there, Kong was coming around, chuffing and looking confused, as Jia had predicted. The M.U.L.E was growing smaller in the distance, its job done.

"There she is!"

Trapper—Travis Beasley on his official documentation—was coming toward her from the surf. He wore a loud Hawaiian shirt unbuttoned over a white tee and sported dark sunglasses. If she hadn't just seen him in Kong's mouth, she might have thought he was a parrot head beachcomber. Or a tourist. Or maybe if she hadn't known him for twenty years.

Was that accurate? Twenty years? Could that be right? It seemed impossible.

"Trapper," she said. "Thanks for getting down here so fast. Nice work."

"You are most welcome," he said, bobbing a little curtsy. He'd grown a beard and mustache, she saw. It was a little redder than his disheveled brown hair. So he wasn't exactly like he was back in the day, but he bore a very strong resemblance to the guy she used to know.

"It's not every day you get to climb inside a three-hundred-foot-tall ape's mouth, is it?"

"Ah," she said. "Are you sure it'll be strong enough?"

"The tooth? That's the same polymer composite they use on the vehicle heat shields. He could chomp through the Eiffel Tower with that."

As if commenting, Kong chose that moment to vocalize an agitated moan.

"Well, good teeth aren't gonna help if Godzilla senses that he's up here," she said.

Trapper took off his glasses and began cleaning them on his shirt, revealing eyes the color of a bright summer sky. Without the glasses, he looked a little older, though, a little more weathered. Like maybe he really had lived through the same years she had.

"Well," he said. "Can't have a Titan with a toothache, can you?"

"Yeah," she agreed.

"Don't worry, a couple of hours, he'll be a bit groggy, but he'll be good to go back down."

That was a relief. The sooner the better, and with any luck, their big lizard friend would be none the wiser.

She glanced at Trapper. She had been a little anxious about seeing him face-to-face for the first time in… a while. But now she was gratified to realize that it was actually pretty good to see him.

"You know," she said, "when I first heard you were gonna be a vet, I thought, no, that is way too boring for Trap. Then you go and become the weirdest vet in the world."

"Yeah, it's basically me and Doctor Dolittle," he replied. "Except my animals are bigger."

"I thought, finally, someone's made him grow up."

"Nope," he said. "Someone tried that back in college, but… it didn't really work."

"Oh, yeah?"

"You know what she said to me?" he asked. "*Trapper, you are not a serious person.*"

"Oh, she sounds *very* smart," Ilene said.

"Ish," he amended. "She's got a PhD."

"Two, actually," she said.

He smiled, paused, as if considering if he was going to keep on in this vein. He didn't, and she was glad. It didn't need to get weird. Instead he nodded toward Jia.

"How's the kid doing?"

"You know," she said. "Struggling. Trying to find her place in the world."

"Yeah, I know how that goes," Trapper said. "She'll get through it. She's got a good mom."

She followed his gaze up to Jia. But the girl wasn't looking at them. She was looking at Kong. Signing.

Rest, she was saying. *You'll feel better.*

Kong responded with a soft sound. Ilene thought it sounded skeptical.

Looks good, Jia continued.

This time, Kong's vocalization sounded... pleased, maybe? He closed his eyes, plainly still recovering from sedation.

She started to turn back to Trapper, not at all sure where to move the conversation to, or whether to continue it at all. Did they really have much more to say to each other? Maybe not.

As it turned out, she wasn't going to find out, because Wilcox, her assistant, chose that moment to appear in the doorway.

"Doctor Andrews? Your, um, *guest* has been asking for you."

Bernie. What now?

"Okay," she sighed.

EIGHT

In the last few decades leading up to the discovery of Hollow Earth, scientists began to suspect that the earliest life on our planet may have evolved not on the surface, but in the chemical stew around deep-sea vents at the bottom ocean. Now that we know more about the world beneath our feet, we must consider that life may have actually originated there, in the Hollow Earth. And when we look at the barren surfaces of worlds even as similar to ours as Mars or Venus, we might also ask if life was ever meant for the surface of planets at all? Or is Earth, in that sense, an outlier?

—Internal Monarch document,
The Subterranean Origins of Life, Hoffman and Li

Hollow Earth Access Point
Monarch Base
Barbados

Bernie, it seemed, had been busy, and he wanted to talk about it. She'd left instructions for him to be shown to the base library. Apparently, he'd been there.

"Please don't take this the wrong way, but can I just say, your research library has many glaring omissions. I had to call in some serious favors on my Discord chat—"

"Bernie, do you have something?" she asked. It had already been a long day.

"Oh, I've got something," he said, waving an overstuffed manila envelope in her face. "I don't fully understand all of it, but I got it. I do, I do. Can you hold this, please?"

She took the briefcase he shoved into her hands. "Sure."

"Thank you so much." He plunged his hand into the folder. "The results from every deep space relay and amateur listening station going back about a hundred years or so."

She glanced down at the papers and the various histograms charted in them, many depicting peaks and valleys, something like a graph of human heartbeats.

"Listening for what?"

He hesitated. "Well," he finally said, "everyone knows that most extraterrestrial civilizations communicate nonverbally, right?"

Oh boy, she thought. "Obviously," she said. She pushed the briefcase back into his hand and continued walking.

"Yeah," he said, sounding relieved. "Obviously. Because they use energy rays. Same as the Atlantean alphabet." He stepped around and in front of her, so she had to stop. "Now this signal you're picking up? Okay. We've seen similar patterns repeated over time, and each spike corresponds with a specific Titan event. Okay, check this out." He handed her the briefcase back. "Hold this."

He held up the folder. "See this?" he said, pointing to a waveform spike. "King Ghidorah." He pointed to another. "First encounter with Godzilla." Another. "Discovery of Skull Island."

"Alright. So what you're saying is that these patterns are some sort of ancient language."

"Well, it seems so, yes."

"And Godzilla is picking up on it."

"Oh," he said. "I can do you one better. I've looked at points of similarities to this waveform, and compared them to—"

Why wouldn't he get to the point? She couldn't take it anymore.

"I mean, what are you saying?" she snapped.

"It's a distress call!" he burst out. "A... a psychic energy SOS. If your daughter is seeing these symbols, then something down there is calling for help."

She took the papers from him and gave the waveforms another look. He was right. They looked like the interference patterns from the Hollow Earth station. And like Jia's drawing.

She'd told Bernie she wanted him because he could think outside of the box. She had just tried to dismiss him because he *had*. Despite his wilder notions, the core of what he was saying—it made sense. It was worth checking out.

"Okay," she said. "Okay. Thank you, Bernie. That's something to go on. I need to talk to Director Hampton."

"Regular soundwaves can't propagate this far without decay," Ilene said, spreading the frequency data on the table for Hampton to study. She'd also invited Trapper and Mikael. The latter was one of their best pilots, and also head of security. Mikael made no effort to hide his skepticism. He had a very, very strong nonsense filter. "This... this is something we've never encountered. And it's getting stronger."

"You got a working theory?" Hampton asked.

"Yeah," Bernie interjected. "Telepathic alien language."

"Some sort of distress signal," Ilene said.

"Signal?" Mikael said. "From what?"

Ilene glanced at the security chief.

"Or from who," Ilene said.

"Well, whatever it is," Trapper said, "this is why Godzilla's on the move?"

"We can't say for sure," Ilene said. "But it seems that way."

Mikael sat down and folded his arms across his chest. With his salt-and-pepper hair, beard, and fierce scowl, he resembled an irritated grizzly.

"Well," Hampton said, "we have to figure this out fast. The wolves are already at our door."

"The government is looking for an excuse to take over Hollow Earth operations," Ilene qualified.

"And the corporations are licking their chops," Hampton said.

"Oh, I bet they are," Trapper said.

"Yeah," Mikael grunted. "Because who wants to be rich and get rid of all the monsters. I mean, that'd be terrible, right?"

Ilene didn't fail to see the disgusted look Trapper directed at Mikael. She felt the same way, but this was not the time to get into it.

"We'd better find the source before D.C. gets wind of this," she said instead.

Hampton pressed her lips together and nodded. "Okay," she said, lifting a finger toward Ilene. "I'm giving you full operational oversight. Take a small team." She turned to the security officer. "Mikael, make it fast and don't let anyone die."

"We'll be in and out of there by nightfall," Mikael grunted as he pushed his chair back and stood up.

"I just want to say," Bernie cut in, "all of this—all of this is incredibly exciting."

Hampton placed a hand on the table and leaned on it. "Who are you again?"

"I'm with her," he said, nodding at Ilene. "I'm her escort." His eyes widened. "Not intimately," he clarified. "Not an *escort* escort—"

Ilene took his arm and guided him away from Hampton. He got the hint and moved off, still mumbling about something. Ilene turned back to Trapper.

"You, uh… you feel like going for a ride?" she said.

"I thought you'd never ask," Trapper replied.

Loudspeakers blared overhead as they approached the launch site: *Attention, all Monarch employees of the Hollow Earth Station. The next launch will occur in T-minus five minutes.*

The first attempt to enter the Hollow Earth by human-piloted craft had ended in tragedy, with everyone involved dying. At that point, they hadn't fully understood the nature of the vortices, of the space-time membrane separating the surface world from Hollow Earth. The second attempt, which Ilene had been a part of, was also fraught with peril, but it had gone—if not smoothly—much, much better, in that everyone had survived. The transition, anyway. The losses afterward had to do with their ignorance of the fauna they would encounter on the other side.

They had learned more in the last few years. More—and generally safer—entrances to the world below had been discovered and mapped. The transition technology had improved. But it still couldn't be thought of as strictly routine. Any passage was still quite dangerous and invariably unpleasant.

Which was why the facility was on high alert, preparing for the launch. Announcements blared from loudspeakers, everyone was rushing here and there, performing tasks they only did now and then but had to do absolutely correctly.

Ilene wasn't worried about that part. They had a good team here.

"There's no response from the Hollow Earth outpost," Mikael informed her, as they moved toward the departure point. "Their radios must be down."

Ilene nodded. That wasn't terribly unusual. Interference was common, which was why Hampton hadn't initially been that worried about the strange frequency graph. Or it could be any number of things, including the electric-cable-eating bugs they'd just learned about. Even so, given everything else going on, it was a bit worrying.

"Well, then that's our first stop." she told him.

"Copy that," Mikael replied.

She nodded, spotting Jia up ahead. She knew what was coming.

I want to go with you, her daughter signed.

She shook her head. *There are a thousand reasons why it's not safe for you down there.*

Something is calling me! Jia said.

Ilene sighed and folded her arms. She couldn't dispute that. It was the entire basis for the expedition. But that didn't change things. Or it shouldn't.

Jia saw her opening.

You belong with me; I belong with you, she reminded her.

Oh my God, I'm such a sucker, Ilene thought.

You're gonna use my own words against me?

Besides, Jia pointed out, *you might need me for Kong.*

That was also indisputable. Jia had a link with Kong unlike anyone else. It was not only urgent they get him to come back to Hollow Earth, but who could predict what would happen with him when they got down there?

An alarm sounded.

"Wakey wakey everyone," Trapper said. "Kong's up."

Almost as if on cue.

Ilene gave Jia her sternest look, like she wasn't totally capitulating. *You will stay near me at all times,* she said.

Jia just smiled. She'd won. She'd probably known she was going to win.

They put on their flight suits, Trapper tugging his over his Hawaiian shirt.

On the way to the H.E.A.V, Bernie caught up with them, of course.

"Hey," he shouted from behind them. "Doctor Andrews, hey! Come on, we had a deal!"

She turned to confront him. "This isn't sightseeing," she said. "It's a reconnaissance mission."

"So I see how it is," he said. "When you need something, it's all *You're so smart Bernie, you're so capable Bernie, I'll subscribe to your Titan blog Bernie,* and then when I *deliver* it, you toss me aside."

"Okay," she said. "Firstly, this could be dangerous."

"What?" He tapped his chest. "I am no stranger to danger."

She cocked her head.

"I didn't mean to rhyme, that time," he said. "But you owe me, okay? I helped *crack* this thing. This could be like last time, when we saved the world. Remember? Hmm?"

She didn't, actually, because they hadn't even known each

other when that actually happened. They'd met after the crisis was over. That's when they'd learned that Bernie really had had a part in defeating Mechagodzilla. Sort of.

But she had made him a promise. And as he said, he really had delivered. He might not fully understand what he was getting into, but *she* did, and had somehow been convinced to take her daughter along.

"You ready to go right now?" she asked.

He twirled about. "Look at me!" he said. "Look at this. I watered my cactuses and everything."

"Cacti," she corrected.

"Cacti. Right."

She nodded. "Mikael?" she called.

"Yep?" Mikael responded.

"Prep a seat for one more."

"Thank you, Doctor Andrews!" Bernie shouted. "You will not regret it!"

"You're kidding, right?" Mikael called after her.

"I'm the plus one," Bernie told the pilot. "Hello."

Bernie's first instinct was to get some footage of the Hollow Earth Aerial Vehicle. This wasn't the old Apex industries model that everyone was familiar with by now. It was the latest design, a little more compact; the cockpit was less like that of a fighter jet and more like a helicopter, and it looked like it was sort of folded up, with the antigravity engines tucked beneath.

He had his camera out when Mikael put his hand on his wrist.

"No," he said.

"But I just—" Bernie started.

"Just. No. Get in *now*, or you aren't going, no matter what

Doctor Andrews says. And no filming in the cockpit. I see that camera on my flight, it's going away, right?"

"Uh… Yes. Okay. My… my bad."

That was okay, he thought. They didn't want people to see the new H.E.A.V. That was fine. He could cope with that. He had seen it, after all. They couldn't take the memory away from him.

Or maybe they could. Shoot. Could they? He made a note to watch out for that.

He climbed inside, noticing that new metal smell, the whiff of ozone and plastic. He found a chair and started fiddling with the straps. He looked around to see how everyone else was doing it.

He wasn't sure what he'd expected inside, but it was like one big wraparound touchscreen, and all of it was booting up. It sounded like a video game. Was that on purpose?

"Oh," he said. "Whoa!" he chuckled. "We're going to Hollow Earth. I. Am going. To Hollow Earth. Okay, okay!"

He finished snapping in and looked around. He was in the shotgun seat, next to the anger-issue pilot. Mikael? Dr. Andrews and Hawaiian-shirt guy were in the back. And Jia. He remembered her. He waved to get her attention. "Hey. Hey!" he said, pointing at her. "You nervous?" He put his hands out and shook them like he was scared, hoping she understood.

She just stared at him for a second, then pretended to yawn.

Yeah. It wasn't her first time, right? The girl was an old hand at this. But it was his first time. He had only read about this stuff, about the g-forces they were about to pull, the space-time distortion of passing through the membrane. But there was nothing to be worried about, right? Or Andrews wouldn't have her kid in this thing.

"Yeah," he said. "Me neither." He glanced around at the

rest of them. "So, is there, like, a safety briefing or something?"

"Yeah, there is," Mikael said. "There's no parachutes. No flotation devices." He gestured at the instruments. "Touch any of this stuff, you lose your hand. And if you die, make sure it's outside of my vehicle."

The pilot fiddled with his instruments. At first Bernie thought it was just a pause. Then he realized Mikael was finished.

"Good briefing," Bernie said, wondering if it was possible to back out at this point. "Great briefing."

"Don't take Mikael too personally," Hawaiian-shirt guy said. Trapper, maybe? Like the guy in the old TV show? "Aggression is his love-language." He reached down and picked up a control of some sort, pushed a button.

Music started, a repetitive guitar riff. Synthesizer, bass coming in.

"Twilight Zone" by Golden Earring. Yeah, of course. The H.E.A.V was starting to move, too. The hairs on his arms and the back of his neck stood up.

Oh, man, this was for real. For really real.

He looked over at Mikael. The pilot looked grim, like he was going on a suicide mission.

"All right, Mikael," Trapper said. "Let's punch it."

Mikael put on his sunglasses. They started to rise.

The vortex entrance looked sort of like a normal, albeit very regular semi-circular bay, surrounded by electrical towers that outlined the circular vortex. As the H.E.A.V rose, so did the towers. Electricity began to arc between them. In the distance, Bernie noticed Kong, who had been lying on the beach, was standing up, like he knew what was happening. Probably he did, right?

"H.E.A.V One, you're clear to launch," a voice on the radio said.

"Let's do this," Mikael said. The H.E.A.V started forward, turning as it went. Bernie suddenly remembered his least favorite part about flying was the take-off, and the turn that followed. He was also not fond of landing, or cruising, or… really any part of it.

It seemed slightly better than being trapped on a mag-lev train racing underneath most of the planet to an unknown destination. He had lived through that, right? This would be fine. All good.

"Try not to swallow your tongue," Trapper advised.

"What?" he blurted. "How do I not do that? That's a thing that can happen? Why is nobody else as terrified as I am?"

They had swung around and were now headed toward the watery center of the bay. Kong was ahead of them, already wading in.

"H.E.A.V, you're cleared for entry," the radio said. "On your count, Doctor Andrews."

"Three," Andrews said. "Two."

"Let's go!" Mikael said.

"Wait, wait!" Bernie sputtered.

"One!" Dr. Andrews finished.

They dove, nose-first toward the water. That would have been frightening enough, but the water was suddenly incandescing, as if they were entering a star.

Then they hit something; Bernie felt the impact as the H.E.A.V strained against it, stretched it like a sheet of latex— and then snapped through. Instantly his weight quintupled, at least. His lungs pressed hard against his backbone.

Jumbles of color and half-coherent images streamed by, like things from his least favorite dreams. He tried to look around, even though it felt like he might break his neck. Mikael was smiling for the first time since he'd met him. He was enjoying this. In his peripheral vision, he noticed Trapper giving him a thumbs-up. He returned it, but then turned the thumb down. What was wrong with these people? They were hollering like they were on a carnival ride. "Twilight Zone" was still playing, but now it sounded like a cover by a band from Sirius B, singing in telepathic mind language and playing instruments of liquid helium. His body was fluid and dissipating, becoming one with the chaos. He looked at his hand. It looked weird, very weird, flattening against the front of the cockpit. No, not flattening. And not just his hand. *Flowing.* Conforming to the vessel he was in. Like…

"I'm… turning… into… water!" he managed.

No one was listening.

There was a burst of very bright light, and Bernie was incredibly dizzy. His body squeezed back together, no longer liquid, but instead of falling down, he was falling *up.*

As the spots cleared from his vision, he saw it wasn't an illusion.

Hollow Earth. The land was below them, heavy clouds above. They were inverted. They were there.

He realized that the systems were making their booting-up noises again, and the screens were flickering on as if they had been off. Had they shut down? Had they really just been falling and not flying at all? If so, he was glad he hadn't known that in advance.

Really glad.

"Systems stabilized," the feminine voice said, as if to confirm his fears.

"All systems good," Mikael reported.

"Everybody good?" Trapper asked. "Bernie, you good?" He was doing the thumbs-up again. Bernie weakly returned the gesture, although he did *not* feel good and might never again.

"That's right," Trapper said, his eyes turning outward to the scene unfolding around them. "Oh, wow."

Trapper's expression of wonder actually calmed Bernie. His terror receded as he took in the strange new world around him. He had seen stills and footage of course, but that was… really not the same. Kong was loping along below them. As he watched, the huge ape went to all fours and really started moving. Like he had someplace to be. For a little while, everyone was quiet. Kong started angling away from them.

"Looks like Kong is headed home," Dr. Andrews finally said. "How far to the outpost?"

"A hundred klicks," Mikael said. "They're still not answering coms."

Just as Bernie was starting to feel easier, some kind of alarm or something went off.

"Birds at five o'clock," Mikael said.

"What?" Bernie asked. There they were, a huge flock coming up from behind them. At first they really did look like geese or something, but then he realized the scale was wrong. Each of them was bigger than a horse. And although they had wings, they didn't look that much like birds. They were featherless, and their wings were long and narrow, reminding him more of the flippers of a blue whale than those of a bird or bat. They had tall, shark-like fins on their backs, far back, almost where the lizard-like tails started. They were yellow and black, sort of tiger-striped. They did have beaks: big, mean-looking ones.

"Vertacines, Mikael," Trapper said. "They're called vertacines."

"Are they a problem?"

"Perfectly harmless," Trapper replied.

That was a relief. They were kind of cool-looking.

"Unless you get 'em riled up," Trapper continued. "Then each one packs about a lightning bolt worth of bioelectricity."

"What?" Bernie interjected.

"The predators know to stay well away. Which—" he started to fool with a touch screen, "—makes them the perfect chaperone, if you have an unbelievably cool bio-mimicry camouflage, which we do."

One of the screens in Bernie's vision showed the H.E.A.V was suddenly tiger-striped, like the vertacines. Mikael banked, taking them into the flock. None of the creatures looked at them twice.

Okay, he thought. That *was* unbelievably cool.

As he relaxed a little more, he realized that "above" him, through breaks in the clouds, he could now see mountains and valleys, plains and forests.

Finally. He was here.

Screw you, GhidoraStan64, he thought. *I'm here. I'm part of this. I always was.*

Hollow Earth Access Point
Monarch Control
Barbados

"Talk to me!" Hampton demanded. The Hollow Earth expedition was barely underway, and already everything else was hitting the fan.

"Godzilla just made landfall in France," Laurier said. "It looks like he's headed straight toward a nuclear power station."

Laurier was young. It was only her second week on this assignment. It was too bad she had to start her tenure with a crisis. Too bad any of them did.

Nuclear power plant, huh? That was bad. It was hard not to think of the Janjira disaster in Japan, or Scylla's more recent destruction of the reactor in India, and the press surely wouldn't miss the opportunity to make the comparisons. Titans fed from energy sources of all sorts, including atomic. Scylla's rampage was only the most recent example of that. Godzilla himself had once been rejuvenated by a tactical nuclear explosion. His earlier clash with the late Scylla a few years back had been over a misplaced A-bomb the six-legged monster was trying to feed on. The MUTOs had not only destroyed the Janjira plant, they had eaten a Russian nuclear submarine and raided a nuclear waste dump in Nevada. Godzilla usually went for naturally occurring sources of energy though. Trashing power plants was not his established MO.

Yet.

She studied the map. He was near Montagnac, a town in southern France near the Mediterranean coast. He had changed course again—the power plant hadn't been in their search cone. It was now.

"Get me someone on the scene, now," Hampton said.

Laurier obliged, patching her into French ground forces following the Titan. It was raining, and night, and the camera footage was jiggling like crazy.

"We've got picture," Laurier said. An image came up, this one an aerial view.

"It's an active nuclear facility. The French military is launching defensive drones."

"Shit," Hampton said, under her breath. Drones? If they did anything, they would only make the Titan angry. That said, this was unprecedented, and their carefully crafted message that Godzilla was not more dangerous than the threats he dealt with was falling apart. There was no big ugly "bad" Titan involved here—nothing trying to munch on the nuclear reactor but the big fella himself.

This had happened before, she reminded herself. Apex Industries had intentionally driven Godzilla into seemingly unprovoked attacks, but in the end, the Titan had been vindicated—in the eyes of many. There were and always would be skeptics calling for nothing less than the eradication of all the Titans. And not just the bloviators on talk radio and cable news, but members of government.

As if that could even be done.

She focused on the footage from the ground crew. Through the driving rain she saw an explosion on a distant hill and lightning climbing up and down a black column boiling into the sky.

The crew was speaking French, but she got a running translation. They were shouting that the reactor was compromised and that they were pulling back because the whole area was irradiated.

"Shit, shit," she said. "See if you can link to French drone footage."

"That's probably a breach of international law," Laurier pointed out.

"Yeah. Probably. Do it. I need to see this. And give me satellite data."

"They're right," Laurier said, after a moment. "There is radiation. But it's dropping fast. He's actually absorbing the radiation."

Hampton took a long breath and then nodded, her suspicions confirmed. "He's charging up for something."

The final fight with Scylla had taken about a minute. Before that, Godzilla had been conflict-free for a while. And he'd had a three-week nap. Vitals showed he was at the peak of health and power.

But Godzilla was capable of storing way more power than he usually maintained at any given time. He didn't do it often, but he had done so spectacularly right before his final confrontation with Monster Zero, resulting in an enormous explosion when that energy could no longer be confined even within his godlike form.

All of the other Titans were quiescent. Kong was back in Hollow Earth. What the hell was he getting ready to fight?

She didn't like the obvious answer, but she didn't flinch from it. Something big, right? Something on the level of Monster Zero. Or worse. But what would that even be?

Unless... There had been an internal document about a hypothetical Titan circulating for years. The great white whale of Dr. Martaans.

Nah. There were plenty of Titans they didn't know about yet. It was pointless to speculate without any evidence.

The drone footage popped up. There was Godzilla, posed like an ancient storm god, surrounded by fire and lightning, inhaling the atomic energy around him. His head turned slightly, and she saw the look in his eye. He had noticed the drones.

Explosions erupted all over him.

"No, no, don't do that," she murmured.

But they had his attention now. Godzilla roared in annoyance and slammed his "hands" together.

The drone footage stopped instantaneously.

"What just happened?" she asked.

"It looks like he generated an enormous electromagnetic pulse," Laurier said. She nodded. "Yes. The drones are down, and satellite shows power outage in a thirty-mile radius around the plant."

"Anything else?"

"Yes. He's back on the move."

Hollow Earth

"Incoming message," Mikael said.

"Put it on," Ilene said.

Hampton appeared onscreen. The picture wavered, and her voice cut in and out. But between the gaps Ilene gathered she was talking about Godzilla. He had attacked a nuclear power plant in France. Predictably, the French had launched missiles at him, which hadn't gone well. Fortunately, the missiles had been launched from drones, so no one had been killed. Yet.

"Godzilla has consumed a huge amount of radiation," Hampton said. "He's clearly preparing for something. I... signal... you to—"

They lost the signal entirely mid-sentence.

She could think of several reasons Godzilla might be seeking out radiation sources, none of them good. The most obvious one—the one that Hampton was keyed in on—was he was building his strength to counter something he perceived as a threat. Kong? But he was back down here. That should be okay now. Did he even know Kong had been on the surface? If he had, wouldn't he know he wasn't anymore?

The timeline bothered her. There was something else going on here. Another Titan. Or Titans.

Mikael turned the H.E.A.V, peeling away from the flock of vertacines.

"Coming up on Outpost One," the pilot announced.

They dropped lower, almost brushing the exotic canopy.

Ilene found she was excited to see the outpost again. In the earliest days there hadn't been much to it. But those had been grand, exciting days watching Kong explore his new home, sharing his sense of wonder and possibility. The new facility was far more sophisticated, not nearly as nostalgic, but much safer. It would be good to catch up with the crew in person. It had been a while. She leaned forward, tracing her gaze up the river valley.

Something wasn't right.

"Oh, God," Mikael exclaimed.

"Well, now, that doesn't look good, does it?" Bernie said.

It didn't. A column of black smoke climbed up from the trees ahead.

"You seein' this, Doc?" Mikael asked.

"Yeah," Ilene replied. "Yeah, I see it. Mikael, take us down."

It looked worse as they drew closer. Although the smoke obscured her view, she could make out the central structure was the source of it. And there was... debris.

The stabilizing fins of the H.E.A.V folded and became landing legs, and the vehicle settled to the ground.

"Wait," Mikael said, as she unbuckled and started toward the hatch. He went to the weapons rack and pulled down a nasty-looking gun.

"Doctor Andrews," the security chief said, "I advise you to leave your daughter in the H.E.A.V."

"Yeah," she said. "I'm with you there." She signed to Jia, who looked worried but to her relief didn't argue.

"Bernie, you stay here too," she said.

"Uh, yeah, I'm good Doc. I'll... ah... watch things here."

She nodded as Mikael opened the hatch and led the way out.

At ground level, the devastation was completely apparent. The roof of the outpost was gone and every piece of machinery in the area had been mauled and jumbled into a heap of scrap.

Her heart sank. She had known these guys. She had founded this outpost. It had been built for safety, to withstand the fauna of Hollow Earth, or at least that's what everyone thought.

Apparently, everyone had been wrong. The building might as well have been made of cardboard.

Mikael consulted his utility pad. "Well, there's no heat signatures," he said. "So much for survivors."

She already saw one of the bodies, crushed by rubble. She couldn't tell who it was.

"Oh, God, have some respect," she said. "These people had families. Who could have done this? I don't understand. We've had this outpost for years without incident. So why attack now? What changed?"

Not far from the main complex, she noticed one building was mostly undamaged. The armory. That meant the prototype might still be okay.

She was headed that way when she noticed Trapper pulling something from the wreckage.

"Hey, Doc," he said. "There's a camera here. You reckon you could pull some footage off that?"

She looked at the hardware, feeling numb. There was some possibility a few of the people here might have escaped into the jungle, but she didn't really believe it. This hadn't been an accidental brush with a Titan or even a predator attack. Whoever or whatever had done this had been very intentional about it. Very thorough.

She nodded slightly at Trapper. It was worth looking at. Then her gaze tracked past him, to the mountainside overlooking the remains of the outpost, where a huge red handprint was smeared.

"Oh, shit," she said.

"Think Kong did that?" Mikael wondered.

116

"That's not Kong," she said. "That's something else."

"Yeah," Trapper said. "Let's get off the ground before that something else comes back."

She nodded in agreement. Mikael's instruments had confirmed no one had survived this. She could check on the armory later.

"Saddle up," Mikael said. "Let's hustle."

NINE

Ever since I was little,
I had always thought to myself:
"Somehow or other, I wish
that I could see a human!
How I would love to kill one!"

—"Song of the Daughter of the Mountain God",
recited by Hirame Karepia of the Ainu People

Kong's territory
Hollow Earth

Kong was confused. He'd broken his tooth. It had hurt. Now
it didn't hurt, at least not very much. And now the tooth
wasn't broken. But it felt different.

It was more than the tooth bothering him, though. He
had been hearing things, seeing things. Not with his eyes and
ears, but in the place he went when he slept. Except he hadn't

118

been asleep. He didn't know what it meant, but he felt… like something was calling him. Something that needed him. But he didn't know who, where they were, or what exactly they wanted.

Jia and the other little ones had come back with him, but he heard the big bug they rode in move away. They were going somewhere else.

He was going home to his caves. To his overlook.

It wasn't far, and after a little climbing he was there. He was looking forward to a rest, and to something to eat. He was starting to feel hungry.

As soon as he entered his caves, he knew something was wrong. The cave didn't smell right. Something had been there. And as he swung down into it, he saw all his things had been moved around, his nest of leaves dispersed, the remains of his prey devoured to the bone.

Not by the food thief from earlier. Something else. Something that smelled like *he* did, but… different.

He continued searching, and after a moment, he saw something on the wall. Marks. Marks like his hand made when he pressed it against something soft, or when his hand was wet with inside-red-stuff. But this wasn't the same size as his hand. He made sure by putting his up next to it.

He had seen prints like this before. Shaped like his, but not the same size. In the place where he found his axe.

His axe! Was it still here?

He went to the boulder he had rolled to block a smaller cave. To his great relief, his axe was still inside.

He liked his axe. It helped him fight. It had been made long ago, by someone like him, from the scale of something like Godzilla. The ancient enemy. Only, he didn't think they were enemies anymore. Godzilla couldn't make sense, like Jia did, not with his hands or his sounds, but Kong thought he understood him. If Kong stayed here, and Godzilla stayed up above, they would not fight. And that was good, because he saw no reason to fight him again. There had been some kind of big fight between people like him and Godzilla. But he thought that fight was over now. He had begun to believe the other apes were all bones and dust, none of them still alive.

But bones did not make handprints. They did not move your things around.

Carrying his axe, he looked further. He followed the sign of the intruders—there had been more than one—to where he had trapped the pack-hunters, but the small crevasse and jumbled rocks from his trap were gone. A much bigger crack had opened there, swallowing everything.

Down inside the new slash in the mountain were long rocks-like-water, like the ones that made the daylight, but they weren't as bright. They glowed only faintly, a pale blue color.

The ones who had come to his cave had come from the place below there. And they had gone back the same way.

He looked down for a moment. Then he jumped, digging his axe into the rocks-like-water to slow his fall.

He landed on the flat surface of a cave floor. His axe began glowing blue, and the rocks-like-water also began shedding light, almost like they were talking to each other. When he approached them with his axe, they shone more brightly.

Apes had lived here, he saw. Or died here. The floor of the cavern was piled with bones. Some were of prey animals. But many of them were bones like those of his parents, with head-bones shaped like his own.

Once again, he had found people like himself. Once again, they were dead.

Except the handprints in his cave hadn't been there the day before this. They were not old, like these bones. Something had made them recently, something with flesh and skin. Something had moved his things and eaten his meat. He grunted. He didn't understand.

Then he heard a sound, as he had the day before. A sound like his own call. Were there more of the loud frogs down here? It might be that. Bones did not make such sounds, he knew that.

Whatever had called out, it wasn't in here. He saw the cave continued on, a big cave inside the bigger cave of the inside-out downside-up place where he had been living. He looked up, back the way he had come. It would be hard climbing back up that way, anyway. He would go forward. He would see what made the sound. He would follow the tracks of whatever these things were.

The cave was blocked by falling water, the kind he liked to bathe in. The sounds came from beyond that. He widened his nostrils, smelling the wet rock, feeling the spray on his skin. It seemed to him that this might be the same water he bathed in up above, but going deeper, under the stone he usually stood on. Had the skeletons behind him bathed here? Had they smelled what he was smelling?

He pushed his axe through the falling water and followed it through.

Subterranean realm
Uncharted territory
Hollow Earth

On the other side, it was still a cave, only much bigger. It was darker, and very misty. He couldn't see very far. Light came from stripes and patches in the rocks, making the mist glow. There were no mountains and forests hanging from the ceiling, no rocks floating in-between, no clouds.

Again he heard the sound. This time, he did not hurry. He became cautious. He remembered his traps. There were plenty of traps he didn't make, that no one had made. The mist could hide many of them. Holes in the rock. Predators waiting in ambush. Cliffs.

As he moved forward, he saw a shape in the mist.

He had seen his own shadow many times in the world above. He had looked at himself in still pools of water. This was a shape that resembled him, but it was taller, thinner. He couldn't make out its face. But he smelled it now, and it smelled familiar. Shadows had no smell, at least no shadow he had met before. They could not be touched; they could not hurt you or help you. They were not family.

He heard another growl, and the form moved toward him. He gripped his axe, preparing to fight. Maybe it was something like him. But he had never met something like him, and he did not know what it would do.

Then he realized the shadow-shape was moving *away*. He almost started forward, but then he realized that something was coming toward him, after all. Something much smaller than the silhouette in the mist.

He understood, then. What he had seen *was* a shadow. The shadow of *this*, made bigger by the haze and light, just as his own shadow had gotten longer in the world above, on Skull Island, when the light of day was low in the sky.

And the thing that made it *did* look like him, just much smaller. It wasn't as tall as his legs. He could see its face now, and that was a lot like his too. And he understood its expression. It was scared. Scared of him.

He lowered the axe, not sure what was happening, what this thing was. It was much bigger than the little ones, but so much smaller than him. It had fur, but lighter than his, red in color. Its head and eyes were too big. It reminded him of Jia, when he had first found her. Small. Helpless. He noticed it had red stripes painted on its torso, the same color as the handprints in his cave.

It still looked afraid, like it wanted to run away. He didn't want it to do that, so he squatted down, trying to appear less threatening. He put one knee on the ground and laid his axe on the stone.

Then he reached out with one hand, the way he did to Jia.

The small ape-thing looked at his hand. It came forward a little, then a little more. It reached out its little hand, too, palm and fingers down, submissive, making faint sounds. It flinched away from him, as if touching him would hurt, but Kong stayed still, and it reached back. Closer, closer.

This was an ape, he thought. Like him. This could be part of the family he had searched for. That Jia had told him might be down here someplace. That he had almost given up hope of finding.

Then the little ape lunged forward and bit his hand.

The pain was nothing. The little teeth stung but didn't draw blood. But it was a surprise. It was his own kind, he knew that now, but it was attacking him. Why? Because it was scared? Maybe because it had also never seen something like itself?

It ran. Kong ran after it.

He charged under a stone arch. The mist ended there, but the cave continued on, much bigger, with a long valley running down it. The small ape dashed ahead, and he kept after it.

Then he heard something thump behind him. He spun around.

It was another ape. But this one was much larger, close to his own size. One of his eyes was scarred white, and his fur was very short, light grey. The hair of his head was almost gone, which looked strange. He held a huge leg-bone in one hand, and his posture was threatening. Like the little ape, he had red stripes painted on him. Kong stared at the other ape, wondering what was happening. Then its mouth widened.

Kong saw motion from the verge of his vision, but not soon enough. Two massive shapes crashed into him from opposite directions. Powerful hands grabbed him and mashed his face into the dirt. He dropped his axe, which went sliding across the ground.

It was a trap. Like the one he had made for the pack hunters. The little one had led him into it.

They held him down, grinding his face against the dirt as the one with the leg-bone club headed for him.

These were apes, like him. His kind. Why were they trying to kill him?

He had searched for so long. For this?

He was Kong. No one attacked him.

Enraged, he reached out and grasped a boulder in his hand, then swung it back and hit one of the apes holding him on the side of the head. The ape yowled and let go; with only one now holding him, Kong managed to stagger to his feet as the other ape put him in a headlock. One-Eye charged forward, swinging his club. Kong spun, so the impact fell not on him, but on the ape clinging to his back. One-Eye's swing overbalanced him and he went past; Kong drove his elbow into his attacker's back, knocking him sprawling. The one he'd hit with the rock was already back up, charging him, this time with a club. Kong intercepted the weapon and caught it, then grabbed the ape's arm and used the double grip to heave him into a flip, slamming him into the ape One-Eye had just clubbed. Kong held on to the weapon.

He noticed that both the apes that had tackled him to the ground also had red stripes across their chest and belly.

One-Eye was back, this time with Kong's axe. Kong stepped away from the swing and clubbed him, knocking him down again. They were all down. He discarded the club and reached for his axe.

The little one came out of nowhere, hurling himself and grappling onto Kong's face, snapping and scratching with his nails. Still empty-handed, Kong reached up to pull him off but the small ape was remarkably strong for its size. By the time he pulled him off, two of the others had recovered and were coming for him. Holding him by the foot, he swung the small ape like a club, striking one his attackers in the head and connecting with the second on the back-swing. One-Eye was next, yowling and lunging at him. Kong kicked him in the chest, knocking him back, and then threw the small ape at him.

One of the other two scrambled back up and charged him, but Kong dodged and punched him in the head, sending him into the dirt at his feet. He raised both fists and pounded him. The second red-stripe flung himself. Kong tumbled, letting the other ape's momentum carry him over and past Kong. The red-stripe fell to the edge of a cliff and over it. The ape scrabbled for purchase but was unable to find any.

Kong should have let him fall, but he didn't. He threw out his hand and caught the red-striped ape by the wrist. Saved from a fatal fall only by the strength of Kong's hand, the other looked up at him, frantic.

Maybe now these apes would see he was not an enemy.

Grumbling, Kong pulled. He was heavy, this ape like him. But he managed to get him up onto the edge of the precipice.

For a moment the red-stripe stayed there, with his head down, as if acknowledging dominance. Kong watched him, panting, then looked to see where the others were.

That's when red-stripe grabbed a sharpened bone-knife from the ground and tried to stab Kong with it.

That was enough. Kong caught his wrist again, this time not to save him from falling. He kicked him in the chest and let go at the same time, barking his fury. Red-Stripe fell, growing smaller as things did when they got further away. Gone.

Kong turned back to the others. He didn't see the small one or the other red-stripe at all. One-Eye was creeping toward him.

Kong glared at him.

One-Eye looked around and saw he was alone. He took a step back, then another.

Then he dropped to all fours, turned, and ran.

Kong didn't run after him. Instead, he found a rock big enough to fit his hand. He weighed it, watching One-Eye get further away. Then he drew back his arm and let it fly.

It curved through the air. Kong kept watching. One-Eye getting smaller, the path of the rock curving downward. When it struck the other ape in the skull, Kong felt an immense sense of gratification. One-Eye fell and tumbled, landing on his face. Then he shook his head and scrambled on, a bit unevenly. Kong watched him go. He was sure he could catch him and kill him. He probably should. But maybe there were more apes. Maybe the others were not bad, like these. Maybe he could follow One-Eye and find them. And if they were bad, if they were all like these, maybe he would kill them all. That way he didn't have to worry about more sneak attacks like this one.

He didn't like the thought. What he had felt when he first saw the small one—he had liked that feeling. But now it was all spoiled.

Something rustled in the bushes nearby. He bolted forward, thrust his hand in, and yanked the small one out. He tossed him to the ground and roared at him. He had done this. He had made all of this happen.

This time, the small one didn't attack him. He backed up and covered his face with his hands.

Without taking his eyes off the little ape, Kong picked up a sharp bone like the one the red-stripe had tried to kill him with. He sniffed it; it smelled of ape. He gestured to the bone, reaching it toward the small one. A question. Where did this come from? Where did *you* come from?

The small one moved his head. It seemed like a refusal. Kong roared again, and gestured in the direction One-Eye had run.

The small one hesitated, but then he turned, head down, and started leading the way.

Hollow Earth

The visit to the outpost was supposed to have been a short stopover to check in on their radio silence and gather any more information they could on the "distress call" they'd been picking up. But after finding the post destroyed and those who manned it all dead, getting back topside seemed like their top priority, thought Ilene. For one thing, the threat level was now astronomical, and they had not only a civilian with them, but Ilene's own daughter. If they had any idea where they should go to investigate the signal, that might be one thing. But they didn't. In fact, for all they knew whatever had destroyed the outpost had *sent* the signal. In the long and often unfortunate history of distress calls, it was sadly true that they were often lures to attract the well-meaning. What if Jayne and her team had figured out what the signal was and attempted to respond to it, unknowingly engineering their own demise?

"All right," Mikael said. "We're ten minutes out from the vortex entrance. We'll be home in no time."

Ilene acknowledged that with a nod, working on retrieving the data from the camera Trapper had found, hoping it contained some clue as to what had killed her people. She found the storage card and plugged it into her utility pad. There were images there. She began scrolling through them.

"You getting anything off that thing?" Trapper asked.

"Just..." Nothing unusual yet. She kept going.

And stopped. "Oh, my God," she said.

"What?"

"Here," she said, unplugging the device, so she could hand it to Trapper. "Take a look."

He took it and frowned at the screen.

"It looks like an ape," she said. "But that's impossible." She saw Jia was looking over Trapper's shoulder. She thought about trying to stop her, but she already knew about the outpost. She had stayed in the H.E.A.V, sure, but she had still seen. And after that, she had asked the inevitable questions, which Ilene had had to answer honestly.

"What the bloody hell is that?" Trapper wondered, studying the still.

"I have no idea," she said. But she did, didn't she? The cave with the throne, the Titan skeletons, the axe, the Kong-sized imprint on the walls. Not to mention the handprint back at the outpost. What she meant was: this ape looked different. Like Kong, but not like him. Every bit of evidence up until today suggested that the ancient Great Apes of Hollow Earth had been gone for years—centuries even. Once again, Hollow Earth had surprised her. Not in a good way. Because while

Kong had proven himself to be a guardian of humanity, this ape clearly was not.

The H.E.A.V suddenly juddered, and interference patterns flickered across the displays. Very familiar interference patterns. The H.E.A.V instantly dropped into a dive, as if Mikael had decided, on a whim, to run them straight into the ground. But she could see the pilot fighting with the controls, trying to override what was happening to the craft by sheer force of will. She was vaguely aware that Bernie was yelling as the ground approached. The whole vehicle shook like it was about to come apart. She glanced at Jia. Her daughter looked oddly calm. Jia had been through a lot.

Ilene closed her eyes. *We'll get through this*, she thought.

And she felt the H.E.A.V pull up. She opened her eyes and saw they were skimming mere meters above the grassland under them. They were lucky it hadn't been forest.

Mikael pulled back further, and the H.E.A.V responded, beginning to lift again.

"What the hell was that, Mikael?" Bernie demanded.

"Calm down, calm down," Mikael snapped back, not sounding all that calm himself.

"It must have been the signal," Ilene said. "The same electrical disturbances were happening at the outpost."

She saw Jia was signing. *It's getting stronger.*

"What kind of signal?" Bernie wanted to know. "'Abandon all hope, ye who enter here' kinda signal? What is that, a warning signal?"

Jia was still waving for her attention.

It came from around there, her daughter said, pointing at the horizon.

You're sure? she asked.

Jia nodded.

"She says it's coming from that ridge point," she told everyone else.

They looked out at the ridge, then back at her.

Right. This changed things. As much as she wanted to get Jia back to the surface, they had only just survived the signal's interference with the H.E.A.V. If it happened again as they entered the vortex or after, Monarch would be scraping them off the walls. It was probably more dangerous to try to return to the surface than to remain here. Besides, if Jia was right—and Ilene had no doubt that she was—they had a chance to figure this out.

"Well, let's go take a look," she said.

"Copy that, Doc," Mikael said, starting a turn.

Mikael did a flyover of the region, but at Ilene's insistence, he kept it short. Flying was clearly no longer the safest way to travel. The area Jia had indicated was heavily forested, so they didn't see much.

Where? she asked Jia.

It's not happening now, Jia said. *But I feel... something. Somewhere that way.*

She nodded. "Mikael, Jia thinks we're close. Find a place to set down. I don't feel safe in the air."

"My thoughts, Doc," Mikael said. "Even though I never thought I'd be using a teen as a GPS."

Ilene wondered about that, too. Why could Jia sense the signal? No one else had heard or felt anything other than the sudden near-catastrophic failure of the H.E.A.V. While the signal clearly affected electronics, as far as she knew the only living creatures who seemed to sense it were Jia, Godzilla, and maybe Kong. She understood the Titans—Godzilla obviously had some sort of global Titan-locating perception, and Kong had something similar. She suspected this signal operated along the same lines as those senses. But why Jia?

Because she was Iwi? Because the Iwi and Kong had been connected by some special link? Something that explained why the Iwi had mostly abandoned spoken language?

Now she was thinking like Bernie. She wasn't sure that was good. Yes, he had been right about a few things. But he was wrong about *so* many. When you fired a shotgun at a target, you were likely to hit *something*, even if most of the shot missed.

The H.E.A.V was an improvement over the earlier models, tailored to meet the needs of Hollow Earth travel Nathan Lind, and later Apex, had only been able to guess at. Setting down in a climax forest didn't present any difficulty.

Once down, Mikael armed himself again.

"Doc," he asked. "You want a gun?"

She shook her head. She wasn't well trained with weapons, and would probably be as dangerous to her crew as anything they might encounter.

"Trapper?" Mikael asked.

"No," Trapper replied. "The only thing a gun will do down here is make us overconfident enough to die even faster."

"Oh, I see," Mikael said. "Well, you don't mind if I hang on to mine, do you?"

"You do you, mate."

"I might..." Bernie started.

"No." Mikael snapped.

"Yeah, okay," Bernie said.

Bernie stopped when the hatch opened and he remembered where he was—and why he was there. He and Sara had always talked about going someplace exotic, like Borneo or the Congo. Well, not always. They had discussed it once or twice. Sara thought it would be fun.

Here I am, sweetheart, he thought, gazing at the alien undergrowth. It looked tropical, sort of. It definitely felt tropical. Slender, pale-trunked trees climbed into the sky, forming a canopy of interlocking leaves—fronds? Climbing vines wound up them, seeking the light from the sunrise crystals on the other side of the world. Couldn't get much more exotic than this, could you?

Just as well he didn't have a gun, right? His camera was his weapon. He pulled it out, checked the charge, and pointed it at the forest.

Mikael was in the lead, followed by Jia and Andrews. Bernie hung back a little, then started filming.

"*The* Hollow Earth," he began, panning through the foliage. "A world untouched by mankind. Is this how Neil Armstrong felt, when he stepped on alien soil? This is one small step for me, and one giant—"

Something loomed in the viewfinder, literally right in his face.

Trapper.

"Who are you talking to?" the veterinarian asked.

"Are you kidding me?" Bernie snapped. "Right down the lens. This—this is a documentary. You just wanna walk?" He gestured for Trapper to turn around. "Just walk."

Trapper shrugged and obliged, continuing to follow the others. Bernie sighed. "Thank you." He checked the camera, and then started again.

"*The* Hollow Earth…"

TEN

And Ahura Mazda spake unto Yima, saying: "O fair Yima, son of Vivanghat! Upon the material world the evil winters are about to fall, that shall bring the fierce, deadly frost; upon the material world the evil winters are about to fall, that shall make snow-flakes fall thick, even an aredvi deep on the highest tops of mountains. And the beasts that live in the wilderness, and those that live on the tops of the mountains and those that live in the bosom of the dale shall take shelter in underground abodes."

"Against the Demons",
the *Vendidad or Vî-Daêvô-Dāta* 2:22,
ancient Avestan religious text

Interestingly for our purposes, elsewhere in the Vendidad we are told that Angra Mainyu the "Evil Mind" who is

"All Death" created the dragon Aži Raoiδita to help the
Daevas (demons) create Winter.

—Internal Monarch document, *Speculations on a
Hypothetical Titan*, Maartens, Chen, and Omar

Hollow Earth

They followed along the top of the ridge, mostly in forest,
occasionally on more open ground where the rocky substrate
didn't have enough topsoil to support large vegetation. To their
right, the land dropped off so abruptly that it became more cliff
than slope.

Trapper had been sidling up to Ilene for a while. She thought
he probably wanted to talk about something, and she was right.
But it wasn't what she had been expecting.

"There's a rumor going around," he said.

"Oh yeah?" she said. "What's that?"

"That Monarch offered you the top spot and you turned
it down."

She shrugged. "I didn't want to spend my life chained to a
desk. I like being out in the field."

"Ah," he said. "A fellow Monster Whisperer."

She smiled. "I wouldn't go that far," she said. "It's just,
you know, I think time's running out. For our planet, for our
species. Everything. And I just… wanted to be able to say that
I tried to do something while there was still time. That at least
we tried."

"I get that," he said. "But… forgive me, okay? But even as
things are, you don't seem to get to the field that much anymore."

"Right," she said. "Well, I…" She glanced ahead at Jia.

"Yeah. You have to think of her. But how's she doing right now?"

Ilene had noticed that, of course. The subdued, angry, melancholy girl she had known for the past couple of years was… gone. Replaced by a girl much more like the one she had first adopted. Injured, yes, but full of life and brimming with wonder at everything around her.

"I mean, look at her," she said. "She loves it."

"That's what I was thinking," Trapper said.

She nodded, not sure what she was feeling. It was good to see her daughter like this. A huge relief, right in the middle of all the danger they were in. But it couldn't last forever. When they left… well, Jia couldn't stay in Hollow Earth.

Trapper seemed to sense Ilene had mentally gone somewhere she needed to be alone, so he dropped back out of her space. A flock of something flew overhead, but at this distance Ilene couldn't tell if they were leafwing relatives or something else. Whatever they were, they either didn't notice their tiny human visitors or didn't think they were worth their time, for which she was grateful.

The insects, however, were enjoying the five travelers a good deal. The main offenders were mosquitos. They looked—and bit—pretty much like the mosquitos she was familiar with in the world above. That wasn't a surprise, really. Mosquitos had existed on the surface since at least the Cretaceous period: they had the fossils, but molecular genetic studies suggested they probably went back to the Jurassic. Maybe the reason they didn't have fossils that early was because they had come to the surface from down here. The data was starting to suggest that most, if not all, surface life had its origins in Hollow Earth. Of course, without genetic analysis, she couldn't know if these were proper mosquitos. The creatures sucking on her exposed skin might be examples of convergent evolution, form following function, the way ancient reptilian ichthyosaurs resembled mammalian dolphins.

Somebody would eventually figure that out. Right now, they were just as annoying as any bloodsucker.

Bernie wasn't disappointed. Well, not exactly. But he had yet to see anything really… impressive. The forest was cool, and everything, but besides the upsy-downsy sky, there wasn't a lot so far to prove that he wasn't in Brazil or Panama. He'd seen some weird birds in the distance, something that looked different from the vertacines from earlier—kind of like bats, actually. But he had expected, you know, *Titans*. Or at least really big, weird monsters. Not too close of course—he had been up close and personal with a skullcrawler once, and as far as he was concerned, he didn't need another near-death experience to complete his monster experience. That box was checked. But it would be great to see something in the distance, a strange beast he could film for his documentary.

Because all he had right now was trees and bugs. And not even crazy-looking what-the-hell-is-that bugs, but just mosquitos, albeit big ones. But at least he wasn't the only one bothered by them, he thought, as Mikael slapped his neck.

"I'm getting eaten alive out here," he growled.

"You must be very tasty, Mikael," Trapper said.

"Smartass," the security chief shot back.

Trapper held up his arm. Bernie saw there was a mosquito clinging to it, already bloated with blood.

"Well, look at that," Trapper said. "I must be tasty too."

"Kill it," the security chief said.

Trapper kept examining the insect. "Only female mosquitos

drink blood," he said. "So they can grow their eggs." Sated, and perhaps shy of all the attention, the bug flew away with an audible whine. "She needs it more than me," Trapper concluded, before he started walking again.

"And if one wanted to keep their blood on the inside of their body, what would you recommend?" Bernie asked.

For an answer, Trapper just smiled.

Bernie was beginning to wonder if they really knew where they were going. If they did, wouldn't they have landed nearer it? How far through this bug-infested jungle were they going to have to walk? Would they have to spend the night?

That was a decidedly unappealing idea, if you asked him. Of course, no one had.

I'm just an observer here, he reminded himself. *Someone else is in charge.*

Although it wasn't clear who. Dr. Andrews had given the order for this hike, but now that they were on it, Mikael seemed to have appointed himself pack leader. He had the gun, and the attitude. It's just—he didn't seem to know all that much about *jungle*. Trapper did, and it was clear that while the veterinarian wasn't the type to directly dominate a situation, he was constantly offering suggestions about how to negotiate the terrain. The little dust-up over the mosquito was just a small example, but Mikael was clearly getting sick of having his authority undermined.

That came to a head just a little later, when for the first time, Trapper actually put his foot down about something. He had gone ahead of Mikael and the rest of them. Bernie saw him slowing, sniffing at the air.

"Wait," he said, holding up his hand in the classic "halt" motion.

"What?" Dr. Andrews asked.

"What's the hold-up?" Mikael demanded.

"Not this way," Trapper said.

"What? Why?" Mikael said.

Bernie wondered the same thing. All he saw was the same forest they had been walking through for hours. A tree in their path had fallen over, roots and all, but they had seen plenty of those.

"No," Trapper said. "We've got to take a detour. There's something here."

"What?" Bernie said. "Where here? Like *here* here?"

Mikael was studying the hand-held instrument he'd been consulting. Some kind of sensor box.

"Nah," he said. "Not picking anything up."

"Something doesn't smell right. And it's not just you, Mikael. Smell that? It's like rotting flesh."

"It's probably just a carcass upwind," Mikael said. "We keep moving."

"Mikael, hold up," Trapper began.

The security chief whirled around and cut him off. "Listen pal," he said. "I'm gonna trust my state-of-the-art thermal over your Ace Ventura hippy-dippy sixth sense all day long. You got me?"

"Well, there's no need to call people names," Bernie said.

"As for *you*, Freakshow," Mikael said, turning to him, "you don't shut it, I'm gonna take that camera, and I'm gonna shove it right up your arse. I'm in charge. We move." He bolted forward.

"Why don't you just listen to somebody—" Bernie began.

"Wait!" Trapper said.

Mikael turned again, livid.

"I said I'm in charge!" he shouted. "I'm in charge!"

That's when the roots of the fallen tree opened a huge mouth, lunged forward, and swallowed Mikael whole.

And started chewing.

Bernie didn't think about running. One minute he was standing still. The next, leaves were whipping at his face and his feet were pounding against the leaf-litter. Everything seemed brighter and unreal, as if he were seeing it by the light of an arc-welder. He was only dimly aware that he wasn't alone, that someone was running with him. And that he had just screamed something about a tree eating Mikael. The pilot's face frozen in an expression of surprise as the "roots" engulfed him and yanked him into... what? A stomach?

Someone else was talking. Trapper. Trying to sound calm.

"We should be alright," the veterinarian was saying. "We should be alright. Those things don't reach that far."

"He was just eaten by a tree!" Bernie shouted. It was ridiculous. Outrageous. Totally horrifying. If a tree could eat you down here, what couldn't?

"What are you doing?" Trapper asked.

I'm panicking, he thought. *Who wouldn't be?* But Trapper wasn't talking to him. He was talking to Andrews, who was fiddling with a piece of equipment.

"I'm calling the base for extraction," Dr. Andrews said.

"One minute he's right there, in my face, and then *bam*. A tree! Out of nowhere."

"I know, man, I know. That's the natural world," Trapper said. "Red in tooth and claw."

"Tennyson," Bernie said, gesturing back the way they had come, panting to catch his breath. "You just watched a man get devoured by a topiary nightmare and now you wanna quote Tennyson? Down *here*."

Trapper laid a hand on his shoulder. "Yeah," he said. "He knew all about it. Come here." He enfolded Bernie in a hug.

Normally he didn't like hugging. No, he still didn't. But it was slightly comforting, and at the moment it was worth it.

"We humans think we took ourselves off the food chain," Trapper went on, now whispering in his ear. "Maybe… maybe the Titans are here to remind us."

"I think…" Bernie patted him on the shoulder. "I think there is something seriously wrong with you."

"Okay," Trapper said, releasing him and stepping back.

"It's not working," Dr. Andrews announced.

"Okay," Trapper said. "We'd better move on. Mourn later." He started off. So did Andrews and Jia.

"But he was eaten by a tree," Bernie said. "I don't want to die like that. Not by a tree."

And yet he followed them. What else was he going to do?

Dr. Andrews had said this would be dangerous. He'd thought he understood what that meant. Maybe she should have used another word. Was there one? That meant incredibly, horrifyingly dangerous? For real, all-kidding-aside dangerous?

Because if there wasn't, there should be. And she should have used it.

Subterranean realm
Uncharted territory
Hollow Earth

Suko glanced over his shoulder at Stranger. He was still following. Suko wasn't sure why. The Skar King had sent him with One-Eye and the others to find Stranger and capture him, drag him back before the Skar King. Suko wasn't sure what the Skar King planned after that, but it would be bad for Stranger. Probably very bad.

But Stranger had killed Stone Fist and he had driven One-Eye and Catcher away. He had dominated Suko. But now Stranger was making Suko lead him to the Skar King. If Stranger wanted to go there, why had he fought at all?

Suko was confused that Stranger even existed. He shouldn't. All the apes lived together. They always had, for far longer than Suko had been alive, for longer than almost anyone but the Skar King could remember. Nothing had changed in a very long time. Suko knew all the apes, even the females that the Skar King kept all to himself.

But now everything had changed. The stone of the caverns had shaken, which happened often enough. But this time the Skar King had risen from his stone seat. He stalked about the caverns, his nose twitching as even he smelled something. He made sounds to himself. He snarled and spit, his hands twitching restlessly at his sides. And he smiled: a terrible, frightening smile. It was always bad when the Skar King smiled.

Suko hadn't noticed anything different. Neither did any of the other apes, but they were all wary of the Skar King's behavior. They all watched and waited to see what it meant.

The Skar King called together all of the red-stripes, his loyal fighters, his personal protectors. By motion and sound he made it known that they were to prepare for a hunt.

Suko was not a red-stripe, so he did not join them. Not until the hand fell on his shoulder and he found the Skar King there, staring down at him with his hard blue eyes. Suko flinched, fearing he would be hit, kicked, or bitten. But instead the Skar King tilted his head and flexed a finger at One-Eye.

One Eye grunted in disapproval. The Skar King hissed at him, and One-Eye fell silent. One-Eye motioned Suko forward. He looked angry, but he wouldn't go against the Skar King. Suko held his breath, not knowing what would happen.

One-Eye painted red stripes on Suko's belly. He blinked. He looked up at the Skar King, but he wasn't watching anymore. He was coiling his bone-whip. Getting ready to hunt.

Suko was a red-stripe now. He was one of them.

Which meant he was going hunting too.

His fear retreated. He began to feel bigger, more important. The Skar King had chosen him.

They started through the usual hunting grounds, but soon they had traveled far beyond any place Suko had been and eventually beyond the travels of any ape except perhaps the Skar King himself. The Skar King went in silence, his eyes burning, his gaze twitching about. When any dared to make a sound, he struck them without warning, and so eventually they all learned to move without chatter or complaint.

After a while, Suko thought he smelled something different. Maybe what the Skar King had smelled, all the way back in the Living Caves. He didn't know what it was, but he liked it. It was… light, without the bitter stench of smoke. It smelled like plants and flowers, and now and then the air *moved* as if it was alive, as if it was coming or going from somewhere.

The smells got stronger until they came to a place where the cave sky had broken. One by one, they climbed up. Up into a different place. Still dark, but bigger—much bigger. And everything smelled new, better. Like water, but not like the still pools and damp mists he knew. This water smelled… alive.

They passed through more caves, but beyond that was jungle, deeper and denser than Suko had ever seen or even imagined. The cave roof was so far away that he couldn't even see it, and now the air was always restless—playful even, growing softer and stronger, sometimes mischievously changing directions. And always more things to smell. Fruit, flowers, carrion, and many other things he couldn't identify. It was frightening. It was wonderful.

He felt lucky to have come. Fortunate that the Skar King had chosen him to be a red-stripe.

The Skar King paused now and then, choosing the trail. Suko could tell he was looking for something.

Finally, he found it. He dispersed the apes into a large hunting circle which then began contracting, driving any prey toward the middle where there was no escape. But there was no sign of prey, at least nothing big enough to feed them all. Instead they came across strange trees made of hard stuff like stone. They broke them, and everything else that didn't seem natural. They were quiet, as the Skar King commanded. Finally they came to the thing in the middle, the thing that did not belong.

Suko didn't see it. One-Eye stopped him from going to the middle, put him on watch against anything that might be coming behind them. But he heard the weird, thin screams in the distance, the ripping and tearing.

As he waited, the world grew light, and he saw, for the first time, how big the cave really was. He stared in wonder at what ought to be the roof of the cave, but wasn't. Instead he saw a reflection, another cave floor covered in forest and grassland. Rivers and streams flowed there, and lakes that must be huge. Between the cave floor he was on and the one above him, rocks drifted, and white clouds of fog. It was frightening; he kept fearing that at any moment he would plunge to his death on that other floor. But after some time passed, and it didn't happen, he began to relax.

In the distance he heard the Skar King calling everyone in, so he went there, curious to see what all the noise had been about. Smoke curled up in that direction, trailing up into the peculiar distance and pooling where the stones floated.

When he reached the place of smoke, he stopped for a moment, trying to understand what he saw. The Skar King and the others had destroyed something, but he wasn't sure what. It wasn't made of trees or branches or stone or earth, but of stuff that Suko did not recognize. In this ruin, there were dead creatures. Small things, smaller than him, yet they looked something like apes that had been stripped of their fur. Suko didn't know what they were. But the Skar King seemed to. And he was… excited.

What was this place, he wondered? Was it the promised place, the place all apes were supposed to go to and conquer? The place the Skar King had been searching for for so long?

The Skar King didn't seem to think so. But he was different now. After a long time being the same, something new was changing inside of him. Every move he made, every gesture reflected that, reflected a *purpose*. Suko was sure of that. He just didn't know what it was.

The Skar King picked through the debris, grunting. Then he stood tall and gestured back the way they had come.

The hunt was over. For now at least. They started back toward the Living Caves.

On the way back to their caves, they found signs of the Stranger. Signs like theirs, but not theirs. It had never happened before. The Skar King was in a hurry to return to the Living Caves, but he was curious about the Stranger. He left One-Eye, Stone Fist, Catcher, and Suko to wait for him. To bring him home, alive if possible. But dead would be okay, too.

Well, now Suko was bringing Stranger home. The Skar King was never pleased, but sometimes he was less angry. And there was the question of what Stranger might do. He was big, and strong, and clever. He wanted to find the Skar King.

The King wanted Stranger captured or dead. He might

be very angry if Suko just led him home still holding his weapon.

So what could be done? Suko began to think.

Monarch Control
Barbados

Godzilla wasn't hard to follow. He left France and bore in a straight line across southern Spain. He looked terrifying; the blue energy that was usually seen in his fins as he charged up to kindle his breath was leaking from his eyes and scales. It reminded Hampton all too much of Boston, but there he had been glowing red just before releasing a terrific energy blast. This didn't seem as extreme, but was nevertheless still very, very worrying.

He reached the Spanish port of Cadiz on the Atlantic.

"The jets are in range," Laurier reported.

Hampton nodded as she watched the images stream. Godzilla was glowing more brightly than before, and the air above him showed signs of heat distortion.

"Tower," the lead pilot reported. "We can't get any closer than this, Godzilla's burning hot with radiation. Whatever he's headed for has him really pissed off."

Hampton nodded, hoping this wasn't going to be a repeat of the Boston incident, when Godzilla had melted half the city.

Godzilla walked to the end of Spain and then he was back in the water, sending up huge plumes of steam, but Cadiz remained largely unmelted.

"Where are you going now, you big iguana?" Hampton murmured.

The sub commander answered her question. "Projected trajectory has him going toward the Arctic Ocean."

What, to cool off? But somehow she didn't think so.

"Do we have intel on that?" she asked. "What Titans are in the area?"

"Pulling it up," Laurier said.

The screen showed a still image of what could only be called a sea serpent complete with fins, long whiskers, and eerie white eyes.

"My God," the sub commander said. "Looks like he's hunting Tiamat."

"Oh," Hampton said. She sat back. "I thought Tiamat was dormant."

"She is. Not a peep out of her since Godzilla thrashed her years ago in the Pacific. She's just been hanging out in the ice."

"Uh-huh." Tiamat had originally been documented beneath Stone Mountain Georgia, establishing Outpost 53. She had awakened at Ghidorah's call and then gone missing for a while. Godzilla had gone on a grand tour a few years back, basically establishing his dominance over the other Titans. He had flushed Tiamat out of some underwater caves below a Pacific island. They had been tracking Godzilla by sub, but didn't get a lot of footage of the fight. Tiamat had seemed pretty nasty; she had pulled Godzilla underwater, and for a while they'd lost track of the situation. Next thing they saw was a visibly wounded Tiamat fleeing the vicinity. Years had passed. Why was Godzilla suddenly spoiling for a rematch?

The briefing on Tiamat came up.

"*Titanus Tiamat, Titan 19. Extremely aggressive and territorial, weaponizing her body of razor-sharp scales. Tiamat's arctic lair sits in the direct path of electromagnetically charged solar winds making it the largest stockpile of energy on Earth.*"

"If Godzilla takes down Tiamat," the sub commander said, "he'll supercharge."

"Shit," Hampton said.

Hollow Earth

Are you okay? Ilene asked Jia, as they pushed further into the jungle.

Jia quirked her lips and lifted her shoulders. Not a shrug.

I don't know, she said. *I'm sorry for Mikael. He should have listened to Trapper.*

Yeah, she nodded. *Me too.*

And for those other people, Jia added. *At the outpost.*

Jia was no stranger to death. She had seen more than her fair share of awful things, and she, like Ilene, was probably still in a little bit of shock over the latest fatalities. She kept catching herself, wondering where Mikael was, and then remembering he just... wasn't.

There was nothing we could have done for him, she said, maybe more for herself than for Jia. Monarch expeditions had encountered tree mimics before. Several species had been described, and this might be a new one, because she had never seen one that looked like roots before. But what they all had in common was that they killed their prey instantly. They were hard to kill, too, and even if they had managed to kill that one, it wouldn't have saved Mikael's life—or him any suffering for that matter. He had probably never known what happened.

Anyway, they didn't have anything with them that *could* have killed it. Mikael's gun was the only one they had, and it had been eaten with him.

She was about to continue the conversation when she noticed Jia was looking up. Something was drifting downward.

It looked a bit like feather-down, but Ilene figured it was some variety of pappus, like the fluffy parachutes that blew off dandelions to spread their seeds. She noticed one or two more, carried on the breeze.

I thought it was ash, Jia signed.

It looks like that, Ilene replied.

I mean when I saw them before, Jia clarified.

When did you see these before? Ilene wondered. But Jia wasn't paying attention anymore. She was pushing ahead, the tree-mimic and Mikael apparently forgotten. Ilene hurried after her, but before she got very far she noticed angular, symmetrical shapes in the undergrowth, the sort of geometric profiles that were rare in nature.

"It's ruins," she said as she realized the truth. Jia already knew; she had knelt at a low stone structure of some sort and was pushing back the vegetation.

"Human civilization?" Trapper said. "Down here?"

Jia had moved on to a square column, carved with odd figures. Ilene leaned in to inspect. Jia got her attention.

These are the symbols of my people, her daughter informed her.

Ilene was already thinking the same thing. Stylistically they were slightly different, the way written English looked different if you compared something penned in the thirteenth century to something printed in the twenty-first. The same alphabet, so to speak. Of course, it wasn't an alphabet per se, but the symbols did carry meaning.

"The markings look older than the ones on Skull Island," she said for the benefit of the others. "Centuries older. But the architecture is consistent with the Iwi."

The feathery white stuff was falling everywhere now, like a gentle snow. It was beautiful, and peaceful—and somehow sad.

Jia looked at all of those things as she took in their surroundings. Now that Ilene was really looking, she saw the remains of buildings everywhere. This had been at least a decent-sized town, if not a city.

What happened to them? Jia asked.

I don't know, she mouthed, shaking her head.

Trapper and Bernie moved slowly, almost reverentially, through the ruins. Bernie was uncharacteristically quiet, as if aware that he was in a sacred space of some kind.

Ilene had long suspected that humans had lived in Hollow Earth. Images found in deep caves, legendary tales from around the world, all suggested that at least some humans had emerged from the ground. The ancient Kong structures they had discovered on their first trip to Hollow Earth had pictures of humans on the walls. She had come to think it was possible that, as other species had moved back and forth between the surface world and the world beneath, so had humans and human ancestors like homo erectus, homo habilis, and homo naledi. But until now, the only evidence for that had been stories and rock drawings.

These were *buildings*, not to the scale of Titans, but at human scale, with obvious similarities to those of the Iwi of Skull Island, a place with perhaps the strongest connection to Hollow Earth on the surface world. The Iwi themselves had told her they came up from below with Kong's ancestors.

They continued to move silently through the ancient settlement. Bernie whispered a little, obviously to himself, and he took a few pictures. But at least he didn't get out his video camera and start a running commentary.

"This site must be thousands of years old," she whispered.

Ahead, Trapper had found a stone staircase and started up it. He paused.

149

"Now, that's weird," he said, indicating the steps. "There's no moss on these ones."

She saw that now. The stone of the stairs and the area above was relatively bare. As if they had been cleaned—or were still in use.

The space at the top looked almost like a sanctuary of some sort, a small stone-paved yard surrounded by walls, most of which were still intact. A shallow oval basin about a meter across was set down into the floor. Eight channels radiated from the hollow like the beams of the sun in a kid's drawing, except they weren't totally symmetrical in arrangement. They were evenly spaced except on one side, where there was a conspicuous gap.

Trapper stepped through the basin and on toward the wall beyond.

"Hello," he said. He pushed back some trailing vines, revealing a bas-relief carving of a winged creature. Even stylized, the creature depicted was instantly recognizable.

"Mothra," Ilene said.

"Queen of the Monsters," Bernie said, "in Hollow Earth."

"Her lineage must go back further than we thought," Ilene said.

A Titan, one of the most mysterious. When Godzilla fought Ghidorah, when all seemed on the verge of being lost—it was the intervention of Mothra that made the difference. If it wasn't for Mothra, Ghidorah might have killed Godzilla. If he had, there was no doubt he would have stripped the globe of life.

Mothra had hatched from an egg that had been kept in an ancient temple in the Yunnan rainforest of China. No one was exactly certain how long it had been there, but it opened into a caterpillar only days before Godzilla's battle with Ghidorah.

The pupa had attached itself under a nearby waterfall and had quickly matured into an adult, mothlike form.

This carving was far too old to be *that* Mothra, but a scattering of legends from around the world claimed the mysterious Titan had been born and died many times, always arriving when she was needed.

This was a temple, Jia signed. *A place of worship.*

It wasn't a question; Jia was fully confident. Ilene hadn't seen her like this in… a long time.

"Yeah," she said.

Something flitted through the air, just past Jia. An insect, a big one. It looked something like a wasp, with two pairs of wings, but it was glowing, like a lightning bug. It made a strange little chittering sound and landed on a protrusion in the wall.

Jia padded toward it. When she got near she reached toward it.

"No, no, no," Trapper said, forgetting the girl couldn't hear him. Ilene shared his concern; it might well be venomous, or— something. But she felt, in that moment, that she needed to trust her daughter.

Jia didn't touch the insect. Instead she placed her hand on the projecting stone and pressed.

The stone moved. It went in, until it was flush with the rest of the wall.

The insect flew away, and immediately Ilene heard the gurgle of water. It came down from above, flowing in steep channels into the grooves in the stone floor, filling the basin at the center.

Jia stared at it for a moment, then started to run back down the stairs. Ilene now realized the apparent gap in the symmetry of the channels was misleading; a channel ran *under* the stones of the temple, shooting the water out and down the stairs. It was that little torrent that Jia was chasing after.

"Hey," Ilene called after her, realizing at the same time Jia couldn't hear her but also aware it probably wouldn't make a difference if she could.

"Whoa, whoa," Trapper called, making the identical mistake.

"It's like some… irrigation system," Bernie said. He did have his video camera out now, as he too ran after Jia. "It predates everything! Mesopotamians, the Lemurians. These guys were the first, man."

Jia ran on, following the newly created stream. The rest pursued her through the jungle until she stopped in front of… something.

It was like a cloud or a cobweb, and yet like neither, a pale barrier that ran through the trees, blocking their path. Jia was still now, contemplating it.

"Now, that's a trip," Trapper opined.

"Great Mulder and Scully, look at that," Bernie said.

Ilene moved closer. Not cobwebs. Not any kind of web she'd seen. And not a cloud, although it seemed to swirl around inside, incandescing with uneven blueish light.

"What could have created this?" Ilene asked.

"Ancient alien astronauts," Bernie said.

Trapper moved up and knelt where the wall and the little canal met.

"Look at this here," he said. "The water's running underneath. This is… this is organic." He slowly extended a finger toward it. When he encountered what appeared to be the surface, his finger stopped and was met by a blue spark. He drew back a little, but looked more curious than hurt or alarmed. He stood up, moving one of his ears nearer.

"Hear that?" he said. "Some kind of bioelectric hum."

He took both hands and pushed against it.

The reaction was instantaneous. The wall of... whatever it was pushed back, flickering with interior lightning, the hum becoming more distant thunder. Vague silhouettes moved within the web, or fog, or... but then she understood. It was a wall, a barrier. To keep something in or out—or maybe both.

"It's like camouflage," Ilene said.

Everyone had stepped back, but Jia strode confidently forward, quickly pushing her hands fingers-first into the wall. Actinic blue-white light poured through, but Jia kept pushing.

"Should she be doing that?" Bernie asked. "She shouldn't be doin' that, right?"

Jia kept pulling, and the slit grew wider, the light pouring through, rendering her face incandescent.

Ilene moved to her side, put her hands in, and pulled with her. The rift grew wider. The light, or electricity, or whatever it was didn't hurt: it just sort of tingled. And the material felt one moment like a sort of spongy fabric and at others like a jellyfish. And as they pulled, the rift tore broader and longer, until they could see through it.

And what they saw was... astonishing, even for Hollow Earth.

Nearby, just beyond the rift, feathery fronds of continuing jungle framed the view. In the distance, Ilene could make out three towers, wider at the base and tapering toward their flat tops, almost like candles. No, very steep pyramids. They looked the same size, by they didn't stand side by side. Instead, one hung down from the land above and one thrust up from the ground they stood on, blunt stalagmites and stalactites almost touching at the narrow ends. In the void between them drifted a line of floating boulders, caught in the zero-gravity borderland between the two major planes of Hollow Earth. Smaller, similar tapering structures descended from near the upper tower, along with what appeared to be a city of some sort. The jungle prevented them from seeing if the lower tower had similar buildings.

From my dreams, Jia said.

"This must be the source of the signal," Ilene said.

"Oh, we gotta check this out," Trapper said.

"Yeah," she agreed.

Together, they pulled the opening wide enough to step through. Bernie, camera in hand, followed them.

ELEVEN

It was I who did command
The dragon god of these hills
To send down the snow
Whereof a few fragments perchance
Were sprinkled over your home.

—poem attributed to Lady Fujiwara,
Man'yōshū or Collection of Ten
Thousand Leaves 11:104, the oldest
surviving book of Japanese poetry

Subterranean realm
Uncharted territory
Hollow Earth

Kong's gaze drew up to the sky as a flock of fliers went
overhead. They looked like the creatures the little ones called
war-bats. He had fought them before. They were tough, but

not really a threat unless they attacked in large numbers. To him, anyway. But they could probably easily kill Small Ape, who kept looking up at them nervously.

Kong vocalized in a way meant to be reassuring. Small Ape mostly looked puzzled. It frustrated Kong that he couldn't communicate better with him. He had tried Jia's hand language, but Small Ape didn't understand it at all. He did understand some of Kong's more basic sounds and gestures, but not others.

But he knew what Kong wanted—to lead him to where the other apes lived. That was enough for now.

They were deep in new territory for Kong. Most of the plants were the same, and some of the animals. But there were smells here he did not know, and that made him cautious. He kept a close watch on Small Ape too, who probably knew these lands better than he did.

Ahead, another group of fliers had landed to search for food. He remembered these from the cave where he found his axe. They posed no danger to him, so he continued to stride forward. He noticed that there were smaller ones among them; the larger ones seemed to be helping them feed. He glanced at Small Ape. Was he supposed to do that? Help Small Ape eat?

Of course, Small Ape had led him into a trap earlier. He wasn't sure he liked Small Ape. He just needed him to find the others.

The fliers scattered at their approach. Seeming to take comfort in this, Small Ape moved a little more confidently, and soon led Kong to a big flat-water place. Small Ape paused, glancing up at Kong, then splashed into the water. He gestured for Kong to join him.

Kong didn't like the smell of the place, but if Small Ape wasn't afraid, there was no reason *he* should be. Small Ape cupped some water in his hands and took a drink.

Kong *was* thirsty. He waded in. The water felt good, just a little cooler than the air. He threw some up on his head and shoulders. That was good, too.

He kept his eye on Small Ape, who was now between him and the shore. He thought the other was starting to look a little nervous. He seemed to be looking at something behind Kong, and he made a little sound—like he had made a mistake? Like he was sorry about something.

A shadow fell over them, and Kong turned just in time to see the huge snake-fish thing rear up above him and strike down with its sharp-toothed mouth. He lifted his axe with two hands and wedged it between the snapping jaws. Small Ape squealed and ran.

Another trap. Small Ape was good at this.

He threw the thing back. It was slick, and smelled like fish, blue striped with yellow, and had a fin on its back. As it thrashed in the water, he charged toward it, wielding his axe in one hand. It arched over him and struck down like before, but this time he was ready, catching its head and shoving it down, lifting the axe to decapitate it. But before he could swing, its tail swept up from behind him and coiled around his axe-arm. Then it yanked him backward. Surprised, his uncertain footing on the squishy ground below the water failed, and he pitched over, the snake-fish pulling him under.

He struggled to pull the coils off his arm, but more looped themselves around his neck. The water was deep here, and the snake-fish was trying to keep him underneath, where he couldn't breathe.

The snake-fish was strong, one long powerful muscle. But Kong was stronger, and he was angry at being tricked again, outraged that the snake-fish thought it could kill him when he had fought far stronger enemies.

He got his feet back under him and pushed, burst back in the air, pulling at the coils with one hand while keeping hold of his axe. The mouth appeared again, darting toward his face.

He brought the axe down, hard, felt it slide through skin and flesh and snick through bone. The coils writhed as if they were still alive, but they were no longer trying to hold him. He pushed them off, grabbed the head, and looked off in the direction Small Ape had run. He saw him there, scrambling frantically through the underbrush, and started after him. When he was close enough, he hurled the axe, watching it turn end over end before burying itself in the ground right in front of Small Ape, who stumbled and fell to a stop.

Then he tossed the head next to him.

Small Ape looked terrified. His eyes darted around for a chance of escape, any escape. Kong glared down at him. Small Ape cowered in a submissive posture—and not a very hopeful one. When Kong reached down, he sank back further, but when all he did was pull the axe from the ground, he looked confused, making small, soft noises.

Kong jerked his head back toward the lake. Small Ape looked in the direction, then started that way. But he couldn't keep his gaze off Kong and tripped. He got up hesitantly, then continued on. Kong followed.

Once there, he dragged the fish-snake's body out of the water, cut off a chunk with his axe, and started to eat. He'd been hungry anyway.

Small Ape watched him as he ate, making hungry noises, but keeping his distance. Kong could tell he wanted some of the meat, but he didn't try to get some, or make any sort of gesture he recognized as asking for it either.

Kong bit into the tubular section, pulling out the slippery insides and gulping them down.

Small Ape picked his own fur and ate something very small he found there.

After a moment, Kong gripped the meat with both hands and held it out toward Small Ape.

Small Ape bristled; he screeched a threat and went into a defensive posture, as if he expected to be attacked.

Kong didn't really remember other apes. He remembered the Iwi. They had shared food with him. He had sometimes given them food. When she was little, he had to find food for Jia.

There had been other little ones through the years.

But something felt wrong about how Small Ape was acting. As if being offered food was a *bad* thing.

Or... maybe Small Ape thought it was a trap, a trick. After all, Small Ape played tricks. Maybe he believed others would do the same to him.

Kong shrugged and tossed the meat at him. Not hard; just to show he wasn't going to fight for it. Small Ape looked at it as if he didn't believe it was there. Then he dashed over, grabbed it, and ran off again. He began tearing into it as if he had not eaten in many day-night times.

He *was* afraid the meat would be taken from him. Kong felt oddly heavy. He had decided that Small Ape wasn't just little, he was young. A child, like Jia. Maybe he would call him Child instead of Small Ape.

He noticed Child was coming closer, for some reason, bringing the meat with him. He sat near Kong and began eating again, slower this time. As if he had figured out Kong wasn't going to take the food from him.

Or it might be another trick that Child was planning. He would have to keep an eye on him.

But for a while, everything was calm, and the two of them ate together, and he didn't mind.

Monarch Control
Barbados

"Director?" Laurier said.

"Yes?" Hampton didn't look up from her monitor. She had been through everything twice now, but she felt that she had to be missing something.

"The sub is nearing the target."

"Yeah," she said. "Godzilla?"

"He submerged a few hours ago. But given his speed and trajectory, he should be there too."

"Speed and trajectory? Don't we have eyes on him?"

"Not at the moment. The energy field from Tiamat's lair is playing havoc with the instruments. The sub and fly-over crew have been playing it safe since the EMP incident in France."

"Bring the sub in closer," she said. "We need to know what's happening there."

Laurier nodded and went off to her station.

"What are you up to, Godzilla?" she murmured. But she knew, didn't she? She just didn't want to believe it. She had been going through every bit of information collected about Tiamat, and especially that gathered in the past few years, since the sea-serpent Titan had been defeated by Godzilla in the Pacific. It looked like Tiamat's first instinct was to just get away from Godzilla. Monarch had tracked her erratic path for months. Notably, at no point during that period had she attacked anything. The working theory was that she was trying to comply with Godzilla's "instructions." After his fight with her, before he himself became quiescent in some caves deep below the Pacific waters, on the outskirts of Hollow Earth, he had seemed to send out some sort of signal commanding the Titans to become dormant. Tiamat looked like she was complying along with the rest of them. She had challenged Godzilla and been put in her place, and now she was doing what the King of the Monsters bid her.

She had found her new, energy-rich lair in the Arctic, and since then she hadn't come out. Hampton had hoped to find some evidence that the Titan had slipped off to trouble the shipping lanes or perhaps trash a coastal village or two, but there was no evidence or even rumors that she had done anything but hang out in her iceberg palace.

Usually, when Godzilla went after another Titan, there was an obvious reason. Scylla had been on a rampage—Godzilla ended it, with extreme prejudice. It fit the usual pattern; get out of line, Godzilla would come along and straighten you out.

But Tiamat had been playing nice. Sure, she could just be charging up, planning a future excursion to New York, Copenhagen, or Sydney. Maybe Godzilla knew that somehow and was just being pre-emptive. Maybe years in her lair had made her much stronger, and *she* was the threat he had been charging up to fight before she became too much to handle.

Or he was just going there to murder Tiamat, steal her energy source and further power up to face what must be an unthinkably dangerous threat.

She hoped desperately that it was the first, but just as she could find no evidence of bad behavior on Tiamat's part, nor could she find any link between Tiamat and the distress call from Hollow Earth.

But they were about to find out in real time, weren't they.

"Sub moving into position," Laurier said.

"Put them on," Hampton told her.

She turned her attention to the flyover images, all blue water and sea-ice, nothing stirring the surface. Tiamat's lair was a massive accretion of frozen sea riddled with passageways, and like most ocean ice the vast majority of its mass was underwater. As one of the other monitors flickered on, she could see part of it in underwater view, courtesy of the submarine's forward cameras. On the other display, the interior of the watercraft was now visible, with Commander Betts firmly in the foreground.

"Fifteen Alpha reporting to base," he said. Then his eyes lifted and met hers through the video link as his side of it came on.

"Director."

"Captain," she replied.

"We're entering Tiamat's domain," he said. "But something's off. Tiamat's energy is distorting our radar. We don't have a visual on Godzilla."

"Can't help you with that," she said. "We've got nothing on this end either."

"We're getting in closer." He nodded to his crew. "Take us forward, silent running, five knots."

The underwater feed brightened as the submarine floodlights snapped on, revealing the hulking iceberg in front of them, growing larger on the viewscreen.

Hampton realized she was holding her breath and let it go. The sub drifted closer.

Maybe he's not there at all, she thought. *Maybe we've misread this situation from the start.*

The underwater view suddenly blazed with blue light; the view of Captain Betts and his crew rattled violently. Filters cut in and the glare dampened, resolving the new brilliance into a blue-white beam.

Godzilla's energy weapon. He was attacking the sub.

No, she thought. *Why?*

But then she realized that the sub commander and his crew

were still on screen, looking shaken, but alive and intact. If Godzilla were trying to kill them, they would already be gone. No, the beam had narrowly missed the submarine and was boring into the submerged mountain of ice. He was trying to get Tiamat's attention.

He succeeded. In seconds the blue beam cut through the entire frozen mass; on the other side an expanding plume of steam and crystals billowed into the frigid waters. Behind the cloud, something broke from the iceberg, like a length of ribbon writhing in the current, but quickly resolving into the Titan which Monarch had given the name Tiamat.

She was named for the ocean goddess of ancient Mesopotamia, but to Hampton she resembled depictions of sea-serpents. Her lengthy, sinuous body was equal parts eel and sea-snake but she also had four stubby—albeit lethally clawed—limbs. A double row of spined, fishlike fins ran down either side of her backbone, glowing with an eerie violet energy similar to Godzilla's blue charge. The four petal-like appendages that had been flattened against her skull opened up, crackling with power, and her mouth gaped open. Godzilla returned the challenge with his own underwater roar, and then they raced straight for one another.

Tiamat coiled her long body around Godzilla and began to rotate her coils. Each scale on her body was sharper than a flake of obsidian and harder than titanium. She was not only constricting Godzilla but cutting into him like a diamond saw. The aerial crew had located the fight now, and from above the outlines of the two Titans, limned in the light of their energy fields, turned beneath the ocean's surface. The view from the sub was a little better; as Tiamat tried to slice Godzilla into sandwich meat, Godzilla bit off a hunk of her flank and tossed it away. The serpent-Titan shrieked and darted her head toward Godzilla, engulfing his entire skull with her cranial appendages; her purple glow increased.

But blue fire ran up Godzilla's spines, and a moment later an explosion blinded the sub's cameras. From the air, though, a blue beam was visible streaking up from below the surface and stabbing into the clear arctic sky.

Then everything went still.

"What's going on?" Hampton asked. The sub's forward camera feed had not come back online, but the view inside the sub remained. Crew members scurried about on fire patrol.

"You guys okay?" she asked.

"We're damaged," the captain said. "Nothing we can't handle."

"Where's Godzilla?"

"I'm not sure," the captain said. "We're trying to get a visual."

"Oh…" Hampton said. "Wait. Never mind."

Tiamat was surfacing—or rather, parts of her were. Lots of them. A heartbeat later, Godzilla breached like a whale, tossed a mouthful of meat that was mostly one of Tiamat's legs, then dove once more.

"Well, that's Tiamat," she sighed. "Anybody still got eyes on Godzilla?"

"Hang on, Base," Captains Betts said. "Re-establishing visual."

The screen came up, just in time to show Godzilla vanishing into a tunnel in the iceberg.

"He's going into Tiamat's lair," Betts said.

"Yeah," Hampton replied. "I can see that. Clear the area. He's going to be a whole lot stronger."

As Godzilla disappeared into the ice, Tiamat's severed head crossed their view, drifting slowly toward the sea floor.

Inside the energy barrier
Hollow Earth

Beyond the barrier, the terrain itself was a lot like outside the barrier. The jungle continued through a scattering of ruins; the water Jia had released continued to flow along in its little canal, and they kept following it. But Ilene felt, well, *watched*. Jia kept looking off as if she was seeing things Ilene wasn't, and even Trapper was on edge. Not usual for him.

Bernie, however, was having a ball. He kept going on about how incredible it all was, how the people who followed his blog weren't going to believe it, but they would *have* to believe. His sheer wonder was endearing, but she wished he would do it all more quietly.

But what did it matter? If there were Iwi here—or people like the Iwi—they probably already knew there were strangers in their territory.

And if there weren't people here, if the buildings they had seen in the distance were just more ruins, then it didn't matter either way.

Bernie's awe was infectious, though. The Iwi of Skull Island had all died, all but Jia. Ilene had tried to help them, but in the end it just wasn't possible. But she had known them as a people, and many of them as individuals. Their culture had been unique and it had been admirable. The chance that some of them were still alive, down here, living in their own way— it was exciting. And what it would mean to Jia she couldn't even guess, but she could see how excited the girl was. Deep in her gut, she knew their lives were about to change.

She desperately hoped it would be for the better.

A few steps later, Trapper put his hand on Jia's shoulder. He held up a finger.

"Wait, wait, wait," he said.

They were emerging from a narrow canyon into a small clearing bounded by closely set trees.

Trapper seemed to be searching for something.

We're not alone, Jia signed.

"Wait, what did she say?" Trapper asked.

"She says we're not alone," she told him.

"See, I knew," Trapper said. "I *knew* I felt something." He drew a hunting knife, flipped it in his hand, flourished it.

"Come on then," he said, louder. "Where are ya?"

Ilene was looking too, but she didn't see anything. If they were Iwi, that was hardly surprising. The ones she knew had been quite good at hiding themselves in the jungle. They'd had to be, given the monsters they had shared their island with. That was likely even truer here.

Then Bernie screamed as if he'd been struck. She spun toward him and saw that someone had stepped out of the trees and grabbed him from behind. And now they were everywhere—behind them, in front of them, all around them. Their bodies were painted and they wore cowls of the same color so they blended in with their surroundings. Ilene guessed they had probably been following them for quite a while, maybe since they had entered the territory protected by the veil.

But now more people were coming, and these were not camouflaged. They wore saffron-colored clothing and carried spears with long, glowing crystalline blades. They contracted around Ilene and her companions like a noose. Trapper had changed his grip on the knife so it was suspended from his thumb and forefinger by the point.

"It's going away!" he said. "See, it's going away."

Bernie had been shoved into the circle with the rest of them.

He still had his camera out, but he had his hands up like the rest of them so it dangled, pointing at the ground.

"Are those... are those Iwi?" he asked.

A woman with a spear lifted its tip so it stood up straight, no longer threatening them. She was looking directly at Jia. Her black hair was pulled back in a tight bun, and she wore a circlet around her head like the one Jia still affected. A blood-colored line of paint ran across her face from ear to ear, and another from her chin to her lower lip. She took a step closer to Jia. Then she nodded in the direction of the city. Jia nodded back.

We're supposed to go with them, Jia signed.

Ilene nodded. "We're going with them," she told the others.

"Nice of them to ask," Bernie said.

They were moving now. Their captors stayed close, the threat of their weapons never very far away. Ilene couldn't shake the feeling that something was happening here, something more than an isolated people reacting to strangers. It was almost like they had been expected.

"I don't think they talk," she told Bernie. "The Iwi had a spoken language, but they almost never used it."

"But you know it, don't you?" Trapper said. "Maybe try a few words."

She shrugged. "Where we all go?" she attempted, in Iwi. There was probably a better way to say it, but it was the best she could do. Iwi verb conjugations were... difficult.

No one reacted. She might as well have been speaking French or Yup'ik.

"So much for that," she murmured.

As they progressed, the ruins vanished, replaced by intact structures that looked like they were still in use. She had glimpses of the pyramid-towers ahead.

Malenka, Jia signed, using the phonetic alphabet.

What?

I think this place is called Malenka.

How do you know?

Jia looked troubled. *I'm not sure*, she replied.

Okay, Ilene thought. *Places have names, even if no one says them out loud.* That sort of made sense. What bothered her more was that she thought Jia wasn't being completely honest with her: not so much that she had lied, but that there was something she wasn't saying.

There was no question that these people had singled Jia out from the start. Was it just the physical resemblance they had picked up on? That Jia looked more like them than Ilene, Trapper, and Bernie? If these people were Iwi, or very closely related to them, that seemed unlikely. It wasn't her experience with them. But they were definitely treating Jia differently. It was probably best not to jump to any conclusions as to why. She needed to keep an open mind, see things as they were rather than as she feared they might be.

Whoever these people were, there were more of them now, and more armed with the crystal spears. That wasn't surprising, either. These people lived in a dangerous world. The Iwi greeted strangers with spears, too, not because they were an inherently violent people. If anything, they were the opposite. But Skull Island hadn't been an island paradise. Meeting something, or someone, new without appropriate caution was just not the smart move.

As Mikael had learned, unfortunately.

They came into a clearing. No, more like a town square. But what a town! For a moment, every other thought was pushed out of her head by sheer wonder.

"Oh my God," she said, sotto voce.

"Oh. My. God," Bernie said loudly.

They were near the base of a gigantic pyramid, the largest of the three they had seen from a distance. It rose much more sharply than any she had seen before. The steepest Egyptian pyramids had slopes of fifty-three and fifty-four degrees. Nubian pyramids were more like seventy degrees. This one looked even closer to vertical than that, which is why from a distance they looked more like tapering columns.

Also, pyramids up on the surface didn't scintillate in the colors of the rainbow. This one did; it seemed to be built of crystals—if it wasn't just one huge crystal. A wide line of blue light started at the center of the base and continued to the summit. Far overhead she could see its twin hanging, point down.

Although the structure in front of them was the largest, there were smaller pyramids all around them. It was hard not to recall the shapes Jia had drawn, and the frequency patterns from the now-destroyed outpost. Were these the physical embodiments of the signal—the one Bernie insisted was a distress call?

She had guessed that this space was a sort of commons, but what did that mean down here? With the island Iwi, spaces like this had been a mixture of social and sacred. They didn't tease the two things apart. Was it the same here?

More people were gathered here, sitting on steps or on the ground. Most of them rose, as if in greeting when the surface-dwellers came in sight. Or maybe it was just for Jia.

These new people weren't armed, and most wore saffron-colored clothing. The designs on their faces were very Iwi-like—colorful arrangements of mostly linear and rectangular patterns, some metallic, resembling gold-leaf. A few of them weren't painted at all. Iwi body adornment was a complex language in itself—one that Ilene had only the vaguest grasp of.

"This is an entire human civilization protected within

Hollow Earth," Bernie said. "These structures—they look like they've been carved from enormous quartz crystals. That must be their energy source."

Trapper said something to Bernie, softly, but Ilene didn't catch it. She was studying Jia. The girl looked over at her.

I can feel their thoughts, Jia said.

That's it, Ilene realized. That's what Jia hadn't been telling her. She was *talking* to them somehow.

They were at the center of an area flanked by four smallish pyramids—two to their left and two to the right. Ahead was a raised circular dais on which a number of people were gathered. Beyond that, broad, wide stairs—like courthouse steps—led up to an opening through which shone blindingly white light. Ilene tracked her gaze upward and saw—in the distant land-sky—a large circular opening, also shining with brilliant, but bluish, light. Specks of floating boulders in the null-gravity zone drifted in front of it. She knew what *that* was, at least, although it was somewhat shocking.

"That's… that's an undocumented vortex," she said.

"Several of them, actually," Bernie qualified.

He was right. There were a number of them. Usually there was no more than one in any given local. This—this was a sort of Hollow Earth Grand Central terminal.

"Routes to the surface," she said. "These could lead—all over the Earth."

"It's incredible," Bernie said.

A man suddenly stepped right up to her face, his dark eyes fixed on hers. Her initial instinct was to flinch from what for her was an aggressive move. But she checked the reflex and returned his stare.

"You should make eye contact with them," she told the others. "It's considered polite."

The Iwi did this. It had always reminded her of the staring contests she'd had as a kid. And yes, they considered it respectful. It could also be extended to become a test. The Iwi figured if you looked away, you had something to hide.

"This... this isn't working for me," Bernie said, trying to maintain his gaze on the man who stood nose-to-nose with him.

Something rang then, like a gong, although Ilene couldn't see the source of the sound. That was followed by rattling as all of the natives raised both hands, fingers spread, and began shaking them, causing the bangles on some of their wrists to sound. They were all facing the stairs and doorway beyond as someone emerged. The woman who had led their capture ascended to meet the new arrival.

It was another woman. Her age was uncertain; she had only a few small markings on her face, but the hand-rattling of the crowd redoubled. This was clearly someone important.

The two women looked for all the world like they were having a conversation, but there was no sound, no signing, no movement of their lips.

"How are they communicating?" Trapper whispered.

"Telepathically," Bernie replied. "Very *Village of the Damned.*"

At this point, Ilene was inclined to believe him. The pieces had been in front of her for a long time. Now the puzzle was coming together. The Iwi of Skull Island had a spoken language, but they rarely used it. She had only been able to find a few older people who were truly fluent in it. She had suspected even then that their language was largely for the benefit of communicating with various other people who had ended up stranded on Skull Island. There was evidence of at least a small Polynesian population that had integrated into the Iwi, and she had identified what she was sure were a few

Spanish and Malay loanwords. Shipwrecks had been washing ashore on Skull Island for a very long time. But down here, with no contact with other humans, any spoken language would have been completely forgotten centuries or millennia ago. It would have been unnecessary.

The woman with the spear stepped aside, and the important-looking woman at the top of the stairs gestured toward someone below, a matronly woman with no face painting. The older woman bowed slightly, and then came straight for Jia. She pointed to the important woman on the stairs, and then reached for the girl's arm.

That was too much.

"Oh, no, no, no," Ilene said, gripping Jia's shoulders, but her daughter was pulled away, and the guards closed in with their spears, stopping Ilene from following. Trapper and Bernie also took hold of Ilene, albeit gently.

"Wait!" she called. "I don't know where they're taking her! Hey! Hey!"

Jia stopped and turned around. She looked confident, calm. *It's okay*, she signed.

They're taking you from me, Ilene thought. *How can it be fine?*

But she nodded. "Okay," she said. She watched as Jia walked up the stairs.

"I…" she said.

"It's okay," Trapper whispered.

"I know, I know," Bernie said. They still held her, but not to keep her from running into the spears. To comfort her. And it did. A little.

"You know the Iwi," Trapper said. "They're peaceful. You taught us that."

She took a breath and nodded. Yes. The Iwi were peaceful.

They only ever acted to defend themselves. And these people looked like Iwi. They acted like Iwi. But what if they were really something different?

She had just seen what looked like a tree's root ball eat a man.

But Jia said she could sense their thoughts. Jia said it would be okay. She had to trust her daughter.

Jia reached the top of the stairs and stood in front of the important woman, who looked intensely at the girl for a moment, then held out her hands, palms up. Jia nodded and placed her hands on the woman's.

For what seemed an interminable period, nothing happened. Then the woman smiled, and Jia nodded. Jia turned, and both of them faced the crowd. They were holding hands. The woman held out her other arm and made a sort of lowering motion. Instantly the guards pulled their spears back and stepped away. The crowd parted for them as Jia and the woman turned and walked into the pyramid.

"Let's go, let's go," Bernie said. But Ilene was way ahead of him, already pressing forward.

As they ran up the steps and into the hall that entered the huge structure, Bernie seemed to be having second thoughts.

"Are you sure we're not going to be sacrificed?" he asked. "I don't want to be sacrificed before I clear my browser history—" He stopped talking as they passed through the hall and gaped at what lay within.

The pyramid was hollow, containing an enormous cathedral-like space. Hanging in the center of it was a crystal, or rather a cluster of crystals held together by bracing. A long cable stretched up to it, dropping all the way to the floor.

As amazing as all of that was, Ilene's focus flipped immediately back to Jia. She caught the important woman's eye.

"Can..." she started.

The woman nodded, as if she understood.

"Thank you," she said, and ran to her daughter.

This is where it came from, Jia informed her.

Ilene looked back at the hanging crystal.

"What's she saying, Doc?" Trapper asked.

"She saying that's the... the beacon that we've been following. It's the Iwi calling for help."

The woman turned to the center of the pyramid and made an elegant—almost dancelike—motion with her arms. A man started pulling on the cable, which was held in such a way that it went around the central crystal and then off to another anchor point across the pyramid. As he pulled, the rope rubbed across the crystal, producing an eerie tone—or rather, a stacked sequence of harmonics that filled the entire space with unearthly music.

"I get it," Bernie said. "Hey, look. We're inside of a giant crystal singing bowl." He chuckled. "I bet the pyramid's shape directs the vibrations up, and it just amplifies them, man."

A little carried away, he bumped into one of the Iwi spear bearers. The man didn't react, but Bernie stopped talking.

"So, wait," Trapper said. "They're sending out this SOS and... Godzilla hears it?"

"Yeah," she said. "They woke him up."

"An SOS for what?" Bernie asked. "They already live in a nightmare monster hellscape. What could possibly scare them?"

The woman turned sharply toward them.

"Hey," Ilene told Bernie. "She can understand everything you say."

"Wait. She understands me?" He looked over at the woman. "And, uh, a nightmare monster hellscape is a wonderful place to raise a family." He reached over and took Trapper's arm. Trapper took his in turn, and they smiled, like a happy couple.

TWELVE

Then a powerful monster, living below in the darkness, became resentful as he heard, day on day, the joy in the hall, the ringing of the harp and clear song of the poet, the telling of the beginnings of all, how the Almighty created the world, formed the bright fields and water all around and reveled in setting the lamps of the sun and the moon to light our radiant world, and bejeweled the earth with trees and leaves, quickened with life every living creature and nation. So men lived in delight and celebrated their blessings. Until the monster stirred, a demon, an evil spirit, a grim fiend named Grendel. March-stepper, dweller in marsh and fen. Miserable creature, he lived among monsters, placed in bitter exile like all the race of Cain, whom God crushed, separated, and drove away from men as vengeance for the killing of Abel.

—Beowulf

Malenka
Hollow Earth

The Iwi—and Ilene was still not entirely certain that the term was appropriate—were not done with show and tell, according to Jia. But the important woman had agreed to give them a few moments before the tour moved on.

This is all okay with you? Ilene signed. *You're comfortable with her?*

Jia nodded, smiling. *I'm fine*, she said. *I'm happy. These are my people.*

I know, Ilene said, *I'm happy for you.* Saying it, she realized that although she wanted that to be true, she actually felt... sad. Which was all wrong, and totally her problem. She would get past that. She had to.

She doesn't mean us any harm, Jia continued. *She wants me to do something, though. I'm not sure what it is.*

Okay, Ilene said, trying not to communicate her own uncertainty. She had decided to trust Jia. So far there was no reason to rethink that. In fact, Jia was the only one of them who had a chance of figuring out what was going on here.

Who is she? she asked, gesturing at the important woman.

She's the queen, Jia replied. Then she frowned. *It's not the perfect word. She's their leader. They consider her the wisest, the most knowledgeable but she's not like—off with their heads! Or anything like that. They all agree she should be queen, but they also believe she was meant to be, if that makes sense.*

Sort of, she said.

The Skull Island Iwi had a word that she had translated as queen, too, but the Iwi term didn't match up well with the English. For one thing, it was gender neutral. For another, "queens" were not born to their positions. They were generally people—and very often women—who had proven themselves to be worthy of their position. It sounded like the same was true down here. Given the deference showed her by the other Iwi, "queen" would probably do as a convenient way of referring to her.

Does she have a name? she asked Jia.

I think they don't like to say her name, Jia replied.

Ilene nodded. That was possible. If a name hadn't been offered, it would probably be impolite to ask. So "queen" it was.

What did she see when you first touched hands? she asked. *Before that, they were guarding us with spears. After they weren't.*

She saw me, Jia said. *My childhood on Skull Island. Me and Kong. Me and you. She knows you're my mother, now. She said it was important.*

Which part?

That I'm from the Iwi above. From Skull Island.

Why?

Jia shrugged. *It has something to do with the thing they want me to do.* She paused. *I think they were expecting me.*

Expecting you? Did they say that?

No. But I feel it. Don't know how, or why.

While she and Jia talked, the Iwi queen appeared to be conferring with other Iwi in their silent language.

"What's going on?" Trapper asked, softly.

"I'm not sure," she said. "Jia thinks they want her to do something. But they have something else they want to show us first."

"Hopefully not their sacrificial altar," Bernie said.

"The Iwi don't sacrifice people," Ilene said.

"That you know of."

"Just... Bernie, no."

The queen had finished her conference and was now beckoning them to come forward.

She says to come with them, Jia said.

"Oh boy," Ilene mouthed. She felt clenched inside. What did these people want with her daughter? If they understood she was her mother, why hadn't they told her? She should be involved with this.

But maybe because she *was* her mother, and they knew she would say no.

She nodded at the queen, hoping that this next round of show-and-tell would involve a little more telling.

The queen led them through a narrow stone passage, wider at the bottom than the top. It reminded Ilene of passages inside some Egyptian pyramids, built to withstand the immense pressure of the heavy stone construction techniques they employed. Here, though, the passages were tunneled through living rock, so the choice was probably stylistic rather than pragmatic. Was Bernie right? Were they inside the prototype of the multitude of pyramids built by ancient surface civilizations?

The stone here didn't glow; the Iwi carried torches to light the way.

Eventually they reached a room that looked familiar, although at first she couldn't parse out why. It was Trapper who got there first.

"It's like the floor where we found the water-guide," he said. "The one with the image of Mothra."

He was right. It wasn't exactly the same, but there was a carved circular pattern in the center of the room and a series of trenches radiating out from it. The inconstant light from the torches suggested carvings on the walls, but she couldn't tell what they represented.

Two of the older women lifted what looked like ceremonial urns and tipped them over a pillar in the very center of the pattern. A glowing blue fluid poured from an urn and began filling up what was not a solid column, but rather another hollow vessel. As it filled and overflowed, it trickled down to flow through the lines etched in the floor, issuing toward square receptacles around the circumference of the room. As this happened, a steady blue light rose to replace that of the torches.

"Oh, wow," Bernie said.

"This whole room is covered in Iwi script," Ilene realized, stepping further in. She knelt to feel the writing on the floor, carved to be read either by sight or touch.

This, she knew well. Whatever the origin and status of their spoken language, Skull Island elders had faithfully maintained their written language, which was largely ideographic, with the symbols representing concepts rather than sounds like the English alphabet. The script here was so close to that of the surface Iwi, it was no trouble to translate.

"It says that Hollow Earth once lived in harmony with the surface world," she read aloud. "There was a balance. The Titans were the guardians of nature, and the Great Apes became the protectors of humanity."

The script on the floor continued on the wall behind her. There, the story became darker.

"But a great evil threatened the peace," she read. "A powerful and ruthless ape, desperate to conquer the surface world, corrupted his tribe and led them into war against the one they called 'The Monster Who Ate A Star.'"

"Godzilla," Trapper said.

She nodded. "There's more. The war with the apes nearly destroyed Godzilla, but after a great battle, he imprisoned the apes in a fiery realm of Hollow Earth. Their false king remains obsessed with reaching the surface. The Iwi call him the Skar King..."

She moved to a bas relief of an ape-like figure. His arms were much longer than his legs, proportionally lengthier than Kong's arms. The image made her think of an orangutan.

It made her think of something else, too. The image recorded on the camera Trapper had found.

"That's the bugger who destroyed the outpost," Trapper said.

Subterranean realm
Uncharted territory
Hollow Earth

Suko had lost hope of escaping Stranger. Part of him didn't want to. Stranger had given him food. No one gave him food. Not even Gnarled Finger, who protected him when he was younger, kept the others from beating him to death, wiped his wounds when they did hit him. Even Gnarled Finger never gave him food until he was himself full and nearly asleep. Even then, Suko had to steal whatever scraps were left. It was the way of the caves. Those who were too frail or injured to fight for food and not clever enough to steal it starved. It was what they deserved, for being weak or stupid or both.

The Skar King did not like weakness. Nobody did.

But Stranger wasn't weak. He wasn't frail. He was strong, very strong, and he had given Suko food.

So he began to think he should not take Stranger home to the Living Caves. Because the Skar King would not like him. The Skar King would hurt him, and then he would hurt Suko.

Suko did not want to be hurt. But to his surprise, he realized he also did not want Stranger to be hurt.

But Stranger was too smart. Suko had tried to trick him. Now he could only do what Stranger wanted, and hope the Skar King would be less angry rather than more. Maybe he could just hide. Maybe no one would know he had led Stranger here. It seemed like less of a risk than to hope he would be rewarded.

They reached a moving long water. It was shallow, clear and cool. Kong didn't think anything big enough to threaten him could hide in it. He signaled to Child that they should rest for a moment. The smaller ape nodded and looked at Kong as if asking permission. Kong nodded, Child bent to the water and brought handfuls of it to his mouth. After a moment he paused, cupped some water, and brought it hesitantly to Kong.

There wasn't much water there, and Kong wasn't very thirsty, but he bent and lapped the little bit of liquid from Child's hands. Then the two of them sat for a moment.

After a moment, Kong turned to Child. He tapped himself on the chest with his knuckles.

Kong, he said, and made Jia's sign. The sound for Kong wasn't the same as what Jia and the little ones made. Ape sounds were different. But for Kong, the sound was his name. He had shared it with little ones before, but never with another ape. Because he had never met another ape.

Child didn't seem to understand, so Kong repeated the sound and then the gesture. Then he extended his knuckles toward Child. *Your name is what?* he meant.

Child blinked, and then he nodded. The smaller ape pointed to himself and made two short sounds close together. *Su Ko.*

Kong repeated the sounds, pointing at Child. Child nodded. *Suko.* Then he pointed at Kong.

Kong, he said. He didn't say it like the little ones did. He said it like an ape. It was the first time Kong had ever heard it like that, like he said it.

Suko.

Kong rose, patting Suko on the shoulder. Then he gestured in the direction Suko had been leading him.

The smaller ape paused. He looked up at Kong and grimaced. But then he nodded, and began once more leading the way. But he seemed reluctant. He didn't go as quickly as before. The further they went, the more Suko seemed to hesitate. Kong encouraged him by growling and motioning with his axe.

The air started to smell funny. As if stone was burning. He knew the scent; in the cave where he had first found his axe there had been burning stone and melted stone that flowed like water. He remembered it had been very hot, though, hotter than the hottest water. That had been a place where some apes like him once lived. Perhaps his kind liked the burning rock. He was not sure why; he preferred the aroma of jungle, swamp, and grassland. The smells that signified food, water, and comfort. Not heat and drought and dust.

Soon he saw the source of the scent. A long water had dug a canyon, cutting the plain in half. On his side was grass and trees and animals. On the other was burnt rock and liquid rock, flowing like streams into that side of the canyon. Black clouds rose from the ground and gathered in the sky. White mist hung in the air above the chasm.

A skeleton bridged the two sides.

Whatever the animal had been, it was very large. The bone of its head alone was bigger than Kong. It was on his side of the ravine. Its spine and ribs hung together and spanned the gorge.

Suko hopped onto the head bone and started across it, gesturing for Kong to come. Waiting for him.

Kong approached the head bone. It was long and low; two long teeth from the top jaw anchored it in the ground. The holes where its eyes should be were small caves. Reluctantly, he followed Suko, who was now out on the spine. When Kong stepped on the skeleton, it began to sway. Below him, the long water boiled from the liquid rock falling into it, sending up white plumes of hot fog.

He paused. Was this another of Suko's tricks? To make him fall? Would the bones fail to support his weight?

But Suko was not all the way across. He was waiting for Kong. If the bones broke, the smaller ape would fall too. Suko was clever; he knew that. Kong might even survive the fall. Suko would not.

Suko was tricky, but Kong did not think he was willing to die to hurt Kong.

So he walked on across the bridge of trembling bone, through the hot fog. It did not break, and a few beats of his huge heart later they were on the other side, amidst the heat and now-ubiquitous stench of burning earth. It tickled him inside of his face, sharp and unpleasant. He did not like this place. But when Suko continued on, Kong followed.

How long they traveled through the mist, Kong did not know. Too long. But eventually they reached another cave opening, and Suko led him through it. Kong hoped it would be cooler inside, as caves often were, but it was not. The burning-stone odor was even stronger within.

The cave went on and on. Light-crystals illuminated the way, although not as bright as the ones in the wider Hollow Earth. But there was almost nothing living here—nothing to eat. To drink? A few pools of steaming water, no more. He liked his cave, where he would be dry if it rained and his things could be kept safe. But his cave had fresh air, a place to look outside. Here, he felt buried. What sort of place was this? The kind of place a skullcrawler might nest. Why would his kind choose to live here?

He was going to find out.

Deeper they went, and Suko seemed to become both more eager and more trepidatious. Kong began to hear things in the distance. Barks, shouts and grunts that sounded familiar. Yet somehow, he did not like the sound of them. They sounded like his kind, but they were bad sounds, somehow. Calls of anger, coercion, pain.

Suko bounded up onto a ridge. Beyond, the cavern opened into a much larger cave, with sharp rocks sticking up from the floor and hanging from the ceiling. The red light of burning stone made everything look covered in blood.

Suko got to the top of the ridge and stopped. He made a plaintive sound.

Kong came up, and now he saw.

They were there. Apes. Not one or two or a hand of fingers or even two hands of fingers, but more, many more. More than he had ever imagined. On Skull Island there had been no other apes, but there had been skeletons. But not this many. This looked like a living-nest of the little ones. But these were not little ones. These were Great Apes, like Kong. He marveled at how different they looked. Some were bigger than others; their fur came in many different shades. Some looked young; others were bent, with patchy fur shot through with white hair. Were these old? He had never seen an old ape.

They were all like Kong, but also all different. The way Jia looked different from her mother, and the two of them different from other little ones.

My home, he thought. *My family*. Could it be?

But something didn't feel right to Kong. *None* of it felt right.

What were these apes doing? They were picking up big rocks, moving them from one place to another. He couldn't tell why. Maybe they were making something? But they didn't look like they *wanted* to move rocks. They looked tired and sullen. Other apes were not moving rocks; they barked and threatened the ones moving the rocks. He noticed these had red stripes, like the ones that had attacked him. Were there two kinds of apes? Those that did things they didn't want to do, and those that made them do it?

He didn't like this. But he had to know more. He started down with Suko.

The bones of another huge beast lay in the cavern, but he saw something else, too. Three ape heads with no bodies. They were stuck on poles, and they were not alive. One of them didn't even have skin or fur; only bone remained. The other two were rotting. He was reminded of when he would tear the head off a predator and show it to the others, to frighten them. But who were these ape heads meant to frighten?

But the way Suko looked at them, he knew. They were meant to frighten the other apes. To let them know that *their* heads could be taken off and put on sticks.

Who would do that? The red-stripes? But who told the red-stripes what to do? He didn't see anything but other apes, but there had to be something. Something that made prey of apes. That made apes live like this.

There had been an enemy. Godzilla, and other creatures like them. Creatures he controlled. Was one of them here, hidden in some cave Kong could not see? Some monster that hurt his family like this?

If so, he would find them and kill them.

So thinking, he started down from the ridge. He thought they would see him, that the red-stripes would challenge him. As he got closer, some of the ones moving rocks *did* see him. But they didn't do anything. Then he realized why.

They thought he was one of them.

The thought stopped him in his tracks for a moment. He had met many things in his life. Some were smaller, some his size, a few even bigger. He had *never* met anything that didn't give him a second look, didn't consider him as either a predator or prey. Not sure what to think, he moved further into the apes.

The smell of them was sour. They reeked of fear and pain.

Ahead of him, one of the apes dropped a stone. He was a little smaller than Kong. All of them were. This one didn't have much fur and he looked like hands that had been in the water too long, but everywhere. Another ape shouted at him, a threat-attack, then slapped him in the head and knocked him down. Then he kicked him. The fallen ape lay there, hurt and submissive.

It was too much. Kong stepped forward and Suko, who had been in a meek, frightened pose since they arrived in this place, suddenly darted forward and grabbed Kong's hand. Trying to stop him.

Kong shook him off. He slammed his axe to the ground and reached his hand down to the fallen ape. The wrinkled ape looked at him. Kong saw fear there, and disbelief. But after a few breaths he took Kong's hand. He helped him to his feet.

The other apes had noticed him now. One of them ran up and began howling in his face, making threatening gestures. He was too close, too loud, and Kong was already out of patience. He closed his fist and clubbed the ape in the face, knocking him to the floor. Then he beat his chest and roared.

He was *Kong*. Who dared yell at him? He didn't care *what* they were.

They all stared at him. He glared back in challenge. None of them moved.

Except one, above, who ran and began chattering to two apes standing in front of an opening to another cave. One of them knocked him down, but the red-stripe pointed to Kong and kept making noise. The other apes turned to look back in the cave—and then stood aside.

Another ape came out. His fur was dark red, and he had very long arms and very short legs. He walked on all fours, but when he came to the ledge looking down on them he drew himself up and straightened his legs. He stood almost like a little one, except his arms reached almost to the ground. He wore chains of bones draped from one shoulder to his other side.

Suko was trying to fold into himself, to disappear. Kong had seen him scared before. Not this scared.

The red ape howled. He slapped one of the apes near him, who in turn kicked another. He stared down at Kong.

Then he put his hands down on the stone and swung out, jumping from the ledge and landing where Kong stood.

All the other apes hooted in fear and submission. They backed up and knelt down, laying one arm on the ground and bowing their heads. The red ape hand-walked up to Kong, aggressive, angry. He circled Kong. Kong didn't flinch. The others were clearly afraid of the red ape. Kong was not. He was shorter, more lightly built. Mostly a pair of arms stuck on a skinny ape. What was there to be afraid of?

So Kong waited to see what Red Ape would do.

Red Ape stared at him. At his mouth. He reached up and pushed a finger into Kong's lip, so he could see the new tooth. He touched it.

Then Red Ape made a sound, a sort of bark. But it almost sounded like what the little ones did when they thought something was funny.

Another ape started doing it too, and then another, until they were all making the noise. What was it Jia had called it? Laughing.

Kong glared back and snorted.

Red Ape stopped his noisemaking and looked past Kong. He was looking at Suko. And he looked angry. He suddenly dashed forward—he was quick for his size. He towered over Suko and screamed at him. Suko cowered.

He was angry, Kong realized. Angry that Suko had brought Kong here.

He was about to do something when another ape intervened. It was an old one, or at least Kong thought so. Wrinkled, losing hair. The old ape grabbed Suko and pulled him away from Red Ape.

Red Ape turned on that ape then. He pushed up to him; the other ape looked frightened, but he stood his ground.

Red Ape glared at him. He howled at him again. Then he turned and began walking away on all fours. But he didn't go far. Instead he kicked back with both feet, hitting Suko's protector in the chest, knocking him back into one of the streams of melted rock. The ape screamed in pain, his fur bursting into flames as he sank and died. Suko screamed too. He looked as if it had been *him* thrown into the burning rock.

Then Red Ape turned back to Kong. His weird blue eyes turned toward Kong's axe, where he had buried it in the ground. He snarled and lurched forward, reaching for it.

Kong slapped his hand away and pulled the weapon from the ground himself.

The other apes began backing up, clearing out of the way.

The Red Ape roared a challenge. Kong roared back.

The Red Ape pulled at the bones he was wearing, uncoiling them into a lengthy strand. It looked like the skeleton of a very long snake, which the Red Ape now whirled around like a vine. A heavy, sharp vine. He slapped it on the ground and the stone surface shattered, sending up a spray of rock shards.

The other apes had stopped backing up, and now they began pounding the floor with their fists.

Red Ape lashed the bone-whip at him. Kong ducked, but he noticed the end of the whip was sharp and blue and glowing like the blade of his axe. He overbalanced and fell, scrambling back up as the bones curled out toward him again. This time he caught the end of the weapon, just above the blue tip. He yanked, trying to pull Red Ape over, but his opponent planted his feet and pulled back. The sharp bones cut into Kong's hand; the pain was so unexpected that he let go. The cuts in his palm welled with blood.

He charged Red Ape, swinging his axe, but once again, the other showed he was quick, nimbly dancing aside as the blue blade cut the air where he had been. Kong was quick, too— he swung again, but the Red Ape ducked. Kong brought a thunderous third cut straight down toward the enemy's head. This time the Red Ape didn't move.

He didn't need to. He blocked the axe swing with his bone-whip. Surprisingly, Kong's blade did not cut through. Kong bore down, forcing the foe to his knees. Red Ape shifted the whip, turning the blade and forcing it into the floor, then dodged and leaped around behind him as Kong was dislodging the blade from the stone. The bones lashed out once more, this time cutting him across the chest. Enraged, Kong lunged forward, raking a big swing at the other Titan's head, but once again, his enemy wasn't there. Red Ape's duck turned into a backward flip, and he kicked Kong under the chin, sending him sprawling onto the hard floor. As he recovered his feet, the whip lashed out again, wrapping around the arm that held his axe. Red Ape jerked, and as the bones cut into his arm, the axe came out of Kong's hand and went clattering away. Then Red Ape somersaulted toward him and flipped over his head, looping the bone-whip around his neck. Now he was behind Kong, and he shoved a foot into his back and began pulling, *hard*, to try and either choke him or saw through his neck. Kong managed to catch the bones with both hands, keeping them from tightening enough to do either, but Red Ape was *strong*.

Not strong enough. Ignoring the pain from the sharp bones, Kong forced his hands between his neck and the whip. Pulled, leaned forward, and used the bones to throw the Red Ape over his head, hurtling him to the floor in front of him.

Rock shattered and sprayed at the impact. Kong wasted no time; he grabbed Red Ape again, picked him up, and threw him back down onto his face. Red Ape rolled back up, but Kong could see he was hurt. Other apes behind him started forward to help him, but Red Ape gestured for them to stop. He stood back, not continuing the attack. Some of the other apes began pounding the floor again. This time Kong thought it might be for him. He pounded his chest and roared his dominance. Red Ape was fast and tricky. Surprising. But Kong understood him now. If the fight resumed, he would kill the other Titan.

Red Ape knew that. But he didn't look beaten. He wasn't submissive. Instead, he took the sharp, glowing tip of his weapon and pointed it.

Not at Kong, but behind him, at a curtain of falling liquid rock. Kong turned to see. Three of the apes were pushing a huge boulder aside. The boulder had bone chains fastened to it, maybe so it could be pulled back to where they were pushing it from. As it slowly rolled forward, it began blocking the flow of the burning stone, just as it would block the flow of falling water. The rock now ran to either side of the boulder.

He distinctly heard Suko shriek in alarm, and other apes echoed the call. Whatever was happening, they were afraid of it.

The parting fall of rock revealed a cave. From the cave, blue eyes peered at him, set very far apart. A shape moved, too dark to see. And although the cavern was stifling hot, and he was facing burning stone, he felt a cold wind. A very cold wind.

The thing in the cave emerged. Four chains held it by a ring on its neck. Each of its massive four feet were also ringed and chained. But it could move forward, and did, coming out of its cage, growling with rage.

Kong had never seen one of these. It was a little like Godzilla, covered in bumps and scales. Spines that looked like blue rock grew from its head and ran along its back. But it stood on four thick legs, not two. It had no arms. Its stubby face ended in a beak, although the gaping mouth also showed teeth. It was thick and wide.

And it was very big. Bigger than Red Ape. Bigger than Kong. Bigger than Godzilla. Bigger than any living thing Kong had ever seen.

And it was angry. Now at the limits of its chains, it glared at Red Ape like it wanted to kill him. But Red Ape didn't look worried. He held up the glowing blue tip of his weapon and pointed it at the four-legged Titan. Then he pointed it at Kong. A command.

The animal screamed, writhed, shook its head and stumbled to the ground. The blue crystals on its skull and back began to glow more brightly. They looked like the tip of Red Ape's weapon, just as Kong's axe looked like the scales of Godzilla.

The air grew even colder. For an instant, Kong's gaze met that of the huge beast, and he felt its—her—pain. The cold Titan was in agony. He hesitated, wondering if he could help her somehow. But her spines were glowing even more brightly as she climbed back to her feet.

When Godzilla's spine glowed like, that, it meant—

Kong dodged and rolled, just as a blue blast shot from the thing's mouth and pierced the air where he'd been. It was near enough that he could tell it wasn't lightning or fire, or whatever Godzilla breathed.

It was like the coldest wind he'd ever felt.

The roll brought him to his axe; he grabbed it and pulled it up in front of him as the Titan exhaled again, blocking the blue light with his weapon, just as he had blocked Godzilla's breath in their battle.

It worked. For a heartbeat. But then he felt the chill run up the axe into his hand and arm. They quickly went numb, and they and the axe were coated in ice. Once again he lost his grip on the weapon. Howling in pain and anger, he used his other fist to shatter the frozen water encasing his arm.

The creature's spikes began to glow again.

Through all the noise of apes shouting and beating the floor, through the pounding in his ears, Kong heard a high, clear call. He looked for it, and saw Suko, far up the side of the slope, pointing to an opening, gesturing for him to come. To come now.

Kong did not run from fights he thought he could win. He did not run from fights he thought he couldn't win. But he *knew* he would not win this, not now. And if he didn't? He had seen how these apes treated one another. He had a sense of Red Ape. They would kill him, and then they would kill Suko for helping him.

As the freezing blast came again, he bounded up the slope, feeling the chill follow behind him. Suko darted through the hole. As Kong felt the fur began to freeze on his back, he hurled himself through. He turned to look back, and saw the entire opening was plugged with water-become-stone.

Ahead, Suko was still chattering at him, asking him to follow. He probably should. There were no other ways out of that place. Red Ape did not seem like one to let an enemy leave the fight.

Where his arm wasn't numb, it had begun to ache. He growled, low in his belly. There would be another fight.

He followed Suko, and together they left the Home of the Apes.

THIRTEEN

Quick the wicked hostess, Louhi,
Sends the black-frost of the heavens
To the waters of Pohyola,
O'er the far-extending sea-plains,
Gave the black-frost these directions:
"Much-loved Frost, my son and hero,
Whom thy mother has instructed,
Hasten whither I may send thee,
Go wherever I command thee,
Freeze the vessel of this hero,
Lemminkainen's bark of magic,
On the broad back of the ocean,
On the far-extending waters;
Freeze the wizard in his vessel,
Freeze to ice the wicked Ahti,
That he never more may wander,
Never waken while thou livest,
Or at least till I shall free him,
Wake him from his icy slumber!"

Frost, the son of wicked parents,
Hero-son of evil manners,
Hastens off to freeze the ocean,
Goes to fasten down the flood-gates,
Goes to still the ocean-currents.
As he hastens on his journey,
Takes the leaves from all the forest,
Strips the meadows of their verdure,
Robs the flowers of their colors.

—*Kalevala*, the Finnish
National Epic, Rune 30

Malenka
Hollow Earth

Ilene shifted, looking for where the Iwi history picked up; the script could be written in almost any direction, and moving from section to section, sometimes the orientation changed without notice.

"Ah," she murmured. "There." She resumed the translation. "Trapped within their subterranean prison for millennia, the Skar King harnessed a terrible power. The ancient Titan, Shimo." She scanned the next bit twice before relaying it to the others. She wanted to be sure she had it right.

"Shimo wasn't just a Titan," she told them. "She's a World Ender. The Skar King controls her with pain. Her power covered the Earth in the last Ice Age."

"So, wait," Bernie said. "All of this is some kind of Hollow Earth... *turf* war?

"*We* reopened the vortex," Ilene said. "We brought Kong

down here. He's been looking for others like himself—going deeper into the Hollow Earth and getting closer to their prison. The Iwi must have known it was just a matter of time and that's why they've been calling for help, and that's why Godzilla's changing."

"He's gearing up for World War Three," Trapper said.

"He barely survived last time," Bernie pointed out. "What's Godzilla gonna do on his own?"

Ilene shook her finger at Bernie. It was a good point, but the answer was there on the wall. "He won't be on his own," she said. "The Iwi believe that at the end of the world, one of their own will return and awaken Mothra—defender of the Iwi and ancient ally of Godzilla. The Iwi believe their savior will be…" She stopped, drew a breath. "An Iwi from Skull Island."

She turned to regard Jia. Jia couldn't have followed everything she said. She hadn't been signing, and she'd been turned away from her daughter most of the time she was talking, so she couldn't have read her lips.

Nevertheless, Jia's gaze told her she already knew all of this. The queen must have been giving her own telepathic translation.

"That seems like a lot to put on one kid," Trapper said.

"And how much time do we have, exactly?" Bernie asked.

"There's no way of knowing," Ilene told him.

Bernie mulled that over for a moment. "The end of the world, huh?" he said. "Can we just… If this Skar King guy wants to rule the surface, why would he destroy it?"

"Yeah," Ilene said. She turned back to the inscriptions. "I mean, the Skar King is said to have one face that is two. One face speaks of paradise. The other promises pain. One tells his followers they will rule everything together. The other promises an end to those things the Skar King hates."

"You mean he's telling his apes one thing, but he has different plans?" Trapper said.

"Maybe," Ilene said.

"Those things he hates," Bernie said. "What does he hate?"

"That's right here," Ilene said. She tapped a symbol of the script.

"What does that mean?" Trapper asked.

"Everyone," she said. "Everything. It can mean the universe—all of it."

"That could... that sounds kind of bad," Bernie said.

"Kind of," Ilene said. "There's some more over here. Let me have a look at that."

Kong knew what death was. And he knew it was chasing him.

He couldn't use his hurt arm for running. It made him slower than usual. That was good for Suko, who was able to keep up with him. It was less good for the outcome of the race. Already he could hear the hoots and calls of his pursuit. How many apes were there? Three? Two hands of fingers? More than that?

The way he was now, with one arm of no use—without his axe, which he'd had to leave behind—he might be able to beat two of them. Maybe.

But if he could make it to his territory, he would have a better chance. And if he lost, at least it would end there.

He wasn't sure why Suko was with him. Why he had helped him back at the Home of the Apes. Suko could be brave, as he had seen. Suko had attacked him, an ape many times his size and strength—twice. But Suko could be a coward too, when he was with the others. Although now that made more sense. Red Ape liked cowards—he killed those who showed courage. Against him, anyway.

Above all, though, Suko was smart. He had to know that in choosing to go with Kong—in choosing to *help* Kong—he had chosen the same death that was now *chasing* Kong. Which meant Suko was now Kong's responsibility.

They crossed the bridge of bones, and the smoking, bitter land of burnt rock was behind them. They still had a long way to go, but at least there would be trees and grass and water. Not that they would have time to stop and drink. Their pursuers were already gaining on them.

He thought of trying to hide, to take them by surprise, but he still didn't know how many there were. No. He could make it back to his cave. There, they would see what he could do, even without the use of his arm.

They charged through the pond where he had killed the fish-snake. They startled a small pack of the same predators which he had fought earlier. They turned their heads, saw Suko. There were only four of them, not enough to have a chance against him, but they seemed to be considering Suko as possible prey.

Kong stopped just long enough to thump his chest and shout at them. They scattered. He chuffed and started running again.

He was slowing down by the time they were back in territory he knew. He could hear the other apes catching up; now and then, as he gained elevation, he caught glimpses of them.

He could count them now. A handful of fingers and two more. Red Ape wasn't with them. It didn't matter. There were still too many of them.

For now. But now he was in his home territory.

He swatted away a stick tied to a vine, releasing the huge rock he had prepared. It swung down from above.

He looked back and saw it crash into the lead ape, shattering bone and sending him flying. The others saw, however, and leaped over or dodged the trap.

A hand and one of them still gave chase. The next ape behind him put on a burst of speed. He couldn't let them catch him here, in the open. He had to make it up the mountain.

The new lead ape leaped at his back, wielding a stone knife. Kong jumped too, catching a vine with his good arm, swinging over the patch of ground below.

The other ape landed on it, and discovered it wasn't ground at all, but sticks and leaves and a scattering of dirt Kong had arranged over a very deep hole. He squealed and was gone.

The others, alerted to the trap, went around it.

Now it was down to a hand of them.

He cast about, looking for Suko, but the smaller ape was nowhere to be seen. Kong didn't blame him. Suko would not last long in this fight. If he survived, they would take him back to Red Ape, who would probably hurt him, *a lot*, before killing him. He hoped Suko was taking this chance to escape to somewhere the other apes couldn't find him.

Up Kong went, to the closed canyon at the top. Here he could fight with his back to the wall and with protection on two sides. He stumbled to one knee as all his strength seemed to drain out through the pain in his arm. He felt dizzy, like after he had awakened with the new tooth. He limped to the back of the canyon and watched hopefully as they rushed toward him, trying not to look at the vine he had stretched just above the canyon floor, just at the level of an ape's shin. Or the rocks above that the vine would bring down when the first of them tripped on it.

They were wary now. They saw they had him closed in. But they still weren't looking down.

Until the one in front did. He barked and held the others back with his hand. Then, very carefully, he stepped over the trap.

Kong prepared to fight. There was nothing else to do.

Then the rocks fell anyway. The apes had a breath to see their fate plunge down on them, but no time to escape it. They vanished under the avalanche, all of them. He waited, ready for any motion, but none came. Kong heaved a sigh of relief, wondering what had happened to trigger the trap, glad it had.

Then he heard a call above. He looked to where the rocks had fallen from and saw Suko was there, looking pleased with himself.

Suko had made the trap work. He had moved the stick the vine was supposed to move. Suko thumped his chest in triumph.

Kong felt the little ape's victory. But his legs wouldn't support him any longer. He collapsed to the ground.

For a moment, he knew nothing. Then Suko was there, trying to lift him, to make him stand.

Yes. They had to leave. Red Ape would not give up. He would send more red-stripes. He might bring the cold-breathing Titan.

Kong felt his new tooth with his tongue, then looked down at the ruin of his arm. He needed a new one. Maybe the little ones could help. He would try to find them. He would follow the call he had heard.

With Suko supporting him on one side, he staggered past the dead apes in their grave of stones.

Monarch Control
Barbados

Hampton watched the topside of Tiamat's ice massif grow nearer as the helicopter approached it. Or, rather, the late

Tiamat's ice lair; it belonged to Godzilla, now. The Titan had gone in hours before, and so far as they could tell, he hadn't stirred since.

"Maybe he's gone back to sleep," Laurier ventured.

"He's just had the Titan equivalent of about a million coffee drinks," Hampton said. "Not exactly conducive to a nice afternoon nap. No, he's doing something else."

"We've got a call from the chopper."

"Put it on speaker."

Laurier nodded. A moment later, a voice crackled through the speakers.

"This is Monarch Air Team to base," it said. "Tracking over Godzilla's location. We've closed the shipping lanes within three hundred miles. Plasma readings indicate he's absorbing *everything* in there. Whatever he's getting ready for, it must be massive."

"Uh-huh," Hampton said. She was watching the data as it came in—energy readings, mostly. They looked... strange. Godzilla's signature was there, of course, but something also remained of Tiamat's energy profile. In fact, that part seemed to be getting stronger and a little weirder. She sat back and watched as the helicopter circled the floating mountain of ice. She glanced at Laurier. "You know anything about the mythological Tiamat?"

"Babylonian, right? A dragon goddess."

"Yeah. The mother of the gods. Her children pissed her off, and she decided to murder them all. They got her first. Butchered her out into parts."

"Nice kids."

"She probably had it coming. Not so nice herself. But it's what they did with her parts. That's interesting. They made the world out of her. They used her ribs to hold up the sky, her tail to make the Milky Way. Her dead eyes, still weeping, became the wellsprings of rivers."

"Okay," Laurier said.

"So Godzilla just cut up *this* Tiamat. He's taken her life, her lair, and according to these readings, maybe part of her genetic code. So what is Godzilla making? What is he creating out of Tiamat's corpse?"

Malenka
Hollow Earth

Ilene watched Jia play some sort of game with the other children in the village. It involved running with streamers of blue and saffron cloth, in patterns that were either very complex or entirely random. At times she thought it might be some version of capture the flag, but she had no idea what the rules were, or *if* there were rules. It wasn't a game she had ever seen played among the Iwi of Skull Island.

What was clear was that *Jia* understood it, and was enjoying it tremendously. It felt so good to see her daughter just for once being a *child*. And yet at the same time she had to hold in her head the prophecy she had just learned of, that Jia was once again to be called upon to save the world. As Trapper had pointed out, that was a huge burden, one most people, much less most children, should not have thrust upon their shoulders.

And yet here they were.

"That looks like fun," Trapper said, watching the kids. "Who's winning?"

"I have no idea," she admitted. He nodded. She could tell he'd really come to say something else. Trapper always knew way too much about how she was feeling.

"How's your head?" he finally ventured. Then met her gaze fully and changed the question before she could answer. "How's your *heart*?"

"What?" she said. "You mean beyond the Iwi believing that that my teenaged daughter will be the savior of all humanity?"

"Yes," he said. "Yes, apart from that."

She nodded. "You know, I made a deal with myself when I became a mother. *I don't care what you have to sacrifice, what you have to give up—you will do right by that little girl.*" She took a breath, not wanting to say the next thing, because that would make it real. But she had to do it. "I just never thought that the thing I'd be giving up would be *her*." Her voice cracked in the last word, and she fought to regain her composure.

"Look," Trapper said. "You don't *know* that."

"Really?" she said. "Trapper, before we came here, she said she didn't belong. Anywhere." She looked back at Jia, where she was smiling and playing. In her element. "If this is the life that she wants—I *have* to give her up."

Sometimes Trapper knew when *not* to talk. He put his hand on her shoulder, instead. It felt good there, at least for the moment.

"You mind talking about something else?" he asked.

"Sure," she said. "Anything else."

He took the hand down.

"All of that stuff in the—shall we call it the library?"

"Temple of Knowledge," she said.

"Okay, fine. Look, I think I followed most of it. Titan war. Rogue apes and all. But this 'World Ender'? Shimo?"

"Yeah," she said. "I've never heard it—or her, I guess—called that. I always thought she was a phantom, to tell you the truth. Just a trace in the rocks."

"I don't follow."

She sighed. "Years ago, a paleontologist, Doctor Magezi Maartens, published a little monograph. It went largely unnoticed. But Monarch noticed. I was part of a team that went to talk to her. I was pretty new at Monarch. I wasn't sure why I was there, because I wasn't a geologist, or a paleontologist, or anything like that. In fact, at the time I was looking at rock art on a little island in the Pacific."

"Titan rock art?"

"Godzilla rock art, specifically," she said. "A cave painting. Godzilla and another Titan. Not one on our books. But *big*—bigger than Godzilla. From what I remember it looked like it might be four-legged, but reared up on hind legs. It had sort of a beaky face, like a turtle. And spines. Not like Godzilla's, exactly, but... similar. It looked almost like it was *dominating* Godzilla."

"That's hard to imagine."

"Sure. Kong tried it and wound up dead—well, technically and temporarily, but you get my point."

"I had the point already. So what did your cave painting have to do with the paleontologist?"

"She had been working on dating the various glaciation events in Greenland, trying to establish a chronology for some fossils she had found there. And she's discovered, well, a sort of layer." She shifted around to look at him. "You know how one of the pieces of evidence of the asteroid impact that killed the non-avian dinosaurs was this thin layer of iridium found everywhere on the planet, all right on top of the last Cretaceous fossils and right under layers of Cenozoic ones? Iridium is really rare on Earth, but common in asteroids. The thing hit, threw up a cloud of iridium, and it settled all over the globe."

"Yep," he said. "That all rings a bell."

"Well, she found a layer in the *ice*. The very first layer of ice laid down on Greenland almost a million years ago, right when it went from being ice-free to encrusted in the stuff."

"Like, right before the last Ice Age," he said.

"Yeah, like that. But it wasn't a chemical layer. It was a pattern in the ice crystals themselves. She didn't know what to make of it, but she had gotten corroborating samples from Siberia. It caught Monarch's attention because one of our researchers had seen a similar pattern."

"Let me guess. From the same period, the start of the Ice Age?"

"No. That was the thing. The Monarch ice samples weren't from a worldwide layer. They were from a localized, singular event."

"Wait. You don't mean?"

She nodded. "Antarctica. Monster Zero."

"You're saying this thing put Monster Zero on ice? And started the last Ice Age?"

She shrugged. "The Iwi script called her the 'original Titan' but I was translating in a hurry. It could also mean 'ultimate Titan' or 'quintessential Titan.'"

"Your cave painting?"

"Might not be related," she said. "The paintings were very old. But I did research with nearby islanders. Some of the elders knew about the painting. They said another, very ancient people made it. And that they called the monster Whose-Breath-Makes-The-Ocean-Into-Stone."

"Sounds related."

"Uh-huh. That's why they sent me. But then years passed. We found lots of Titans. But never her."

"'Cause she was down here."

"That's what it looks like. Trapper, there has been more than one Ice Age. Some were a lot worse than the last one. There was one where everything was frozen to the equator. Life on the surface almost didn't survive it. What is Shimo really capable of?"

"I think you just said it."

"But if that's true, what can Godzilla do?"

"But it's not just Godzilla, right? And that raises another big question. I may be crazy here, but didn't Mothra, um, die? In Boston a few years back? And not just technically dead but, you know, blown to bits? Kablooey?"

"There is that," Andrews said. "And just days before that she was an egg in an ancient temple in Yunnan Province, China." She shrugged. "Mythologically, Mothra is sort of eternal. She's born, she dies, she's born again. She comes when she's needed. Monarch was never sure how long that egg had been in that temple. It could have been hundreds or thousands of years. Or where it came from, for that matter. But in the Iwi texts, there was a phrase I wasn't sure how to translate, so I just blipped over it. But it used the same word as was used when they were talking about Shimo. It might mean the original Mothra, or the First Mothra, or just the most *Mothra* Mothra."

"So, like the mother of all Mothras?"

"Could be something like that."

"Huh," he said. Then, for a while, neither of them said anything. They just watched Jia play.

"You know," Trapper said, softly, after a little while.

"What's that?"

"I… I had better check in on Bernie. He might…"

"Oh," she said. "Yeah. He could be getting us all in trouble as we speak. Good thought."

"Right," he said. "We'll talk later, hey?"

"Sure. Hey."

Bernie realized he'd been neglecting his whole reason for being down here—his documentary. The initial meeting with the Iwi had been a little anxiety-inducing, but now everything seemed good. Nobody seemed to care where they went or what they did. Or what they filmed.

He had come upslope from the village to get a good shot of the stalagmite-stalactite pyramids, but then he'd seen some Iwi working at something that could help him prove a point.

Trapper had trailed along with him, almost as if he didn't fully trust Bernie not to get into some kind of trouble—ironic, since he'd been the one waving a knife at these guys earlier.

Trapper seemed to also be watching the Iwi, gathered around a massive cut-stone block. A sound like the distant chime of a bell settled over the valley.

"Why is it, when I hear that funny tone, does everything feel lighter down here?" Trapper asked.

As he said it, three Iwi men lifted the block without apparent trouble and began to carry it away.

"That thing must weigh a ton," Trapper said.

"Yeah," Bernie said. He kept filming; Trapper's question gave a chance to narrate a nice voiceover. If it didn't come out right, it would at least remind him to go back and dub in a better version.

"Yeah. See, I don't know how they can do it, but somehow they're able to move their pyramids' positions, which disrupts the gravitational pull down here. An entire civilization built off the manipulation of gravity." That was good, he thought. He wouldn't have to do another take.

"God, I wish I was streaming this live!" he said.

Trapper pulled something out of a ration bag and popped it in his mouth.

"What are you gonna do with that, Bern?" he asked as he chewed.

Bernie sighed. "Look," he said. "I know what you're thinking. But you don't understand. To have been through what I've been through, seen what I've seen and to have absolutely nobody believe you?" He shook his head.

Trapper gazed around. He had a chip in one hand. Or a crisp? A snack. He gestured with it.

"This place," he said. "This place is special, man. It's magic. How long do you think it'll stay like that if you start posting that? If you look at any isolated tribe, or community—how many of them survive contact with the outside world?" He waved the crisp at him again. "You know what I think the brilliant thing is? You already saved the world once. They can't take that away from you."

Bernie nodded, then raised the camera and pointed it at Trapper. "Can you say all of that again? The last part? So I have it on footage?"

"What?" Trapper said.

Trapper obliged him, finished his snack, and walked off. His repetition was less heartfelt. Or maybe, on hearing it twice, it just didn't sound as good.

"I mean, it's true," Bernie said to himself, as he set up the camera to film himself doing a little exposition. He framed it so the pyramids were in the background. "No one can take it from me. But a little credit would be nice."

But would it? Half the trolls would never believe him, no matter what. It's what made it all so infuriating. It was like trying to climb a hill of sand, where when you took a step forward you slid back two. But he was down here now. It would be different after this. It had to be.

Sure he had everything framed right, he closed his eyes to clear his mind, then started the camera.

"So you see those pyramids behind me, right, Titan Truthers? Those are the real things. The template. The pyramids of Egypt, the Mayan and Toltec pyramids, the ziggurats of Mesopotamia. Oh. There's lots more, all over the world. People have been trying to explain that for a long time. We've talked about Atlantis, Lemuria, Mu, how their civilizations spread ancient technology—alien technology—all over the world. Then, boom! They sank and vanished. Only maybe they didn't ever sink. Maybe they were never continents on the surface at all. They were down *here* all along. Because I promise you, what you see behind me came first. And all those other places on the surface—just imperfect copies. The same form, but without the function. You ever hear of the cargo cults? In World War Two, indigenous people of the islands around New Guinea came in contact with the U.S. military, with technology and canned food and, just, things they had never seen before. After the war, the military left. The natives started building airstrips, life-sized models of planes out of straw. They carved headphones and wooden rifles, and marched like they had seen the soldiers do. They were trying to get them to come back, to bring more 'magic' stuff. So when you see the Great Pyramid of Cholula and you wonder 'what were they going for?'" He turned and lifted his chin toward the huge crystalline structures. "It was that."

He looked back at the camera, then switched it off.

"That was pretty good," he told himself.

The Iwi men were back, moving another rock. Maybe he should get some more footage of that.

Sometimes, sometimes his imagination went off without him. That was usually good, Inspirational. But as he turned the camera, he suddenly felt not so much like an intrepid filmmaker, but more like those dads at one of those big corporate theme parks. Recording stuff while his kids rode the rides. And he suddenly imagined a hundred people like that, a thousand, all here, chopping this place and its people into easily digestible images and making little out-of-context comments for the folks back home.

He lowered the camera.

"Trapper," he murmured. "You really, truly suck."

FOURTEEN

When the thousand years are over, Satan will be released from his prison and will go out to deceive the nations in the four corners of the earth—Gog and Magog—and to gather them for battle. In number they are like the sand on the seashore.

—Revelations 20:7–20:8

Hollow Earth

One-Eye smelled blood. Some of it was his own, but some belonged to the other apes. He was in the dark, in pain. What had happened? He struggled to recall as he pushed at the weight covering him. His back and sides ached where rocks pressed against him, but what lay on top of him was softer, furry. Still warm.

The Stranger. He had killed two apes in the hunting party with his traps. There had been another trap, but One-Eye had noticed it in time. When the rock fell, he had pulled his companion Knob over him, providing him shelter from the falling rocks.

It had worked, he realized. Knob was on top of him, dead. One-Eye was alive. Because One-Eye was smarter and faster than Knob.

He gathered his strength and pushed, heard a rock tumble. He pushed again, and again, until Knob shifted and more rock tumbled and he saw light, until he was out, standing again. He puffed.

The Stranger was still in sight, though distant. He could just make out his head through the trees.

One-Eye kicked at the rocks, walked around them. The rest of the apes that had been with him were all dead, so they would be of no help to him. He stood and heaved in lungfuls of fresh air, trying to decide what to do.

Twice One-Eye had attacked the stranger, twice with greater numbers. Both times he had lost the fight. The Stranger had done well against the Skar King. He had survived Shimo.

No, One-Eye would not follow the Stranger to fight him. But he could not go back to the Skar King, either. He had failed twice. The Skar King did not take failure well. One-Eye needed to bring the Skar King… something. He wasn't sure what. But he wasn't going to find it here.

One-Eye decided he would follow the Stranger, to see where he went. What he did. Maybe the Skar King would want to know that. If he could bring that knowledge to the Skar King, perhaps he would be forgiven. Or at least not beaten to death. He had his doubts, but it was better than going back completely empty-handed, and better than trying to live in exile.

He set off following the bigger ape, noticing the smaller tracks as he did so. Suko. Suko was still helping the stranger, still with him.

He growled in anger. He had a plan now. If he caught Suko alone, he would snatch him, bring him back for the Skar King to punish. That would surely earn him forgiveness. Maybe the Skar King would spend all of his anger on Suko.

Malenka
Hollow Earth

Jia had gone off someplace with the kids. Ilene sat alone, considering things.

The trip to the Iwi Temple of Knowledge had been informative, but the queen hadn't brought her there merely for a history lesson. First and foremost, it had been to convince her why they needed her daughter here, now. That it wasn't just the Iwi who needed her help, but everyone on Earth. The distress call hadn't been just for Godzilla, but for Jia, too. Intellectually, she understood. Emotionally, this was all much harder.

And although she didn't believe that the queen was trying to deceive her in any way, a lot was still missing, and not just about Shimo and Mothra. There was too much she didn't know about Jia's *actual* role in all of this. How was she supposed to summon Mothra? Was it dangerous? How dangerous? Would she have to be there when the Titan war started? A fight involving maybe dozens of Titans, including one that had changed the very nature of life on Earth at least once, if not many times. One that looked like she might be bigger and more powerful than Godzilla?

She would never get the battle in Hong Kong out of her head, when Godzilla and Kong had gone three rounds. The collateral damage, the chaos. This would be far, far worse.

She thought back to the cave painting. She hadn't said anything to Trapper, but at the time she had first seen it, the image had an... emotional effect on her. Who painted those two Titans? What had they felt? But she thought she knew. Awe. And fear. It came through in every line of the long absent artist's composition, each shade of pigment.

In the painting, Godzilla had been shown using his powerful breath-beam. She hadn't seen it in action back then—not in person, anyway—but she certainly had now. He had used it to violently evaginate Scylla into a city-sized bug splat only a few days ago.

But in the cave painting it looked like Godzilla's most powerful weapon wasn't doing anything to the other Titan at all. Except maybe making the larger Titan angrier. In fact, she thought Godzilla looked... worried. Now that she had first-hand experience with him, she found that impossible. Godzilla was like a tropical storm and could no more worry than a hurricane could. But whoever did the cave painting—maybe they had transferred their feelings onto Godzilla. Maybe *they* were worried he was going to lose.

Whatever. She needed to go back to the Temple of Knowledge and go over the texts more closely. And she needed to get some answers from the Iwi. Which meant finding Jia and interrupting her good time.

She was working her way up to do that when a sound, something like a big horn, began echoing through the city. It sounded very much like an alarm of some sort.

She intended to learn what that was. Just as soon as she found Jia.

Jia wasn't hard to find. She was with the queen and a number of other Iwi, all in a hurry. Jia nodded as she joined them.

What's going on?

I don't know, Jia said. *They're opening something.*

Already ahead, she saw a group of the Iwi were pushing some sort of wheel. No. Not a wheel, exactly. The axis it turned on was arranged vertically, and it turned horizontally. Like the capstan that raised the anchor on a tall ship. The capstan—if that's what it was—was overgrown with vines, as if it hadn't been used in a long, long time.

They're opening something, Jia had said. But what? She hadn't seen any gates, or drawbridges—anything like that.

But in the next instant she got it. They were opening the sky. Or at least the energy curtain that kept their civilization protected.

And coming through the mountain-sized gap in the field—was Kong.

Ilene had seen Kong beaten up before. And just now, he was *very* beaten up. He had one arm clenched against his chest, as if he couldn't use it. Although the tree line hid him from the waist down, he was clearly limping, badly.

She glanced at Jia and saw her daughter was on the verge of tears.

It's okay, she signed. *Kong is tough. You know this. He'll be okay.*

This isn't a tooth, Jia signed back. *And if the Skar King is coming—it could be too much for him. I need to see him.*

The queen approached and put a hand on her shoulder. With a nod of her head, she indicated that they should follow her.

The queen guided them up a steep cliffside path to a level, rocky shelf overlooking the valley. From there, they had a better view as Kong approached.

"Oh my God," Ilene said.

Kong wasn't alone. A smaller ape with reddish hair was helping him walk. Smaller was a relative term, of course. The other ape was still bigger than any land mammal usually found on the surface world.

He found his family, Jia signed.

I see that, Ilene replied. It seemed like everyone was discovering where they belonged. But thinking back to what they had just learned about the other apes down here, was that a good thing?

"Is that a mini-Kong?" Bernie asked as he and Trapper climbed up from behind.

"How'd those guys find this place?" Trapper wondered.

"He must have sensed Jia," Ilene replied.

Kong swayed, staggered and fell. The little ape hooted in consternation. Ilene's heart fell. Kong was in even worse shape than she'd thought.

Jia stepped forward, her face twisted by concern. Kong groaned, then raised himself slowly to a sitting position, extending a finger longer than a car toward the girl. On hands and knees, Jia lifted one hand and leaned out to touch the tip of the huge digit.

Kong slowly sank back. He raised his hand and signed.

I lost home, he said. Then he groaned and lay back against the cliffside.

Jia rocked back on her haunches and cast a look at Ilene. *What can we do?* She didn't sign it, but Ilene got it anyway.

She shook her head. *I don't know.*

Kong pulled his arm up, and she now saw why he was favoring it. It looked burnt, sort of, but the fur wasn't singed.

"That looks bad," she said.

"It's worse than bad," Trapper said. "Those aren't burns. It's frostbite."

Frostbite. Kong had been hurt by something cold.

The small ape—she saw now it was actually a very young

ape, a juvenile at best—touched Kong's injured arm and made a plaintive sound.

"What was it?" Trapper said. "The power to cover the Earth in a new Ice Age?"

"Yeah."

"Who does *that* sound like?"

Ilene glanced at the queen. She seemed stricken. She also knew what it meant. Trapper had asked earlier how long they had. Not very long, it looked like. The little ape was evidence that Kong had found more Great Apes. He seemed to have also met the Skar King—and Shimo. And she had done *this* to him.

"I'd better go take a look," Trapper said.

As he started down the cliff, Kong's little friend began screeching, then turned and ran off through the forest.

One-Eye watched as the strange cloud-web parted and another place was revealed, with weird, colorful mountains going up from the ground and hanging from the sky. Beyond and above he saw... the way up. The holes in the land-sky that led to the Surface World. The place the Skar King dreamed of. The place denied him for so long. The place he hated and desired.

And One-Eye had found it. One-Eye knew where it was.

Now the Skar King *needed* One-Eye.

He squinted. There were things there, many of them. Like the little ape-creatures with no fur they had killed at the strange shelter. These, too, were ancient enemies, prey to be hunted by the Skar King. But besides Stranger, there were no others of the size to oppose them. Not like last time.

One-Eye turned away and began running through the jungle.

The Skar King was never grateful. But he could be less angry. And this could make him much less angry. At One-Eye, anyway.

Trapper made his way down the cliff and approached the big guy. Kong growled.

"I know, I know," he said. "Nobody likes a dentist." He got his pocket doc out and began taking temperature, pulse, blood pressure—all without touching Kong. Handy, that, when you were dealing with something that could crush you without ever noticing.

Ilene was still up on the cliff, but they had two-way radios that fortunately weren't affected by the interference that kept them from contacting Monarch—probably because of the short range involved.

"Trapper," she said. "He looks really hurt."

"Yeah," he agreed. "It's not great. I'm seeing nerve damage, significant tissue loss."

"So what are we saying?" she asked. "He's not gonna last a day in here with only one arm."

"Communications with the surface are still out," he said. "But if I can get back to the outpost, I think there might be some supplies that we can use."

"I don't think a massive cast is gonna solve the problem."

"I wasn't talking plaster of Paris," he replied. "I was thinking more along the lines of… uh… Project Powerhouse."

"You can't be serious," she said.

"Oh, I'm deadly serious," he replied. "That prototype was almost finished when they pulled the funding."

He waited through the pause as she thought it through. "All right," she said. "So what are you still doing here?"

"I love you, too, Doc," he said. Then he grinned and looked over at Kong. "Just hang in there, old boy. I'll be back in a jiff."

Up on the cliffside, Ilene was coming to grips with the fact that she had just given the go-ahead for a project that Congress had shut down in no uncertain terms. There would be hell to pay for that, and she would be the one paying it.

But then again, Congress probably wouldn't be convening if D.C. was buried under two kilometers of ice. First things first.

She turned to find Bernie right in her face.

"Project Powerhouse?" he said. "What is—what is that, exactly?"

If Trapper succeeded, Bernie was going to find out soon enough. If they survived this fight, probably everyone would. Not telling him would only ensure he asked her about it again every five minutes.

"After Mechagodzilla, we realized that there were some threats that even Kong couldn't face," she explained. "So we started working on some minor augmentations."

"Oh," Bernie said, nodding. Then his eyes snapped back up. "Wait. What kind of augmentations?"

She smiled. "I'll bet you can get there on your own."

"No," he said. "Really? Apex tech."

She nodded. "Simmons was crazy, but he was also a genius. The problem with Mechagodzilla was that he used one of Monster Zero's skulls to channel energy he didn't fully understand. So it went rogue and killed him. But the cybernetic aspects of his work—the nuts and bolts of building a Titan-sized mech—he was way ahead of his time. We figured we could find a use for some of that."

"What was left of Mechagodzilla was disappeared," Bernie said. "Every scrap of it. Moved to Area 51."

"Area…" She frowned. "Aren't you listening? No. What was left of it went to our labs, none of which, I promise you, are in Nevada."

"So Project Powerhouse was based on mech tech. But it's not another robot. Something for Kong."

She shrugged. "Anyway. Making one of the strongest Titans even stronger didn't go over so well, so we got shut down. Lucky for us, the prototype had already been transported to Hollow Earth for testing. It's stored in the armory—at Outpost One."

"The Outpost the Skar King and his apes trashed."

She nodded. "They wouldn't have known what it was. And if anything survived that mess, this thing probably did. The armory looked more-or-less intact. We can hope. That's about all we've got right now."

One-Eye found that running was harder than he'd thought it would be. His injuries tired him, and he could not keep up the pace he wanted. That worried him—the Skar King would not accept his weakness as an excuse for being slow to bring him the news. Nevertheless, he spent more of the trip walking than running.

When he drew near to the Living Caves, it dawned on him that the Skar King only had to *think* he had nearly killed himself running, so when he knew he didn't have far to go, he ran as fast as he could, trying to ignore the pain. It would seem as if he had never let his wounds slow him down.

That was how he arrived, his legs shaking, lungs heaving. The dutiful red-stripe, ignoring all pain to serve his master.

When One-Eye arrived, pushing through the other red-stripes, the King was eating.

Predictably, on seeing him return alone—without the others, without Suko or the Stranger's head—the Skar King was furious. He was always angry, but at the moment he was angry at One-Eye. So before the Skar King could kill him, he began trying to explain, in the way apes did, with short single-thing-and-do sounds, with gestures.

The Skar King's anger was great; it was like a mountain of stone. But his hunger for what lay above on the surface—and his grievance at having been denied it for so long—that was something that could break a mountain. As the King understood—about the place, the holes in the land-sky—that mountain of anger toward One-Eye shattered and reformed into a much bigger one. He dashed his food against the wall. He rose to his magnificent height, full of fire and fury. And as he howled, One-Eye remembered. It wasn't just the Skar King's grievance, it was all of theirs. They had been beaten. They had been imprisoned, all because they wanted what was theirs. What they had been promised. *They*, the apes were the mountain of rage, and the Skar King was the peak.

For so long, their wrath had meant nothing, had been good for nothing. They had turned it against each other, and it had made them strong. Ready. Each ape was a weapon in the Skar King's hand. But they were no longer tired. No longer defeated. No longer was their rage turned inward. Like the soft-hot red rock that burst from the ground, they had been released, and they would burn everything in their path.

No more would the very air scorch their throats. No more eating scraps and pushing rocks. When the Skar King took back the World Above, all of his apes would be kings. Even One-Eye.

After that, things happened very quickly. They had been ready for so very long. They gathered their weapons. Shimo was brought from her prison, her shackles removed and replaced with chains that the Skar King could use to control her as he rode upon her back. The many wives of the Skar King were moved to a deep cavern and put under guard.

And for the first time in more time than could be counted, the army of the Skar King marched.

Monarch Control
Barbados

Lunch came around and Hampton told her staff to take it. The break room was only about thirty seconds away, and whatever Godzilla was doing, he seemed to be taking his time. She stayed at her desk and poked her way through the conch samosas from the food truck near the front gate, studying the data streaming back from the submarine and aerial reconnaissance. The energy levels continued to increase, and the signature continued to become weirder.

Laurier came back early and fiddled around at her post.

"You eat already?" Hampton asked.

"I guess I'm not that hungry," Laurier replied.

"You okay?"

Laurier nodded, but her expression said otherwise.

"You're doing fine, you know," Hampton said. "I was going to tell you that in your performance review."

"I... thank you. I just feel... maybe a little out of my depth?"

"No? With Godzilla?"

"With all of it," Laurier said. "If we make a mistake... if *I*

222

make a mistake… the consequences…" She flapped her hands a little.

"You think anything we do or don't do makes any nevermind to these Titans?"

Laurier's eyebrows arched. "You don't? Isn't that why we're here?"

Hampton shrugged. "There's a lot more to the equation here than the Titans. Mostly, there's people. Governments and the people who run them. Corporations. Taxpayers. Their fears, their delusions, their hubris. Ours, too. Monarch isn't immune, either. A lot of nonsense in our ranks as well. We thought we could contain these monsters. We tried to put a leash on Scylla just a little while ago. You saw how that turned out. Godzilla's doing something, that's plain enough. You think we can stop him?"

"No," she said. "That's what worries me."

Hampton sat a little straighter in her chair. "I met Godzilla once, did you know that? Not like this, over a monitor, but actually face to face."

"I didn't," Laurier said.

"Honolulu," Hampton said. "It was Godzilla's coming out party, wasn't it? He showed up to fight the first MUTO. Between the tsunami he brought ashore with him and the fight, he did as much or more damage to the city as the other monster."

"It must have been terrifying."

"My room was on the twentieth floor of a hotel," she said. "I didn't even know what was happening until the MUTO scraped one side of it off, and my room was suddenly open-air. So, yeah, pretty terrifying. The floor was tilted, and I was hanging onto the bathroom door, trying not to fall to my death. The MUTO was still there, you know. I was sure he was about to finish the job and knock the whole building down. He was coming straight for me. Well, not me, personally, but, you know. And then Godzilla blindsided him, knocked him away from the hotel. The fight went off in a different direction."

"I can't imagine."

"Here's the thing," Hampton said. "There was a second there when all I could see was Godzilla. He looked right at me, or at least I thought he did. That's when I really thought I was dead. And he could have knocked the MUTO in any direction, including straight into me. But he didn't. He pushed it the other way."

"Are you saying he saved your life?"

Hampton shrugged. "I didn't know what to think. I still don't. I mean, he did, but did he mean to? Maybe he didn't even see me. But maybe he did, and he made a choice. I'll never know, and even if I did I could never know why. What does Godzilla see when he looks at one of us? A lot of people died in Honolulu. A lot of them died because of Godzilla. I lived because of him."

Laurier stared at her, clearly trying to think how to respond.

"It's just this," Hampton said. "He's responsible for me being here, doing this job. And that sort of makes me feel responsible for *him*. For whatever he does, good or bad. I'd like to think he's a force for good, but good and bad have nothing to do with Godzilla. He is what he is. And on balance, despite the damage he's caused, he's done more to help humanity than to hurt it." She sighed and rubbed her eyes. "Nobody is objective about Godzilla. Least of all me. I almost turned down this job because I know I'm not completely clearheaded when it comes to him. In the end, I decided I should be here for the same reason. But I'll tell you this—you can study a hurricane all you want. But you can't change its course or weaken its windspeed. But you can sure as hell figure out where it's going and get people out of the way."

"But he isn't a hurricane. The military almost killed him once. With the oxygen destroyer."

"Yeah. That's a good point. And we saved him from dying at least once," Hampton replied. "But we've never been able to tell him what to do. And we never will. No more than I'll ever know if he took pity on me that day."

"So…"

"We do our jobs. We do our best."

Laurier nodded. "Thanks."

"You've got a signal there," Hampton noticed.

Laurier blinked and looked at her board.

"It's the helicopter."

"Put them on and get everyone back in here. You're doing okay, Laurier. Just hang in there. You'll be good."

"Thank you, Director," she said. "Putting them through."

"Monarch Base," the radio voice said. "We've got movement inside of the ice mass."

She could see it; flashes and light like lightning within a thunderhead, if the cloud were ice and the lightning was of a weird red-violet color. The ice began to distend until it exploded, Godzilla erupting from it, stretching his huge frame upward, opening the jagged lines of his maw to scream at the sky.

"Oh my God," Hampton said. "He's changed."

"Yeah," Laurier said, studying the screen. "The computer is still analyzing, but his dorsal plates seem to be charged with Tiamat's energy. His molecular density has increased, too."

His spines looked bigger, too, Hampton thought. Craggier. And they were glowing constantly, as were the gill slits on his neck—and his eyes.

"One god eats another," Hampton said, "and gains her powers for himself."

"It looks like he somehow incorporated Tiamat's DNA into his."

"Same thing," Hampton said. "Now we know what he was doing in there. Now what will he do with it?

Laurier shook her head slowly, her expression stunned.

FIFTEEN

How you have fallen from heaven,
morning star, son of the dawn!
You have been cast down to the earth,
you who once laid low the nations!
You said in your heart,
"I will ascend to the heavens;
I will raise my throne
above the stars of God;
I will sit enthroned on the mount of assembly,
on the utmost heights of Mount Zaphon.
I will ascend above the tops of the clouds;
I will make myself like the Most High."
But you are brought down to the realm of the dead,
to the depths of the pit.

—Isaiah 14:12–14:15

Hollow Earth

Suko had never been alone before. At least not for long. He had his hiding places in the Living Caves, of course, but even there he was never out of earshot of the others, never so distant or isolated that he couldn't smell them. In the last few days he'd been with the Stranger he now called Kong. There was a difference, though. With Kong, he had come to feel... not afraid. Kong had hit him, thrown him—but only because he was attacked. He never struck out randomly, for no reason, the way the Skar King did. The way One-Eye and most of the others did. In the Living Caves, never being alone meant always being afraid. With Kong, not being alone meant—something different. Something better.

He had not wanted to leave Kong. But when he saw the little ones, the apes-without-fur that were so clearly part of Kong's family—when he saw how they cared for him—he knew he had to. Partly it was his fear that they would learn he had been with the ones that killed other members of their troupe, even though he himself had not. But that was a small reason, and not enough to send him alone into the jungle.

What worried him was One-Eye.

When he and Kong had made their way to the hidden place, he thought he had caught a glimpse of One-Eye in the distance, following them. He hadn't alerted Kong; in his injured state, he feared One-Eye might win if he and Kong fought. And he thought he might be wrong. The rock fall might have killed all the apes chasing them, and what he thought he saw was just a trick of light and shadow. But One-Eye was tough, and clever in an awful way. If any of them had survived, it would be One-Eye.

Now Suko had to be sure. He retraced his steps to the place where he and Kong had entered the valley. There was still a small gap in the veil there, small enough for a red runt like him to pass through.

After that, he found his fears confirmed. One-Eye had left a big trace, easy to follow. And it led back the way they had come, to the Living Caves.

He thought that might be enough. He could go back and try to let Kong know. Then he wouldn't have to be alone.

He almost turned back, but he knew he shouldn't. He knew if he learned more, it would be more helpful.

And so he went on, alone, and discovered something.

It wasn't so bad, being by himself. In fact, he was beginning to like it. It made him feel free and… he wasn't sure what else. Like he could do things.

One-Eye was moving slowly. Perhaps Suko could catch him before he reached the Skar King. Maybe he could trick him, kill him before he could tell what he had seen.

He would try. Not just because Kong might be pleased. But because somehow he felt it was the thing he ought to do. He picked up his pace, determined. One-Eye's signs grew fresher.

The Skar King wanted the surface. But Suko wondered what the surface could have that this place did not. Compared to the caves of their exile, the bigger world was much better. Full of food. Water everywhere, and no burning stone to singe the back of the throat. To Suko, *this* seemed the perfect land for apes. You could wander forever and never see the same place twice. Or you could settle near a river and eat fish and snakes all day.

The Skar King would not see things that way, though. The Skar King thought only of what he wanted, long ago. What he had been denied. He dreamed of inflicting pain, of revenge, of dominating everyone and everything. The Living Caves were not enough for him. This outside cave, as big as it was, was not enough for him. Whatever the World Above was like, that would not be enough for him either. And he would punish everyone and everything for his disappointment.

So it would be better if he caught One-Eye and pushed him off a cliff or something, before the Skar King learned anything from him.

Eventually, in the distance, Suko heard a call. At first he thought it might be One-Eye, but then he heard another, different voice, followed by more. He climbed up the side of the gorge for a better view, hiding in the leaves of the thick bushes there.

He'd thought he had more time. One-Eye must have traveled faster than he'd thought, and the Skar King must have been prepared to leave when he got there. Because they were marching. All of them, except the females, who were probably still locked in the Skar King's harem compound. One of them was probably his mother, although he had never known which one. There were none with red hair.

Of all the apes of the caves, only two had red hair. The Skar King and him. When he was younger he'd thought that might mean something. He had dreamed that one day the Skar King would claim him. When he had been chosen to be a red-stripe, no matter that he was little, he had almost believed that time had come, or was near. But then the Skar King killed Gnarled Finger for protecting Suko. Then he tried to kill Kong, who had been kind to Suko. Now, Suko did not care about the Skar King, except to believe he must be stopped.

He saw them now. The Skar King sat on Shimo, the captive, the destroyer. Sometimes he felt sorry for her, because he knew that she did not care about the Skar King or his plans. She only wanted to be free of the pain he caused her. The pain he controlled her with. The pain he controlled *everyone* with.

230

None of them could escape it. The Skar King had always been, he always would be, and he would always be the owner and the bringer of pain.

So Suko had once thought. But now he thought something else. He thought that Kong would have beaten the Skar King, if it were just the two of them. That was why the Skar King had released Shimo to fight Kong. That was why he brought many apes to fight one. The Skar King feared Kong.

But Kong was not alone. Kong had Suko now. And Suko would run ahead. He would tell Kong the Skar King was coming. Even hurt, Kong would know what to do. If he didn't, at least Suko could die with Kong. It was better than being in the Skar King's army.

He felt a sudden cold wind as the branched and leaves hiding him began to frost over. Shimo was bringing ice with her, leaving a trail of dying jungle in her wake.

Suko raced back through the jungle, pushing himself until his arms and legs and lungs burned.

On the jog to the H.E.A.V, Trapper had a few worries about being killed and eaten, but the Iwi queen sent four of her camouflaged guys with him. He liked them; they saw things the way he did. Rather than fight threats, they avoided them. And they were way better at noticing them than he was. Unless they were having a go at him. They detoured five times, but he never saw anything to explain why.

His second worry, that the H.E.A.V might not start, was also unfounded. He wasn't as familiar with the controls as he wished, but all he had to do was fly a straight line to the ruined outpost, and his piloting skills were plenty good enough for that. The Iwi didn't accept his offer of a joyride, so he had some concerns about them being killed and eaten on the other end, but he suspected that the smell of the apes still lingered in the ruins of the outpost and would put any other predators or scavengers off from coming there for a while.

His third fear, or course, was that what he was looking for had been trashed along with everything else, but the armory was set apart from the main building. It had been compromised, but not as badly as the main compound. He figured that was because there hadn't been anybody there. The apes had been bent on killing, not just random destruction.

And that—that was a bad sign. The Great Apes were meat-eaters, but even though he hadn't counted the corpses, there were enough around to see that the attacks and murders hadn't been about food. Animals that killed just for the hell of it— there was usually something wrong with them. Badly wrong. There were some exceptions. But the most notable animals that did that as a matter of habit were humans.

A few more moments of searching brought tremendous relief. Not only was the prototype there, and intact—there was also a M.U.L.E to carry it with.

As anyone could tell you, a Titan doctor wasn't much use without a M.U.L.E.

With a grin, he put on some music and got to work.

Ilene lost communication with Trapper not long after he got the H.E.A.V in the air. All they could was wait.

And eat. The Iwi brought them some food. She knew better than to try and figure out what it was, even though it seemed to be mostly vegetables and fungi. It was pretty good; something in it tasted a little like mint, and something a bit peppery. Jia seemed to like it, or at least not hate it, but she was so distracted by Kong, who had fallen into a restless sleep, that Ilene couldn't get her to talk much. She understood; it was difficult to see Kong in this condition. She couldn't help but remember when the big ape's heart had stopped during his fight with Godzilla. Kong was strong, determined, usually so robustly *alive*, one sometimes forgot that he was mortal. That they could lose him. But right now, that reality was being tossed right in their faces. What if Trapper couldn't find Project Powerhouse? What if it had been destroyed or stolen by the Skar King? Assuming Jia could do what the Iwi believed she could do, would she then have to face the Skar King, his apes, and a world-ending Titan with just Mothra on their side? Would Godzilla come? The Iwi beacon had been calling him for a while now, but he still wasn't here. She remembered the rock art. Could it be that even Godzilla feared Shimo? They seemed to have some sort of history.

Bernie ate the Iwi meal with a fair amount of enthusiasm. He took selfies and filmed his food and made audio notes about putting together a Hollow Earth cookbook. He asked her what she thought about that.

"Sure," she said. "Take two cups chopped man-eating tree and fifteen clean giant river leeches. If unavailable, substitute tofu and anchovies."

"I'm not saying it's a perfect idea," he said. "But you can get all kinds of stuff online."

"Of course," she agreed.

He nodded. "Hey, Doc?"

"Still here."

"So I guess we're figuring Kong ran into this Shimo character."

"It seems likely," she said. "He encountered something intensely cold. In case you haven't noticed, there isn't a lot of that down here."

"Yeah," he said. "Not much. Um. It doesn't look like Kong came out of that meeting the winner."

"Well," she said. "We haven't seen the other guy, have we?"

"No," he said. "That's true. True. Maybe he took care of the Skar King and Shimo and all of them already."

"That'd be nice," she said.

"Right. And Jia wouldn't have to do the thing."

"That would also be nice," Ilene said.

"But you don't believe it."

She shook her head. "Not from the way Kong's acting. If he'd won a big victory, he'd be showing it, even hurt like this. I think he's worried. And I think the Iwi are more concerned now than ever."

"That's my impression too," Bernie said.

Her eye caught movement in the sky. Not a war-bat or a leafwing.

Not the H.E.A.V either.

It was the distinctive, blocky, yellow-and-black M.U.L.E.

"I think the party is about to start," she said, as Trapper maneuvered the M.U.L.E over the sleeping Kong.

A boxy yellow-and-black object dropped from the M.U.L.E. An instant later it began to unfold into a new configuration. Four braking jets started to burn. Mounted on gimbals, they also functioned to steer the device, which made a beeline for Kong's damaged limb, killed its momentum with a final flare of its jets, and dropped straight onto Kong's arm.

The Titan's eyelids fluttered as the package snapped and whirred, fitting itself to the Titan. High above, she heard strains of music. She was almost certain it was "I Was Made For Lovin' You" by Kiss. Which… it was Trapper.

"What do ya think of that?" Trapper's voice on the radio asked.

"That's one hell of an augmentation there, Trapper," Bernie answered.

Kong's eyes closed again.

"Yeah," Trapper said as he started to set the H.E.A.V down. "Only the best for Mister Kong. You should see the jetpack mod."

Bernie cut his eyes toward Ilene.

"He's kidding," she said. "I think."

It's an arm, Jia signed.

An exoskeletal arm, she agreed. *It will help fix his real arm. But it will make him stronger too.* Kong was still sleeping. *He might not like it, though*, she said.

He'll like it, Jia said. She sounded confident.

Kong subsided back into his fevered sleep. Trapper emerged from the M.U.L.E and started up the path toward them.

"So this arm," Bernie said. "It's not, like, an evil arm that's gonna take on a life of its own, is it?"

"Probably not," Ilene said.

"*Probably* not?"

"A very low chance, the engineers said."

He blinked, opened his mouth as if to ask something else, then closed it again, shaking his head *no*.

You're trying to be funny, Jia signed. *You're scared.*

She quirked a half-smile at the girl. *Yes, I'm scared.*

Trapper will fix Kong, she said.

That's not the only thing worrying me.

I know, Mom, Jia said. *But I'll be okay, too. Don't worry about me.*

I'm trying not to, she replied. *But you have no idea how difficult that is.* She sighed. *I believe in you, Jia*, she said. *I may be scared of this thing they want you to do. But don't think for a second I doubt you can do it. I know you can.*

Thanks, Mom, Jia signed.

Trapper arrived a few minutes later. He took a second to recover his breath.

"What now?" she asked.

"It's configuring," he said. "Shouldn't be long."

"Lucky the M.U.L.E was still intact," she said.

"Yeah," he said. "Not to worry, though. I brought the H.E.A.V along too. There was plenty of room in the cargo hold."

She nodded. That was good. They could have always gone back to the outpost for the H.E.A.V later, but if they were going to be fighting and dodging Titans, the M.U.L.E was a bit too slow and clunky.

Far below, something clicked in Kong's new arm brace.

"All right," Trapper said. "It's ready to go."

The arm went to work on its new wearer. Gigantic hypodermic needles emerged and plunged into the Great Ape's veins.

"Those injections should heal the frostbite nicely," Trapper said.

Ilene nodded. Even if Kong ripped the thing off, he would be in better shape than he had been.

Kong growled. He grimaced and opened his eyes. He'd felt *that*.

He began to rise.

"All right, there he goes," Bernie said. "He's moving."

Kong reached for a rocky ridge to pull himself up with his new, enhanced arm. Ilene watched, almost holding her breath as he grabbed the rocky ledge, pulled... and it shattered, putting him off-balance so that he fell. Kong looked back and forth between his hand and the cliff, looking confused.

"Well, it's a bit rough and ready," Trapper allowed. "But it should hold."

"Looks good, Trapper," Ilene said.

"Damn good," Bernie agreed.

But what really mattered was what Kong thought.

The ape picked himself up and stood to his full height. He brought the mechanized arm brace up to where he could examine it.

"He's either gonna love it, or he's gonna rip it off with his teeth," Trapper said.

Kong stared at the augmentation another few seconds. Then he pumped it into the air and bellowed to shake the valley.

"I think he loves it!" Bernie shouted.

Jia smiled wide.

Kong brought the arm back down and studied it intently. Ilene thought he did look pleased. And something else: something a little harder, a little more dangerous. Like maybe he was ready to make whoever had hurt him pay.

Off through the jungle, a loud hoot sounded. Something like one of Kong's calls, but higher in pitch.

The little ape was coming back, gesturing excitedly to Kong. He ran up to the bigger ape and began pulling at his newly enhanced arm, gibbering and pointing back toward the way he had come.

Kong seemed to understand. His eyebrows lowered and his face set in a scowl. Then he lifted his hand and made some signs.

"Skar King," Ilene translated. "He's coming. And he's got an army."

"If they find this place, they'll take the surface," Trapper said. "Godzilla can't fight them all."

Jia was signing to Kong; Ilene didn't notice in time to see what. But the Great Ape reacted with a loud, assenting grunt.

"Hey, hey!" she said, talking as she signed. "What did you tell him?"

I told him we need help, Jia replied.

Kong made another sign, and then he was in motion, shivering the earth with his footfalls. The juvenile ape dashed after him.

"Did Kong just say what I think he said?" Trapper asked.

Godzilla, Jia signed, using the gesture she had made up years before.

"Godzilla!" Bernie said.

Ilene stared after the apes as they ran up the sides of the world toward the vortices above.

Kong gestured at the smaller ape running beside him. The little one hesitated, but then broke paths with Kong, who continued alone.

Kong is protecting him, she thought. The two of them were friends, or something. She wondered how Kong's new companion fit in with the Skar King. There was a story there for sure. Kong had a history of protecting those weaker than himself, bonding with them. Was the little ape some sort of adoptive son?

"Where's he going?" Bernie asked.

"Godzilla won't come down here unless Kong brings him," she said.

"Okay, but the last time those two met up it was almost the end of Kong."

"He's taking a hell of a risk," Trapper said. "If Kong invades his turf, it could start a war."

"That's a suicide mission," Bernie said.

"If Kong draws him down here, then we can make their stand in Hollow Earth, then there's a chance that Godzilla and Kong may stop Skar King and Shimo from reaching the surface."

"Warriors like Kong, they don't die of old age," Trapper pointed out.

"Right," Bernie said. "Sometimes they get beat to death by a real big lizard. I was there the last time they got rambunctious."

Ilene shared their concerns. Godzilla seemed to be ignoring the Iwi distress call. At the very least he was taking his sweet time to answer it. Kong going up there—it might just complicate things.

But that was out of their hands, now. And Jia was right. If the Skar King, and Shimo, and who knew how many apes were on their way, they needed help. They needed Godzilla.

The queen had moved to stand by Jia. Now she placed a hand gently on the girl's shoulder.

What now? Ilene wondered. But she was afraid she already knew. The clock had run out. As the queen and Jia started back toward the pyramids, she took a deep breath and followed.

Trust your daughter, she thought. *She'll be okay.*

Small with distance, Kong leaped into a vortex and vanished.

SIXTEEN

Nibalut Benangniya
Iya tengah tidur
Iya sampay aken niperluken
Sampay laguniya agan nimulaken

Wrapped in her threads
She sleeps
Until she is needed
Until her song begins

—"Lagu Ngendget", a song from *Pula Anak*,
recorded by Chen Yue circa 1975

Cairo
Egypt

Keith smiled at the cab driver, trying to think of how to say what he wanted, but to his dismay, he drew a blank.

The driver finally said something Keith didn't understand. Outside the cab, the crowded Cairo street was alive with motion, color, and sound.

"Ah…" Keith said to the man. "Do you speak English?"

Before the driver could answer, Fiona leaned forward. "Men fàdlàk," she said. "Momken tewàSSàlni Haram?"

The driver nodded. "Yes," he answered in English. "I will go there. Seventy pounds."

"Forty," Fiona said. She said something in Arabic Keith didn't catch. They went back and forth for a moment. Finally the driver nodded and started driving through the narrow street. The pedestrians largely ignored him; Keith kept flinching, afraid they were going to hit someone.

"How much did you settle on?" he asked. "I couldn't follow that."

"Fifty Egyptian pounds," she said, sitting back. "It's a fair price, I think. Especially considering this cab has air conditioning."

"Clearly you picked up more of the language than I did in the crash course," he muttered. "I couldn't understand anything he said in Arabic."

"I don't think he's Egyptian," she replied. "Syrian, maybe. Different accent."

"Still," he said.

"Hey, I'm good with languages," she said. "I like them. They make sense to me."

"You know," he said, "I tried to learn Ancient Egyptian as

a kid. My aunt had a book on it. It took me years to admit I'd never get it."

"This the same aunt who told you the scary stories?"

"Yeah," he said. "They weren't scary, though. They were freaking *terrifying*. Gave me nightmares. Stories about Duat, the Egyptian underworld, and all the monsters that waited there to tear apart the souls of the unworthy. Except in her stories, Duat was, like, directly underneath my bed, and opened up every night. I used to lie awake, convinced I could hear Apep crawling around below me."

"Apep?"

"Huge snake-god-demon, Lord of Chaos. Tries to devour the sun every night when he goes through Duat. He sometimes causes earthquakes when he moves."

"Sweet dreams indeed," Fiona said. "This aunt, she wasn't Egyptian, I take it?"

"No," he said. "Far from it. Just a crazy old lady who was way too much into Egyptian mythology and scaring little kids."

"And yet here we are, in Egypt. And you know all about this stuff."

"Right. Well, I started learning about all things Egyptian as an act of self-defense. I figured the more I knew about it, the less afraid I would be of her stories. That I would see them for what they were."

"Did it work?"

"Yes. Sort of. Intellectually. But the monsters you have under your bed never really go away. Not emotionally."

"I'm surprised you didn't become an archaeologist, if you were so interested."

"Me too," he said. "That was my dad getting into my head. And tuition. I… oh my God!"

They had finally broken out of the city, traveling southwest.

The sun was rising, a great golden globe edging up from the east, illuminating the tableau that had just come into view, the great pyramid complex of Giza. For a moment he was so wonderstruck he couldn't say anything.

"Oh, look at you!" Fiona said. "You look like a little kid. Is this what you were like as a kid?"

"It's just so… these are the oldest wonders of the ancient world. Thousands of years old. I've seen hundreds of pictures of them. Documentaries. But we're really here. They're really there."

"I like this side of you," she said. "I'm glad I get to see it."

"It's dumb, I know," he replied. "How many tourists come gawk at them every year? How many are here just today? And yet somehow I feel… It's like I'm the first person to see this. That it's just for me." He shook his head. "Dumb, huh?"

"A little," she said. "But it's also very sweet." She leaned around him for a better view. "What's that? Is that supposed to be happening?"

He saw what she meant. A huge plume of dust had just erupted near the Menkaure pyramid. As he watched, it continued to grow. It didn't look like a sandstorm, or a dust devil, or anything like that, though. It was too localized, with no discernable rotation.

"Maybe a show for tourists?" Fiona wondered. "The curse of the mummy, or something like that? Like in the movie, where he could control sand?"

"I don't… I don't think the Egyptian government would allow anything like that," he said. "It looks more like—look, it's a sinkhole!"

He could see it now, the vast depression forming. An empty aquifer collapsing? A gigantic tomb that had somehow gone unnoticed?

He noticed the cab had stopped. The driver was on his phone, shouting into it frantically.

The plume of dust suddenly incandesced blue. Keith saw the light was coming from below.

Then an arm came out of the hole. At first the distance and scale fooled him. The arm didn't look that big. And it looked strange; dark, but with a yellow and black pattern that looked almost like a machine.

And then a face came up from the dust. A monstrous face. A face from his nightmares.

His heart pounded and his chest felt tight. He knew the signs of a panic attack. But this was real. That wasn't a sinkhole. It was an entrance to Duat, the night world, the vast dark caverns the sun must negotiate after it set in the west. And this—this thing crawling out of it could only be one of the ancient gods of Egypt.

And he knew which one.

Babi, his aunt had said. *The baboon-headed god, the earliest incarnation of Ra. He waits there in the dark bottomless pit of the underworld. Waits there to pull you down and eat you alive.*

"Babi!" he gasped aloud. "The Bull of Baboons, god of the underworld, bloodthirsty devourer of entrails…"

"Umm, honey," Fiona said, taking his hand. "I don't know that much about Egyptian mythology. But… isn't that Kong?"

"Ah…" the dust was subsiding into the sinkhole, and what had come out of it pulled itself to its feet by gripping the pyramid and stood to its full height. Now in profile, Keith saw the face wasn't that of a baboon at all, but of a Great Ape.

"Oh," he breathed. "Yeah. Thank God. It's just Kong."

Kong shook himself as if getting his bearings, and then began striding toward the Great Pyramid of Khufu. When he reached it he turned and roared. The cab shuddered as if they were in an earthquake. The Titan raised his arm, which definitely had something black and yellow attached to it. He called again, an unmistakable threat and challenge.

"I think we won't be sightseeing today," Keith told Fiona.

"Speak for yourself," she said. "This is way more exciting than I thought it would be."

Monarch Control
Barbados

Laurier jumped up and strode purposefully to the display.

"We're reading a massive bioelectric spike outside of Cairo!" she said. "Energy like that is going to attract every Titan on the planet."

"No," Hampton said from behind her. "Just one."

She looked for another moment at the signal emanating from Egypt. "I want visuals," she said. "And someone find me Godzilla."

That part wasn't so hard. There were already dozens of cellphone videos online, and two stations in Cairo quickly joined them in filming Kong's surprise appearance.

"How did he get there?" she wondered. But the answer was obvious. Aerial footage and the signature itself made it clear that a vortex had opened in Giza. Another undocumented one.

"Found him," Laurier said. "Godzilla, I mean."

"I knew who you meant," Hampton said. "Yeah, there he is."

On the friggin' Rock of Gibraltar. Posing, shrieking at the sky. Answering Kong's challenge. He scintillated, beautiful and terrifying.

"Try to get through to Doctor Andrews again," she said.

"Something weird is going on down there. I have a feeling we need to know what. Like, right now."

"On it," Laurier said.

As Hampton watched, Godzilla arched toward the water and dove headfirst from the cliff, plunging into the Alboran Sea, sending a small tidal wave crashing through the straits.

"He's swimming towards Cairo," Meeks said.

"Yeah," she replied. "No kidding."

Malenka
Hollow Earth

The Iwi—most of them, anyway—were evacuating the city, taking refuge in the surrounding jungle.

The queen and Jia were deep in conversation about... something. Ilene tried to push back on her feelings of being left out; this wasn't about her. Or it shouldn't be.

Jia nodded at the queen, then signed to Ilene.

We have to go, she said.

Ilene's throat closed, but she forced herself to breathe. She nodded.

The Skar King was on his way, with an army. Kong had gone up to try and lure Godzilla down.

That left Jia's part. Waking Mothra.

The queen and her entourage led them back to the base of the temple pyramid. Jia vanished into one of the smaller ceremonial buildings with the queen, and when she came back out only moments later, she was transformed. Now dressed in a yellow mantle, the queen then painted a yellow stripe on her forehead, bisecting Jia's headband. But it wasn't just the new clothes that made the girl seem different. It was the way she held herself, full of confidence and purpose. She looked every inch an Iwi.

Ilene had never been so proud, nor so terrified. It felt like a turning point; from this moment on, Jia would be less her daughter with each turn of the planet, each beat of her heart.

But what she could become—it had to be worth it. If she survived.

She had to survive.

"Are you sure about this?" Trapper asked.

"No," Ilene replied. "But she is."

"Yeah. I guess I can see that."

Ilene tried to smile. Tears burned at the edges of her eyes.

A hand touched her shoulder. The queen. She stared directly into Ilene's eyes, and she did her best to hold that gaze.

What's she saying? she asked Jia.

That we're right where we need to be, Jia replied.

Ilene nodded at the queen. Their gazes remained locked for another few seconds. Then the other woman turned back to Jia. They conferred briefly in their silent language.

Then Jia stepped out alone and began ascending toward the lower platform of the pyramid. She paused at the top of the stairs and looked back at Ilene.

I love you, Ilene signed. *So much.*

Jia was still for a moment. Then she ran back down the short flight of steps and into Ilene's arms. Ilene held her, her tears bursting forth, and finally she felt Jia hesitate. Jamming down a sob, she pulled back a little and shook her head. She didn't speak or sign, but she knew Jia understood. Maybe she wasn't telepathic like the queen, but she and her daughter knew each other.

You can do this.

Jia tried a little smile. She started back up the stairs. This time she didn't look back. She continued to the base of the pyramid and started up the stairway to the top, so steep it was almost a ladder.

"So we are absolutely sure she can pull this off?" Bernie said.

"It's why Jia was called here. Only an Iwi from Skull Island can awaken Mothra."

"Uh-huh," Bernie said. He sounded skeptical.

"I've got a dozen books on parenting," she told him. "Not one of them mentions ancient prophecies."

"I'm sensing some one-star reviews in your future," Bernie said.

"So many reviews."

Jia was climbing more quickly now, and distance had diminished her form. But where she touched the pyramid, it glowed white, so it was easy enough to track her.

Near the top, Jia's face turned back toward her briefly.

"She's gonna be alright," Ilene whispered.

"Uh-huh," Bernie agreed.

"She's gonna be alright," she repeated, anyway.

Jia reached the top of the pyramid. A glance down showed how dizzyingly high she was, but she didn't fear falling. In fact, she felt light, as if she weighed little more than a feather. The last part of the climb had been the easiest. She was nearly at the boundary between up and down, where gravity changed the direction of its pull. The top of the pyramid that either rose up or hung down—depending upon your perspective—from the other side was right above her.

The queen had told her she would know what to do, but now that she was here, she wasn't sure that was true. She knew she was supposed to awaken Mothra, but she didn't see any

Titans. Just the pyramids and the upside-down world. The queen had said that an Iwi from Skull Island would be the one to do this. Was there some clue in her childhood? But try as she might, she could remember no stories about Mothra, nor, in fact, anything that reminded her of this.

But then she remembered the moths and her aunt Oa. She remembered liking them. She remembered telling Oa that they could sing, and her aunt asking what she meant by that. *Moths don't sing*, she had said.

But they do, Jia had replied.

She blinked. She had just dreamed about that a few days ago, hadn't she? But it had been such a small dream, quickly overwhelmed by the visions that had brought her here. She had already forgotten it again. But she was thinking about it now. Why? Considering it, it didn't even make sense. Even if a moth could sing, how could she have heard it? She couldn't hear. And if they sang the way the Iwi talked, why couldn't her aunt hear the song too?

And yet, she realized, she was hearing it now. Not the same song, exactly, but a very similar one. Low, then high, rising and falling—not in her ears or in her mind, but on the fine hairs of her arms and back of her neck. On her skin and gently tickling in her bones. Like the pulse of wings moving air. Something secret, hidden, but yearning to be known.

It's not because I'm from Skull Island, she realized. *No one else on Skull Island could hear this. It's because I'm me and I am from Skull Island.*

She felt easier, relaxed now. She allowed the song to fill her. She remembered the dance of the moths. She reached out into the music and placed herself within it. The tingle of the song climbed up her body and focused in her hand, and it grew stronger. She reached out, and light danced on her fingers.

In response, more light appeared, swirled from her hands and from the empty space in front of her. It formed radiant streams and rivulets and then a shape, suspended between the two pyramids, bridging the gap between them. Like strands of silk, wrapped tightly in a familiar form.

She had seen a chrysalis before, the cocoon in which a caterpillar became a moth. This was a large one. A very large one. She smiled as shape and color moved within it, as the silent melody grew to fill everything. She felt the energy pulsing within; she felt peace, like watching clouds on a moonlit night. And she felt a purpose and intent that seemed eternal.

Mothra, she thought. *I'm here. It's time.*

In no particular hurry, the chrysalis began to split, and wings emerged, immense, beautiful beyond anything she had ever seen before.

Between the summits of the pyramids, Mothra's wings unfolded in soft radiance. A low chittering noise filled the valley as the Titan awakened.

Ilene had seen stills and footage of Mothra, from Yunnan province and the Battle of Boston, but she had never seen her in person. The difference was astonishing. Godzilla was like a remorseless god, a primal force, beyond human ken. Kong was more personal, somehow. Despite his immense size, strength, and temper, you also felt he was comprehensible. More human.

Mothra was neither of these. She was even more alien than Godzilla, in a way, and far less relatable than Kong. But there was a magnificence there that transcended her mere form. This wasn't the same Mothra as before—she couldn't be. And yet she was, somehow. She was like life itself: always changing, always evolving, but always *living*. Whatever it was that made trilobites and bacteria and tigers and Godzilla all a part of the same world, the same universe—Mothra felt like that thing. And when the great Titan took wing with Ilene's daughter on her back and headed toward the vortex Kong had leaped though, her fear for her daughter was nearly eclipsed by wonder. And by hope.

Nearly. Her hands were shaking.

"She really bloody did it," Trapper said.

"So if she's going up there, what are we doing down here?" Bernie asked. "Last I heard there was a giant monster squad on the way."

The queen turned to him and motioned with her hands. She pointed at the pyramids and then formed their shape, and a circular flowing motion. Ilene didn't understand it.

Bernie did, though. His eyes went wide.

"Gravity," he said. "Gravity! The pyramids and gravity. I got it!"

Ilene didn't understand, though. "Tell me on the way," Ilene said to Bernie, as the queen and her people started moving.

"Umm," Trapper said. He seemed excited. "While we're throwing random shit at the wall, permission to take the H.E.A.V and rally some reinforcements."

"From the surface?" Ilene said. "No, there's no time."

He shook his head. "No. This idea is way weirder than that."

SEVENTEEN

O inundation of the Nile, offerings are made unto you, men are immolated to you, great festivals are instituted for you.Birds are sacrificed to you, gazelles are taken for you in the mountain, pure flames are prepared for you. Sacrifice is made to every god as it is made to the Nile. The Nile has made its retreats in Southern Egypt, its name is not known beyond the Tuau. The god manifests not his forms, He baffles all conception.

—the *Hymn to the Nile*,
circa 2100 BC

Monarch Control
Barbados

The Ancient Egyptians had considered the Nile River a god: the source of abundance, of soil and water for crops. For millions of years, it had been swum by crocodiles and hippopotamuses, monitor lizards, and perches over six feet long and weighing over four hundred pounds. For thousands of years, human watercraft had traversed its surface, from the canoes and papyrus rafts of the Stone Age to Egyptian and Roman barges, and later still steamships and vessels burning gas and diesel.

Now Godzilla entered the storied river and plowed upstream, one god swimming within another.

Hampton watched his progress, trying not to pick her nails.

"Kong's just waiting there," she muttered. "What the hell is he up to?"

The downtime they'd had while Godzilla made his way across the Mediterranean to where Kong was stomping around Cairo had now officially been frittered away. All attempts to reach Dr. Andrews had met with failure. Whatever was going on down there was still generating a massive amount of communications disruption. She was reluctantly considering the possibility that Andrews and the others might be in need of rescue—or worse, might be beyond rescue entirely. She had ordered another H.E.A.V prepped, but it would be at least a couple of hours before it was ready, and even then, readings suggested the vortex was less stable than usual.

Her only, very small victory in the last few hours had been in talking the Egyptian military down from unleashing hell on Kong, who was currently just sort of hanging out—or worse, trying to somehow prevent Godzilla from entering Egypt. Whatever was going on, she argued, it was between the two Titans, and if they didn't somehow attract the Titans into a major city, like Cairo, maybe they would be content to work out their aggressions in the desert.

* * *

Giza Plateau
Egypt

Kong had known Godzilla would come. He was counting on it.

It was taking longer than he'd thought it would.

He had always had a sense that Godzilla was out there, even when he was younger on Skull Island. He had sensed the Titan near the island many times, without ever knowing exactly what he was. He hadn't cared. There were plenty of enemies to face as it was. Whatever he sensed out there past the storm didn't concern him if it never came ashore. And it never did.

Godzilla apparently felt the same way, because as soon as Kong left the island, Godzilla came for him, determined to kill him. They fought on the open sea, which did not go well for Kong. He wasn't much of a swimmer—and Godzilla was a very good swimmer.

Later, they fought again, and they fought together against the weird thing that looked like Godzilla, but smelled like the machines of the little ones.

Godzilla couldn't talk. He couldn't do hand-talking. He could only make scratchy-mean-nothing noises. But he and Godzilla had understood each other. Below was for Kong. Above was for Godzilla. That was how it had to be.

That had been fine with him. It was still fine with him. He did not want to live up here, especially in this place, where the bright light was so sharp in the sky, the air so dry, with sand in all directions and no jungle anywhere.

Since their agreement, he could feel where bad-breath-lizard was even more strongly than before. It was an itch in his head, usually easy to ignore. He had chosen the hole in the sky where he felt Godzilla strongest, but when he arrived, Godzilla wasn't there. So Kong waited by the hole. They would need that to go back below, to fight the Skar King and his army. Godzilla would understand that.

He had helped Godzilla fight the Machine. Godzilla would help him fight Red Ape.

Now he felt Godzilla was close, and soon, in the long water, he saw his spines. They looked different. Brighter. A different color. But it was the same Godzilla. He could tell that much.

He waited. When Godzilla burst from the water and slapped his scaly feet on the dry ground, Kong forced down his instinct to reply with a threat by beating his chest or vocalizing. He would show Godzilla that he hadn't come to fight.

But Godzilla charged at him. The Titan wasn't slowing down. He wasn't here to find out what was wrong. He was here to fight.

Kong held out one hand, signaling for Godzilla to stop. With the other, he gestured to the hole.

This is why I'm here, he was trying to say. *We have to go down there.*

Godzilla wasn't paying attention. Still resisting a threat-call, Kong threw both arms up as Godzilla crashed into him, knocking him back into the little four-sided mountain behind him. It collapsed under his weight and he went right through it. He skidded across the sand and his back hit another of the little mountains.

He was just getting to his feet when the Titan came at him again. Kong hadn't even hit him yet, but he wanted to. Why wouldn't Godzilla pay attention?

Still trying to avoid a fight, Kong threw a handful of sand into Godzilla's eyes and dodged aside. The Titan missed him and careened into another of the hills, breaking it with his little head.

Godzilla shook it off and charged him again, his mouth gaping open to bite. Kong shoved his new machine arm between his jaws. It was his first time using the arm in a fight, and it felt good. Strong. The Titan's teeth didn't cut through it. He didn't have his axe, but this arm was good, too. And he couldn't drop it, like he'd dropped the axe.

Godzilla was heavy. Very heavy. Kong tried to dig in his feet, but the sand slid beneath them, and Godzilla drove him back against a four-sided hill. Then Godzilla lifted him up off the ground and fell over backward, so Kong went way up in the air—and then slammed back to earth. It hurt the breath inside of him. For a moment he didn't see anything, and when he did, it was to see Godzilla lifting his foot to bring it down on his neck, like last time.

No.

Kong rolled aside, felt the impact ripple through the sand. Enough. Enough of this.

Godzilla snapped at him again, but this time Kong didn't try to resist the urge to fight. He unleashed it. He hit the Titan under the chin with his yellow arm and was gratified when it sent his antagonist staggering back.

You want to fight? Kong roared. He punched Godzilla again: Godzilla stumbled and landed on his back. Kong came down on him, pummeling him with both fists. His opponent tried to bite him, but Kong caught his mouth with his new arm once more, driving the Titan into the sand. Kong heard a hum and felt the crackle; Godzilla opened his mouth, and it was glowing. He knew what this was. If he didn't stop it…

Kong drove his yellow-arm fist straight into Godzilla's mouth.

The lizard pitched back into the dirt. Kong expected him to get right back up, but instead he lay still. Not dead.

He glanced at the hole. This was his chance.

Kong chuffed, heaved himself to his feet, and took Godzilla by the tail. He started dragging him toward the hole. Maybe he would figure it out when they were down there.

He had almost reached the hole when he realized Godzilla's tail spines were glowing again. He looked back and saw the Titan's eyes were shining and his mouth was opening.

Kong dropped the tail and ran, trying to get behind one of the little mountains before the bad breath found him.

The bad breath came after him. It cut through the mountain, chasing him so he had to throw himself forward and roll as it singed by. He came back up and thumped both fists on the ground, ready to spring in any direction.

But he didn't see Godzilla. He couldn't see anything. The dry sand filled the air, and everything was dull yellow. His gaze flicked around, searching...

There. Godzilla was right on him. He tried to meet the attack but didn't have time. Godzilla head-butted him in the chest and his feet lost purchase; he fell back to the dusty ground.

The Titan slammed his feet down again, and this time Kong didn't have time to move. The clawed foot smashed into his chest. Before Kong could move, the foot went up and down, stomping on him repeatedly. Then Godzilla pressed down on Kong with all his weight and reared up to his full height. His spines flashed like purple lightning. Kong raised his yellow arm defensively, hoping it might help, wishing now more than ever that he had his axe. He squirmed, but Godzilla had him pinned. He would never get free before—

Something happened. A sound, a burst of light. The air itself became hard, harder than any wind, banging everything around.

It pushed Godzilla off him, knocked him over as if he weighed nothing. A strange song filled the dry air.

Still on his back, Kong saw wings above him. He had seen many things with wings, fought many of them. But this was something he had never seen before. It reminded him of the dim light of the night, it reminded him of a flower opening. It was huge, strong enough to knock Godzilla down, and yet Kong somehow did not feel threatened.

Godzilla was standing back up. But he was not looking at Kong. He was looking at the new thing with wings. It had landed on a hill of stone that had a sort-of face on it. It reminded Kong of some kind of cat. The winged one was clearer now; it had many legs, and he now realized it looked like a very small night flier, the kind that was drawn to light. Something was drifting from the sky—ash, or winged seeds or tufts of grass.

He looked over at Godzilla and saw... something. Kong did not know this giant flying bug. But Godzilla did. Kong could tell. It felt like they had known each other for a long time. Like family, even though they looked nothing alike.

And then he noticed something else, a little one, standing on the stone-hill-head. Jia. She smiled at him, but her attention was on Godzilla. She did not move her hands, but Kong thought that she was telling him something.

Godzilla leaned toward Jia, but he did not open his mouth. Then he lifted his gaze to the winged one.

Godzilla pointed his face to the sky and screamed. He knew now. He understood.

Kong roared. The winged one flapped her immense wings and rose between them.

Monarch Control
Barbados

Hampton sat back in her chair. She tried to take a deep breath and let it go slowly. What was it? Draw in green air, release red air. The tension was supposed to go out with red air, or something like that.

I need to try yoga again, she thought. *Or tai chi.* Or more realistically, maybe a whisky sour.

"Well," she said, to no one in particular. "That got very weird very quickly." She looked up at the ceiling and closed her eyes.

"That was Mothra, right? Someone tell me I haven't lost it. That was Mothra. Of course, Mothra is dead, right? Turned into little starlight sprinkles? We all remember that, too, right?"

"I'm checking bioacoustic and bioelectric data," Laurier said.

"Yeah. Do that," Hampton said. "Meanwhile, play that last part back. To where the bug shows up. About half speed."

Laurier obliged.

The cameras had been focused on Kong and Godzilla, but the playback made it clear that Mothra had come up out of the same vortex as Kong. That meant she had come from Hollow Earth.

"Stop it," she said. "Move that back about six seconds and make it still."

"It's a match," Laurier announced. "The same signatures as Mothra, with an error range of three percent."

"Maybe just the same species?" Hampton muttered.

"It's impossible to say, with a sample size of two," Laurier said. "But if we compare any two members of well documented species—Skullcrawlers, for instance—the error range would be much bigger. More on the order of fifteen or twenty."

"Sure," Hampton said. "So it's somehow Mothra. Fine, why not?" She pointed to the screen. "Enlarge that."

They were looking at the Sphinx of Giza, one of the few monuments still unscathed by Titan brawling. Someone was standing on its head. A person.

"Can you get better resolution on that?" she asked.

"That's as good as it gets. We may get some other footage that's better."

But Hampton was pretty sure she knew who it was. Jia.

"What the holy hell is going on down there?" she wondered.

"Put all Monarch locations and participating governments on high alert," she said. "I have a feeling things are about to get even weirder."

Malenka
Hollow Earth

The Iwi queen led them into the temple pyramid. Inside, it was mostly hollow, its surfaces intricately carved. Reflected light shimmered from what Ilene thought at first was a vast pool of water, but something about it didn't look right: the way it rippled. It seemed more... viscous than water. Columns stuck out of the pool at regular intervals and climbed up toward the dark upper reaches of the structure. They didn't go all the way up, though. They weren't supporting anything, which led her to wonder what they were for. Were they merely decorative? It seemed unlikely.

Trapper had gone after whatever mysterious allies he had in mind. The Iwi warriors were tracking the approaching army of monsters. Word was that they were very close indeed. Jia had flown off on Mothra. And she was here, wondering what their part in all of this was.

She glanced over at Bernie, who had been mumbling something about gravity for a while.

"All right," she said. "We're underneath the pyramids. Now what?"

"Gravity," Bernie said. "Iwi technology. We've known for years that ancient temples like Teotihuacan in Mexico were built over lakes of mercury," he said. "But no one has ever understood why." He smiled. "Iwi technology. Yeah."

That's mercury, she realized. As Bernie spoke, the queen approached the drop down to the pool and made a circular gesture. Several other Iwi carrying a wide metal bowl with long handles came up as well. They tilted the bowl, and a red fluid began pouring into the lake of liquid metal.

"It's a fail-safe," Bernie went on. "A defense mechanism. If anything ever breaks the veil, they can trigger an overload explosion that can knock the invaders off course using gravity. Through a chemical reaction this liquid metal becomes an engineering mechanism forcing the two electromagnetic pyramids together, causing an antigravity shockwave, but only for a few minutes. After that everything that goes up will come crashing down."

The queen regarded Bernie and nodded. *Yes.*

"It may buy us some time to stop this Skar King," Bernie concluded.

Flickers of electricity like miniature lightning began playing upon the columns. Ilene could feel the charge on her skin, smell the sharp tang of ozone.

The columns began to rise out of the mercury, reaching ever higher.

"It's working," Ilene said.

"Yes," Bernie agreed.

The expression on the face of the queen changed suddenly. She gestured toward the entrance, and everyone started running outside. Ilene and Bernie followed. Ilene had the distinct feeling that it was bad news.

The veil over the Iwi territory was glowing, forming a bright blue dome. But even as she watched, it faltered and flickered. And in the distance it shattered, melting into nothing as it collapsed.

And in that gap stood pure horror.

She hadn't had a firm picture of the Skar King fixed in her mind. She had been imagining something a lot like Kong. And he was that, in the broadest outline—another Great Ape. But he was thinner than Kong, with longer arms and legs, reddish in color. Kong was an ape that had no precise analogue among smaller, surface-dwelling apes. He resembled a gorilla, but that was superficial. In fact, the way his body was put together, the way he was able to carry himself comfortably bipedal, was more like a human or an early human ancestor. The Skar King more closely resembled an orangutan. But she had known orangutans, worked with them. They were peaceful, kind, extraordinarily thoughtful creatures, usually slow moving, very deeply intelligent, and probably the most solitary of the surface-dwelling Great Apes.

The Skar King, even at first glance, was none of these. Cruelty sat on every angle of his body, showed in every gesture. His gaze was pure malice, as if anger and grievance had burned every other emotion out of him, if he had ever had them at all. Even at this distance, the mere sight of him chilled her to the marrow.

We can't win, she thought. *We can't beat that.*

So terrifying was the Skar King that at first she didn't notice the mass of apes following him. Dozens, at least. All Titans nearly as big as Kong and Godzilla.

And then there was what stood next to the Skar King. The biggest Titan she had ever seen. The biggest Titan anyone had ever seen, dwarfing even Godzilla and Monster Zero.

It was the color of polar ice, a quadruped supported by massive pillars of legs, her forelegs longer than her rear. She looked reptilian, like Godzilla, but from a very different lineage. Her thick, broad shape and beaked mouth made Ilene think of some prehistoric turtle, a dinosaur like an ankylosaurus, or a a species of dicynodont, the beaked therapsids of the Permian period. Shimo was probably none of those things, but like the other Titans the result of convergent evolution so convoluted that taxonomists were still trying to work out what exactly any of them were.

But Ilene knew, just looking at the monster, that it was the Titan the Iwi spoke of. The World Ender. The bringer of Ice Ages; the ice dragon who had somehow frozen Greenland over, not in years or months, but in minutes or hours.

Shimo.

Above, the tops of the pyramids were drawing nearer.

"This looks pretty bad," Bernie observed.

"You still think the gravity thing will buy us time?" she asked.

"I... hope so," he said. "Because. Wow."

"Glad you came down here to save the world again?" she asked him.

"Let me get back to you on that," he said. He nodded at the army of Titans. "Come on," he said. "Come a little closer." He looked back up at the pyramids. "Any time now," he said.

But the Skar King paused. He cast his terrible gaze across the Iwi territory, and then his eyes turned up to where the pyramids were converging. Then he swung himself up on Shimo's back, riding her like an elephant. He pointed at the pyramids and Shimo roared, opening her beak, and a beam shot from it— not unlike Godzilla's breath, but purest white. It struck the closing gap between the pyramids. The air around the beam shimmered with cold, and a chill settled over everything, like a cold front arriving, even though Shimo's breath was high above them. The wave propagated much more quickly through the air than it should.

Ice condensed instantly from the humid atmosphere, bridging the gap that still existed between the two pyramids.

Stopping them from touching.

The Skar King either knew about the Iwi gravity weapon or he was suspicious of the moving buildings. Either way, Bernie's gravity wave—the thing that was supposed to hold off the monsters until Godzilla, Kong, and Mothra returned—wasn't going to happen at all. Or at least not soon enough.

"We're not going to make it," Ilene said. "There's not enough time. We need something to slow them down."

"Well, what else can we do?" Bernie snapped.

The answer came from the sky-tearing sound of the H.E.A.V arriving, along with a screeching horde of...

Vertacines.

Trapper's very weird idea. He had disguised the H.E.A.V as a vertacine again, but rather than blending in with the flock, he had used the aircraft to lead it here. Now he dove toward the Skar King's army, and his aerial escort followed close behind.

Trapper's voice crackled over her earbud. "It's vertacine mating season!" he shouted.

Each one of them had a lightning bolt's worth of electricity, she remembered. Now she saw it was true. As the flying creatures blew through the apes and Shimo like a wind, the Titan army responded by attacking them, triggering the vertacines' survival instincts. The distance suddenly lit up with blue arcs of electricity. Shimo roared and stopped blasting the pyramids with cold, instead sweeping her ray through the hundreds of winged tormenters. Where her breath touched, wings seized up instantly, and the frozen fliers plummeted to the ground—but there were so many vertacines it hardly affected their numbers. Apes howled and swiped at the flying beasts with about as much effect as taking a bat to a swarm of bees.

Way to go, Trapper, she thought. Now and then he really did come through. But although the apes appeared hurt by the voltage, and a few even dropped, most seemed merely annoyed by the attack. The vertacines didn't want to be in this fight. They were just passing through, but at least they were wreaking havoc, creating the pause they needed.

But the yellow-and-black-striped creatures were already turning upward, away from the valley, which meant their respite was at an end.

Above, the newly formed ice cracked and shattered without the continued pressure of Shimo's breath. The tops of the pyramids drew closer together. Ilene already thought she felt lighter, as gravity held less sway. Higher, in the land-sky, one of the vortices suddenly shimmered, and something shot from it, like a comet or a meteor streaking through the atmosphere. It vanished from view but a few seconds later Ilene heard the impact. Her ears popped, and all the trees bent; loose rocks on the ground jumped into the air and almost seemed to pause before falling back down. The shockwave spread across the valley in a widening circle, carrying leaves, branches, and dust along its bow-wave. It swept through the Skar King's army.

A brief hush followed, as if the world was taking a breath.

Then the ground began quaking in pulses—one, two, one, two, followed by the ear-splitting jet-engine screech that could only be Godzilla. But his wasn't the only familiar war-cry, because on top of it was the enraged roar of an angry Kong—

possibly the strangest and most awesome two-part harmony she'd ever heard.

Kong had done it—he'd brought help. And although the fight was now two against many, she couldn't help but feel more hopeful.

The Skar King and his apes charged forward, the King still riding Shimo, and now dozens of monstrous battle-cries filled the winds.

Godzilla and Kong broke through the cloud caused by their descent, charging side-by-side, straight for the Skar King.

The Skar King kicked Shimo, spurring her on.

The H.E.A.V came screaming around and dropped to the ground just in front of them. No longer marked like a vertacine, Ilene was glad to see it. The ground on which they were standing was about to becomes the front line on the battleground of gods and monsters, and absolutely not a safe place for tiny mortals like her or even the Iwi queen.

The back hatch of the H.E.A.V popped open, revealing a smiling Trapper.

"Your carriage awaits," he said.

Bernie shouted something, but Ilene wasn't paying attention. Instead she ushered the Iwi queen and her bodyguards into the H.E.A.V.

"Get in, buckle in, you beautiful people," Trapper said.

Trying to show the queen how to do that, Ilene checked to make sure everyone was in. When she was certain they were, she swept her gaze toward the other side of the world and the vortices there. Where were Mothra and Jia? Why hadn't they come back with Kong and Godzilla?

Focus, she thought. Trapper was waiting on her mark.

"Three, two, one—" she said.

The invisible hand of acceleration pushed her back as the

craft shot into the air. Trapper pulled the H.E.A.V's nose up hard, and instants later they were nearly at the altitude of the pyramid summits. There was almost no gap between them now.

Below, the charging Titans were closing the space between them, as well.

Things were about to go tremendously nonlinear, to say the least.

EIGHTEEN

"I have not heard before of Ragnarok," said Gangler; "what hast thou to tell me about it?"

"There are many very notable circumstances concerning it," replied Har, "which I can inform thee of. In the first place will come the winter, called Fimbul-winter, during which snow will fall from the four corners of the world; the frosts will be very severe, the wind piercing, the weather tempestuous, and the sun impart no gladness. Three such winters shall pass away without being tempered by a single summer. Three other similar winters follow, during which war and discord will spread over the whole globe. Brethren for the sake of mere gain shall kill each other, and no one shall spare either his parents or his children.

"Then shall happen such things as may truly be accounted great prodigies. The wolf shall devour the sun, and a severe loss will that be for mankind. The other wolf will take the moon, and this too will cause great mischief. Then the stars shall be hurled from the heavens, and the earth so violently shaken that trees will be torn *up by the roots, the tottering mountains tumble headlong from their foundations, and all bonds and fetters be shivered in pieces. Fenrir then breaks loose, and the sea rushes over the earth, on account of the Midgard serpent turning with giant force, and gaining the land. On the waters floats the ship Naglfar, which is constructed of the nails of dead men.*

—the *Younger Eddas of Snorre Sturleson,*
translation by I.A. Blackwell

Kong's rage built as he charged alongside Godzilla. The Skar King was riding Ice Breath and he was shaking Kong's axe in one hand. *His* axe. The other apes came behind him. The apes for which Kong had searched so long, that he had hoped would be his family. But they hadn't been what he hoped, and now he had to fight them.

Of course. He had been fighting since he could remember. It was what he did.

He hoped Suko was safe, that he'd found a good place to hide.

They were almost on the enemy. He flexed his arm, the pains of his battle with Godzilla forgotten. He roared again, threat and promise.

He had almost forgotten how big Ice Breath was. She was bigger than Godzilla. Bigger than anything Kong had ever seen that was alive. And although the Titan beside him was screaming and rushing to the fight, Kong had the sense that Godzilla was… not worried, exactly, but maybe not sure. Like in the fight with the Machine Godzilla, when the metal monster was winning.

Except they hadn't even started this fight yet.

Red mist rose before his eyes, as they at last met Shimo and the Skar King. The Red Ape sprang from Cold Breath's back, and Kong vaulted onto Godzilla's back, used the elevation and speed to leap higher, arcing to meet his foe in midair. The jump carried him further than he had expected; he didn't weigh as much as he had a moment before, as if he were further up in the sky, where everything floated.

He drew his yellow arm back, timing his blow as the Skar King prepared to swing the axe. Below, Godzilla and the other Titan howled at each other as they prepared to collide.

And then, suddenly, everything turned. Kong felt like a huge hand had grabbed him and thrown him away from the Skar King, who also went tumbling wildly through the sky. Land and sky-land whirled around him; he felt like he was pulled in every direction at once. He was falling, but not falling down—or up. He was falling everywhere.

The pyramids crashed into one another with such force that their summits splintered into crystalline shards, borne away on pale blue spheres rapidly expanding away from point of contact. Before Ilene could draw another breath, it overtook them. The g-forces pressing her into her seat suddenly vanished, replaced by the dizzying sensation of free fall. Bernie yelped and Trapper swore. The Iwi queen somehow kept her face placid as everything outside the windows somersaulted into chaos. The cloud of boulders that marked the transition between the two "downs" were now freely whirling around everywhere, along with Great Apes, Godzilla, and Shimo.

The H.E.A.V—aside from the exclamations of its passengers—was exceptionally silent. Its brightly lit consoles and internal lighting were absent.

"The engine's out!" Trapper shouted. "The shockwave did something to our power... battery... thingy."

She shot him a look.

"Hey!" he said. "I'm not a mechanic! I went to vet school!"

"Well, you better do something," Bernie said. "The gravity could come back any time now."

"I'm trying!" Trapper said, working furiously at the dead controls.

Ilene pulled in a breath, wondering if this was what it was like being in outer space. Weightless, tumbling aimlessly, struggling to find a point of reference.

A floating ape the size of a skyscraper whizzed past her field of vision.

Probably not. There was probably literally nothing else like this. Anywhere.

She couldn't do anything to help Trapper. She couldn't really do anything. She tracked her gaze around, feeling queasy. Still no sign of Jia or Mothra. But the exercise helped her get her bearings. If she moved her gaze against their rotation, she could focus on and decipher what was happening outside. It was better than running a preview in her head of their inevitable plummet to oblivion when gravity came back.

Godzilla had adjusted quickly to the situation. Of course, she realized, moving in all of this must be something like swimming, which was exactly what it looked like Godzilla was doing. He was bouncing from boulder to boulder with his hind legs, sometimes catching one with his arms for leverage to propel himself forward, sweeping his tail to-and-fro — not to propel himself, but to stabilize his flight—and to club away the Great Apes stupid enough to come near him. For a creature of his size, he was weirdly elegant.

Godzilla was different, wasn't he? His colors, his spines,

everything about him had changed. He was more… crystalline. And glowing more magenta than blue. It wasn't the first time he had undergone a transformation, but to her it seemed the most dramatic. What exactly had been going on on the surface while they had been down here?

She hoped she would get to find out, although right now it wasn't looking that great. Trapper was still trying to cajole something out of the vehicle, but it was just a metal box caught in a tornado.

She kept her focus on Godzilla.

Kick her ass, she thought, as the Titan launched himself directly at Shimo.

Kong seemed to getting the hang of things, too. But the Skar King was adapting as well. Jumping and swinging from rock to rock, they pitched toward one another.

Suko was tired of hiding. He knew Kong was protecting him, but even with the new monster he'd brought back through the sky, it was clear that Kong was outnumbered. Before he had only fought the Skar King and Shimo, and Shimo had nearly killed him. Now all of the other red-stripes would fight him too. The monster was terrifying, but he was smaller than Shimo, and Shimo would do what the Skar King commanded. She would freeze the whole valley and everyone in it. He did not think Kong and the monster would win.

Even so, he knew which side he was on. He belonged with Kong. And if Kong fought, Suko would fight too.

He took a deep breath, then beat his chest and howled. No one heard, but it made him feel better. Stronger.

As Suko charged out of his hiding place, everything went crazy.

His feet no longer stuck to the ground. In fact, the land pushed him away, sent him flying into the air. He screeched in fright, failing to find purchase that wasn't there, but that only made him spin head over legs.

At least the same thing was happening to everyone else. In the distance, Kong and the Skar King were both tumbling aimlessly. So was Shimo, and Kong's monster. And the rest of the apes.

The ground was getting further and further away from Suko and the sky-ground was getting closer. He thought this must be like flying, so he tried waving his arms and legs like a flier, but that didn't do anything that he could tell. A huge boulder drifted past. He reached for it, but it was too far away, and he couldn't control where he was going. A smaller one came closer, and he managed to grab it. It wasn't much, but it gave him a sense of steadiness, of a small amount of control.

Another big one went by. He pushed himself off the smaller rock, which went flying off behind him, but it had the intended effect, propelling him straight toward the larger rock. He hit it a little harder than he intended to, but managed to cling to it. He screeched, this time not in terror. But in amazement.

It was frightening, but it was also… fun. And now he had an idea.

He got his bearings. The boulder he was on was moving away from Kong. But now he thought he knew what he was doing. He picked out another rock moving the right way and launched himself toward it.

Kong had been in the in-between sky before. It hadn't been like this, but the feeling of being light, not pulled on by the ground—that was familiar. He fixed his gaze on the Skar King and tried to swim toward him. It didn't work.

Then a flying rock bumped into him, sending him in a different direction.

That made sense. He looked around for another rock. One came near enough and he grabbed it, pushing himself toward the Skar King.

The other ape was figuring it out, too. He turned to face Kong as he approached, pushing off another boulder with his hind legs, pulling back Kong's axe to hit him with it.

Kong roared and met the axe with his yellow arm. The blow shocked up through the metal, but there was no pain. It deflected the axe easily, but the impact knocked the two apes apart.

But the axe wasn't the Skar King's only weapon. He unwound his bone-whip and lashed it at Kong. He blocked that with his new arm, too, but the bones wrapped around it and pulled tight. Then the Skar King yanked, pulling the two of them together. Kong was fine with that. But before he could get close enough to strike, the Skar King kicked him in the chest with one of his long legs. Kong grunted and lurched away. The whip was still wrapped around his arm, though, so he pulled himself back. The Skar King, off balance, tried to swing the axe again, but Kong punched him in the face and then again under one arm. He unwound the bone-whip with a twist of his arm and followed with another punch. Then he reached for the axe, still in the Skar King's hands.

An ape hit him from behind, hard, then grabbed him around the waist with his lower legs while hitting him for a second time in the back of the head. Kong's grasping hand closed on empty space instead of the axe. Both of his arms were busy, but he couldn't let go of the Skar King to fight the second ape.

He felt teeth clamp on his neck. But the next instant he heard a dull whump and the hold on him instantly loosened. The ape behind him grunted in pain and let go.

His last punch had sent the Skar King flying beyond his reach. Kong growled, looking for a stone to help him maneuver, reach the Skar King, kill him, and take back his axe.

"We should be flying!" Bernie said. "We need to fly! We're going to fall any second now."

"I hear you," Trapper said. "And I'll hear you when you say it for the fifth time. But the power still isn't on. If you have a solution, I'm happy to hear it."

"Make it fly," Bernie said.

"All right then," Trapper said. "Suggestion noted. Maybe try and enjoy the ride? You don't see this every day."

No, you don't, Ilene thought. She was trying to watch Godzilla. Their rotation had become regular, so it wasn't that hard, she just had to keep turning her head and try not to throw up from the motion sickness.

It was hard to comprehend the sheer scale of what was happening. Godzilla was almost unthinkably huge for a living creature. Next to Shimo, he looked merely middle sized. Like a humpback whale next to a blue whale. They rammed one another; Shimo snapped at Godzilla's neck, but Godzilla reared back, rolled up, and kicked Shimo with both hind legs, knocking the two saurians in opposite directions. Godzilla recovered first, twisting and slapping a nearby ape with his tail, thrusting him back toward the World Ender. Shimo fetched against a boulder and clawed at it. Their trajectories were not quite lined up: Godzilla sailed past Shimo, who struck him solidly with her enormously thick tail, sending Godzilla once more plunging out of control.

Bernie yelped. Ilene tore her gaze from the Titans in time to see why—one of the Skar King's apes was heading straight toward them. Even if the H.E.A.V had been working, there wouldn't have been time do anything but brace for impact. Which wasn't going to help at all.

Blue radiance overwhelmed her vision and a high-pitched keening cut through the metal walls of the cockpit. For a split-second Ilene thought it was just her brain processing the shock of the fatal collision, but then she realized the ape hadn't hit them. Something had hit *it*. It flew off as if struck by a giant, invisible tennis racket. An instant later, Mothra shot by. Ilene had a brief glimpse of Jia on the Titan's back. Something spewed from Mothra, striking another of the apes and wrapping it up in what appeared to be silk. Then the huge insect and her daughter were again out of her field of vision.

Jia was back. She was okay. And she had just saved their lives. Of course, the H.E.A.V was still at the mercy of gravity, still very much out of control. She craned her neck, trying to relocate Mothra, and instead saw Shimo launching herself toward Godzilla. This time the World Ender didn't wait to close the distance. Instead, she unleashed the energy that had begun the last Ice Age directly at Godzilla, who was hurtling toward her, head-first. There were no floating boulders nearby, no way for him to change course. The icy beam struck him full in the snout. Ilene watched in horror as ice immediately began forming on him, crusting his face and neck. His fierce glow sputtered and subsided, overwhelmed by Shimo's power.

But then Mothra was there again, her wings beating into the freezing ray and into Shimo's face. The ice-Titan hesitated; the beam faltered. Godzilla's eyes glowed through the ice, an eerie red color. He flashed red-violet, and the ice shattered and sloughed away. He shrieked, and the two Titans hit with enough force that the shockwave knocked the H.E.A.V on a new trajectory.

You could never count Godzilla out. Just when you thought you understood him, he proved you wrong. Especially, it seemed, with Mothra by his side.

Suko hooted in delight when the rock he'd thrown hit One-Eye in the head. The older ape let go of Kong and went reeling through the air. Suko slung another of the smaller stones and was rewarded when it hit the howling One-Eye in the chest.

But One-Eye saw him now. He fetched against a boulder and steadied himself, killing in his eyes.

At least Suko had distracted One-Eye from Kong. But now One-Eye was coming for Suko. Fast.

Suko sprang in the other direction. He knew he couldn't beat One-Eye in a fight. But he could keep him from interfering with Kong. At least until One-Eye caught him and broke his neck.

The Skar King's whip uncoiled toward him, the sharp glowing tip seeking his heart, but Kong slapped at a nearby boulder, breaking his path to the left so that the bone weapon cut the air just over his head. He twisted and flipped inside the range of the deadly lash and swung his yellow arm at the Skar King. The other ape wrenched the axe up, deflecting the blow with the flat of its blade. With his other hand, Kong caught the arm holding the whip, stopping the Skar King from turning head over heels, and punched him again, this time in the jaw. Then he backhanded the axe.

The weapon flew from the Skar King's hand. The Skar King snarled and stretched for it, but Kong used his hold on his enemy's arm to pull himself ahead. His hand closed on the weapon's handle.

But before he could try and turn to use it, he was suddenly heavy again. And falling.

So was everything else.

Suko called a taunt back at One-Eye and was rewarded with a snarl of frustration. The other ape might be bigger and stronger, but he had a harder time changing direction than Suko did. Suko would wait for him to jump, and then dodge on the next rock. One-Eye was getting angrier and angrier, but it wasn't making him nimbler.

Suko glanced back, saw One-Eye gathering to push off a boulder. This would be easy. He could probably keep ahead of him forever like this. Suko began to think he might actually survive.

One-Eye jumped. Suko waited.

And then the rock he had been planning to push off from fell. So did he. He squeaked in terror.

One-Eye was also falling, but he had already jumped. Suko watched him come, helpless to get out of the way. Then One-Eye caught him around the throat with both hands. Suko tried to suck in a breath, but he couldn't. He flailed at One-Eye's arms, trying to pull the chokehold loose, but the half-blind ape was too strong. And by the look on his face, he didn't care that they were both falling to their deaths, just so long as Suko died first.

They hit the ground sooner than Suko thought they would, and somehow they weren't dead. One-Eye let go of his throat. As he gasped for air, Suko realized they were still falling. They had hit the top of one of huge light crystal formations. They bounced again, then both went tumbling down onto the lower slope of the translucent stone. Suko scrabbled for a handhold, but the crystal was slick, and there was nothing to grab. Still, he managed to slow down a little. One-Eye was ahead of him, going faster. The other ape's back legs went over the edge, and for one joyous moment Suko saw the bigger ape was going to fall off.

But then One-Eye swung his arm up and caught Suko by the leg. Suko clutched at the glassy rock, and for a moment, everything stopped; him at the edge, One-Eye dangling over the jungle far, far below, supported only by his hold on Suko.

Then Suko started slipping.

The H.E.A.V stopped tumbling and fell like a stone. Bernie started screaming. The Iwi queen looked concerned. Ilene stared out the window as her guts climbed up into her throat.

That was a *long* way down.

Then weight returned, so quickly she was slammed back in her seat. At first she thought they'd hit something, maybe one of the pyramids, but then she realized that something had wrapped around the cockpit, and they were again surrounded by a nimbus of soft blueish light.

Mothra was back, and she had caught the H.E.A.V in midair.

Ilene realized she had stopped breathing. Relief was a wave, washing head to foot. As the Titan settled the H.E.A.V on a flat rocky ledge, she started to laugh. Not because anything was funny, but because she needed to.

"Remind me to buy your daughter a birthday present this year," Bernie said. "No price limit."

Kong was still falling. So was the Skar King, although the Red Ape was far ahead of him. Between them were Godzilla and

279

Cold Breath. They had plunged across the middle sky and were now nosediving toward one of the blue holes. Maybe the one he'd come and gone though. Maybe a different one.

Either way, they were all going to the same place.

As he fell into the hole, Kong swung his axe, trying to slow his fall by digging into the wall. It bit into the stone surface as he intended and then stuck there, so that it was yanked out of his hand. He continued falling, vainly reaching for the weapon. His weapon. That he had just gotten back.

NINETEEN

The ancestors lived in a subterranean, dreadful realm
The ancestors left that underground, terrible realm
All came out.
On a path of beautiful water they departed the deep and
* horrible realm.*

—a legend of the Guayaki, indigenous
people of Paraguay and Brazil

In 1882 Telêmaco Borba collected the origin story of the
Kaingáng People of Southeast Brazil. Like many other
indigenous people of the region—and around the world—they
believed their people had emerged from below the surface of
the Earth. Twin brothers—Kamé and Kairu—then divided up
everything in the world between them; every plant, animal,
social division, and so forth were either Kamé or Kairu. The
sun, for instance, was Kamé, while the Moon was Kairu. Kamé
made jaguars and Kairu made snakes.

Lizards, it was said, were from Kamé. Monkeys from Kairu.

—from the notebook of Dr. Chen

Monarch Control
Barbados

Hampton drained the remaining coffee in her cup.

She wasn't fond of coffee. She'd started drinking it in grad school to stay awake, always with tons of cream and sugar, but she'd never actually developed a taste for it. She thought of it more like medicine than a beverage. But right now, it was medicine she needed. Even with four cups in her, she found herself nodding off as she scanned the monitors.

"How's the prep for Hollow Earth going?" she asked Laurier, more to stay awake than for the answer.

"The vortex keeps fluctuating," Laurier said. "It doesn't seem to be entirely stable."

"Do we know why?"

"Maybe because of the vortex opening in Egypt. The membrane is all of a piece. When mass passes through it, it affects the whole thing. We've never seen anything quite like this." She paused. "We're also getting some weird gravitometric data."

"Specifically?"

"Flux in the Earth's gravity."

"What? How big?"

"Not big at all, globally. Nothing anyone would notice without the right equipment. But it suggests some localized event which might be pretty intense. Like if you drop a rock in a pond. We're far from where the rock was dropped, so we see only the tiniest ripples. But at the source—"

"Yeah, I get it," Hampton said. "And that probably relates to what's going on with the vortices, too, right."

"Maybe," Laurier said, cautiously.

"No, absolutely," Hampton said. "Crank up the sensitivity of our sensors. If there's even a slight variation in the membrane anywhere on the planet, I want to know when and where immediately. And I want fast reaction forces prepped and manned. That means butts in jets, Ospreys, ships—not near them, *in* them. At all locales. Something comes through a vortex, I want us there before yesterday."

Hampton sighed and lay back, feeling the sun on her skin. It was such a relief to finally be able to get some sleep, to relax, have a drink.

She reached for her glass without opening her eyes, found the straw with her mouth and took a long sip.

It tasted horrible. Like coffee. Shit, it *was* coffee. And cold at that.

"Director?" someone said. "Director, something's happening."

"What?" Her eyes snapped open, not to tropical sunlight, but to screens and displays.

"Ah, dammit," she groaned. "What? How long was I…"

"Only a few minutes," Laurier said. "But the enhanced scan you asked for—it's turned up something."

"What? Where?"

"Brazil. Rio de Janeiro. Or more specifically, Guanabara Bay."

"Great," Hampton said. "Perfect. Do we have eyes there?"

"Yes, we do," Laurier said. "There's still a small team in the old Tingua Preserve containment area, where Behemoth was, back when. Observation capacity only, but they do have some drones. They're already in the air." She gestured as four screens came up, Rio and the bay beyond from several different directions.

"Is there anything there yet?" she asked.

"No. But it looks like a vortex is about to open."

For the moment, Hampton might have been looking at a travel advert for Rio, detailing the famous views. A long, beautiful beach filled with sunbathers and wave-frolickers, Sugarloaf Peak rising from the foot of the bay, the iconic Cristo Redentor, his upraised arms blessing the city from atop Mount Corcovado. The fourth view was above the bay, looking straight down from about six thousand feet. From that view, she could see a perfect circle out in the Bay that looked different from the surrounding water. Brighter. And very still. No waves or swells as in the surrounding sea. It was obviously a vortex, but… weird.

"What is that?" she asked.

"Ice," Laurier replied.

"Ice?"

"The ocean temperature right there is plunging."

"That's not normal, even for a vortex. Not that I've ever heard of."

"No," Laurier replied. "Me either."

The frozen spot flickered brighter, and then erupted in a spray of shattered ice, as a gigantic form—no, two forms—burst up through it. One was nearly the color of ice, thick in every dimension. The other was smaller, lankier, all arms and legs and a dull red color.

"Bioelectric signatures—" Laurier began.

"Let me guess. Off the charts."

"Way off."

The big one landed back in the bay, the red one crash-landed on the beach, plowing a Titan-sized rut through the sand. The thousands of beachgoers were already streaming away in every direction.

Poor Rio. It seemed like just yesterday when Behemoth had trashed half the city. They had only just finished rebuilding. Now they had two more Titans showing up out of nowhere.

"Two unknown Titans, to boot," she muttered aloud. "Anyone got a profile on either of these?"

"Not in our database," Laurier said. "Although that one sort of looks like Kong."

One of the drones was closer to him now. Laurier was right; it certainly was not Kong, but it was very Great-Ape looking. The red color was its fur. It had lifted itself to stand and was staring up curiously at the sky, blocking the sun with one long-fingered hand. Then its eyes fastened briefly on the drone, and she shivered at the awful glower in its pale blue eyes. Its mouth stretched in what might be glee, although she knew that with most Great Apes that expression was actually a threat.

If Red was roughly the size of Kong, the other thing was far, far bigger.

"The dragon-looking one? What the hell is that?"

"It's bigger than any Titan on record," Laurier said. "We've got nothing matching it in our database. But... uh... it's cold."

Hampton could see it better now, too. A sort of four-legged dragon turtle thing. Still in the water, ice was forming around it and spreading at an alarming rate, especially given how warm it was in Rio.

Red had some sort of whip wrapped around him. It looked to be made of the vertebrae of a very, very long snake. He unwrapped it from his torso by the small end, which terminated in what looked like a glowing, ice-blue crystal. He howled and pointed the crystal at turtle-dragon.

The bigger Titan responded immediately. It opened its beaked mouth, pointed it at the sky. A lance of white energy struck upward. The effect was nearly instantaneous; clouds began to condense around the beam, spreading to block the sun. Shadow fell across the bay.

"Did that ape—did he just tell the other thing to do that?" Laurier asked.

"Maybe?" Hampton said. But something had been creeping up in her from the back of her brain. "Oh, shit," she said. "I think I know what that is. That's the Hypothetical."

"What?" Laurier asked.

In response, Hampton entered a passcode and navigated through the menu on her computer. She found the file and clicked on it.

"Yeah," she said, reading through the entry. "This is sub-optimal."

Laurier peered over her shoulder. "Is that a cave painting?"

"Yeah, see? Godzilla and something else." She pointed at the new Titan on the monitors. "*That* something else."

"What is it?"

"We call it the Hypothetical," she said. "We've been piecing little bits and pieces together about this thing for years. We hoped she wasn't real, or that she died long ago. No such luck, I guess."

"She?"

"We call her she. A lot of the myths that might be based on her had her as a female. But who knows?"

"What do we know about her, then?"

"Put it this way," Hampton said. "You can stop worrying about global warming."

The sky continued to darken and the circle of ice on the bay expanded. Then the Hypothetical dropped her... *cold breath?* level to the ground and swept it across the city. In an instant, the nearest buildings were sheathed in ice.

"Yeah," Hampton said. "This is really worrying."

"Incoming," Laurier said. "Two more signatures."

"Of course," Hampton said, as another Titan splintered through the ice. "At least we know this one."

Kong.

The big ape didn't waste any time getting his bearings. He recovered from the gravity reversal and charged straight at Red, who never even saw him coming. As Kong swung a haymaker at Red, Hampton noticed that he was wearing something on his arm, like a brace—no, wait, she knew this. An augmentation. Project Powerhouse. Sure, why not?

She saw Senate hearings in her near future. Assuming any of them survived all of this.

"Strike force?" she asked Laurier.

"On the way. But the nearest is almost two hours out."

"Brazilian military?"

"They took a big hit from Behemoth a few years back. There's some chatter about scrambling fighters, but we don't have anything on radar yet."

The Hypothetical abruptly shot up out of the water as something violently shot up from beneath her. As the spray cleared, Hampton identified the familiar silhouette of Godzilla.

"Inform the local military of what they're up against," Hampton said. "Advise they wait for our assistance and focus their efforts on evacuating Rio. If they push back, put me on the line with them. Tell them Godzilla is here now. As the man once said: 'let them fight.' 'Cause we really don't have a choice."

No worries about that, though. They were certainly fighting. The question was, how much of a tussle could Rio stand?

Red staggered back from Kong's strike. He spit out a tooth, which bounced and smashed through a storefront.

Godzilla put his head down and hit Hypothetical like a bull, sending them both crashing through the buildings along the waterfront and in the city proper.

Meanwhile, it had begun to snow. In Rio.

Malenka
Hollow Earth

One-Eye yanked Suko's leg. Whether the larger ape was trying to use him to climb up or pull him to his death, Suko wasn't sure. And it didn't matter. It was going to end up the same. He turned and locked gazes with the bigger ape. One-Eye glared back, nothing but malice in his stare. Suko grinned back fiercely. *I'm not afraid of you.*

Suko cocked back his other leg and kicked One-Eye in the face as hard as he could.

And One-Eye fell. He fell a very long way.

Suko watched for a few heartbeats to make sure he was really gone, that the broken body far below did not rise again. Then he looked up, where Kong and the others had vanished into a blue hole. He started climbing.

Kong and Red had taken to the skyscrapers, using them to swing into and away from each other. It wasn't exactly elegant, but there was more finesse involved than the brawl going on between the two reptilian opponents.

Red swung around a building, lashing at Kong with the whip, but Kong evaded it, leaped feet first and kicked Red in the chest, knocking him supine. Kong jumped high, coming down on Red with a double-fisted blow, but before he could land it, Hypothetical's tail slapped him away.

There's got to be something better to call this thing, Hampton thought. "Hypothetical" was unwieldy.

As Kong struggled to stand, the Ice Dragon—no, strike that, Hampton didn't like that name either—charged straight at the Great Ape. But this time it was Godzilla who came to the rescue, tackling the four-legged monster before she could take a bite out of Kong.

"Well, I guess we see what the teams are," Hampton said.

Godzilla and Hypothetical rolled through the city, a pair of juggernauts flattening everything in their path.

But, maybe for the first time, Godzilla was a middleweight fighter in a heavyweight brawl. The larger Titan flung Godzilla halfway across Rio. When he crashed to a stop, he lay still.

Impossible, Hampton thought. Was Godzilla stunned? Injured? Either way, he was vulnerable, wasn't he? But the Ice Monster—nah, not that either—didn't stop to savage her fallen foe. Instead she went banging back toward Red and Kong.

Red used his bone lash like a bullwhip, wrapped it around a skyscraper, tearing a several-story chunk of it loose, hurling the wreckage at Kong with another deft turn of his arm. Kong punched through it using the augmented arm he *absolutely* was not supposed to have. Red stepped through the cloud of debris, flung out one of his unreasonably long legs, and kicked Kong in the chest. Kong backpedaled, trying to keep his balance, straight into Hypothetical, who promptly snapped her toothy beak at Kong. Kong managed to make the bite land on his enhancement, so the ice Titan didn't shear through his flesh and bone, but the World Ender had an unshakable grip. It reminded Hampton of an alligator snapping turtle. She'd once heard if one clamped on you it wouldn't let go until the next time lightning struck. Who had told her that?

It didn't matter. Monster H—yeah, that was better, not as cumbersome as "Hypothetical" and a nod to Monster Zero—scrubbed Kong across the pavement on his face, used him to shatter a few buildings, then began whirling him around in a circle before throwing him a few hundred yards to fetch up against more high-rises.

As he was getting up, Monster H opened her mouth, and the now-familiar white beam speared out.

"I think you're right, Director," Laurier said. "The red ape. He's controlling the big one somehow."

Hampton saw what she meant. Red was looking on. Almost like he was gloating. Or laughing. She saw the blue crystal on his whip again, and realized it looked a lot like the spines sticking out all over Monster H.

Kong pushed his augmented arm into the beam, using it as a shield. It seemed to work—he at least wasn't covered in ice yet.

Kong slowly began to press forward against Monster H's freezing breath.

"Get 'im," Hampton said. But if Monster H had bested Godzilla, what chance did Kong have?

"Wow," Laurier said. "Look at that."

"What?" Hampton asked. Then she saw Godzilla towering up from the wreckage. "Oh, yeah," she said. "He's up. Thank God for that."

"He's not just up," Laurier said. "Something is happening. His energy signature—all that radiation he's been storing up—nobody has ever seen readings like these." Hampton saw it now, even without instruments. Godzilla's new fuschia glow was building up from his tail, setting his entire body ablaze with barely contained energy. His eyes were twin stars, weeping glowing nebulae. All the hairs on Hampton's neck pricked up.

"Yeah," she said. "No one has ever seen this, period."

Godzilla reached his forelimbs wide, and for a moment Hampton feared an explosion, like the one the Titan had released in Boston.

Instead, radiation jetted from his open mouth, brighter, stronger than ever before, boring through the air in a corkscrew pattern, straight toward Red. At the last instant Red noticed and dove frantically away, tumbling through a few buildings before leaping back up and snapping his bone whip at Godzilla.

Godzilla, still visibly burning with power, didn't try to dodge. He didn't try to block the blow. He caught the lash between his powerful jaws, right near the end, where the blue crystal was. With a jerk of his head, he pulled Red off his feet and began to whirl him around. Red clung to the whip as if he couldn't let it go, despite the beating he was taking. But finally he could hold on no longer, and the centrifugal force sent him careening through downtown Rio.

Hampton winced again at the destruction, hoping most of the buildings were empty by now. At this rate she was going to develop a tic before the fight was over.

"Look!" Laurier said.

Red pulled himself from the rubble, turning his gaze frantically until it fell on the shard. He ran toward it.

"That *is* it," Hampton said. "He needs that to control Monster H."

Godzilla seemed to have figured that out as well, sending his blazing breath at the red ape—forcing him to dodge away from the shard, clamber over buildings, and leap from roof to roof to avoid Godzilla's attack. He tumbled across the broken city and came up next to the blue crystal, snatching it up and holding it up high, a triumphant sneer on his face.

Until Godzilla's atomic breath struck his hand and sent the shard flying once more.

With a roar, Red went after it.

Kong pushed his way toward Shimo; the cold was starting to seep through his yellow arm. But without it he knew from experience it would be much, much colder. He remembered the awful pain well, the surprise. But he also remembered that Shimo had been in pain. She was in agony now, he could tell. But he didn't know how to stop her pain, so he would have to stop her. If he didn't, she would kill him.

Godzilla had just knocked the blue crystal from the Skar King's hand. Kong remembered how the Skar King kept Shimo chained. Why did she do what the Skar King said? She hated him. And she was far more powerful than him.

Was the shard part of her? It looked like it. Is that how the Skar King caused her pain?

But right now, the Skar King didn't have the shard. He could not tell her what to do. But Shimo didn't know that.

If Shimo froze him, though, it wouldn't matter. He grunted and pushed forward, ignoring the cold, closer and closer to the other Titan, until they were nearly eye to eye. He was sure, then. She was trying to stop whatever was hurting her. She didn't care about Kong; he was just in her way.

He forced his yellow arm into her mouth, shivering as the cold finally began creeping up his arm. Then he boxed her with all the strength he could find in his other arm. Her head snapped back. The cold stopped.

Godzilla almost seemed to be grinning. As Shimo stumbled from Kong's punch, the Titan blew out his burning wind, striking her in the head. Then he rushed forward and slammed into Shimo. The two Titans rolled off though the city.

Kong looked back to where the Skar King had dropped the shard. Maybe if he had it, if he could show Shimo that the pain would end, she would stop fighting.

Behind him, he heard the thunder of titanic feet as the Skar King arrived. Kong glared at him and realized those blue eyes were staring past him, at the shard.

Kong leaped forward, toward the blue sliver. But the Skar King was fast, and caught his legs so he belly-flopped on the ground. Kong howled in rage and pulled himself forward, but the Skar King drew himself up Kong's back and wrapped one long arm around Kong's windpipe. Kong's breath rasped in his throat as he struggled forward. Godzilla and Shimo were still locked in battle, but Kong had a bad feeling about it. Godzilla was strong, the strongest thing that Kong had ever fought—until now. Shimo was stronger.

He dug his fingers into the earth, but he couldn't break the Skar King's grip. The edges of his vision were starting to fade.

He thought he heard a hoot-call, a familiar voice. He thought he heard Suko. But that was impossible. Suko was safe, hiding back in the Iwi territory. Wasn't he?

No. Suko was here, running toward them, carrying something —Kong's axe.

Kong tried to roar, but his breath was cut off. Suko cocked the axe back over his head—it was nearly as big as he was—and he chopped straight down into the ground.

No, not the ground. The blue crystal.

* * *

"Kong's figured it out," Hampton said. "He's going for the shard."

Godzilla and Monster H were still wrestling. In his supercharged state Godzilla was doing better, but it still seemed like a toss-up to Hampton. Before Kong could reach his destination, Red grabbed him from behind and got him in a sleeper hold.

"There's a fifth signature," Laurier announced. "It came through a few minutes ago. It's a smaller spike, so I didn't notice it at first."

"Another one," Hampton said. "This is turning into a real party." What would it be? A lobster Titan? A colossal crab, maybe? Apparently, everything eventually evolved into crabs.

But she didn't see anything on the screens.

"There," Laurier said.

"You're right," Hampton said. "That *is* little. Comparatively, I mean. Must be on our side. Magnify that."

The view zoomed in.

"Is that a mini-Kong?" she wondered. "Wait, is that Kong's *axe*?"

The words were hardly out her mouth when the small ape swung the axe. Right down onto the shard.

The detonation was a hemisphere of blue energy, quickly expanding with incredible force. It swept Red from his feet and sent Godzilla and Monster H hurtling in different directions. Kong, already on the ground, skidded back across the asphalt. The remains of nearby buildings flattened like sandcastles hit by an incoming wave.

And for just a second, everything was almost still.

TWENTY

When he got home, Nĭ'ltsi (the Wind) whispered to him:
"Hakáz Estsán (Cold Woman) still lives." Nayénĕzgani
(Monster Slayer) said to Estsánatleh (Changing Woman):
"Mother, grandmother, where does Cold Woman dwell?"
His mother would not answer him; but Nĭ'ltsi again
whispered, saying: "Cold Woman lives high on the
summits of Depĕ'ntsa, where the snow never melts."
Next day he went again to the north and climbed high
among the peaks of Depĕ'ntsa, where no trees grow and
where the snow lies white through all the summer. Here
he found a lean old woman, sitting on the bare snow,
without clothing, food, fire, or shelter. She shivered from
head to foot, her teeth chattered, and her eyes streamed
water. Among the drifting snows which whirled around
her, a multitude of snow-buntings were playing; these
were the couriers she sent out to announce the coming
of a storm. "Grandmother," he said, "a cruel man I shall
be. I am going to kill you, so that men may no more
suffer and die by your hand," and he raised his knife-

club to smite her. "You may kill me or let me live, as you will. I care not," she said to the hero; "but if you kill me it will always be hot, the land will dry up, the springs will cease to flow, the people will perish. You will do well to let me live. It will be better for your people." He paused and thought upon her words. He lowered the hand he had raised to strike her, saying: "You speak wisely, grandmother; I shall let you live." He turned around and went home.

—*A Navajo Legend*, collected and translated by Washington Matthews, 1897

Rio de Janeiro
Brazil

Kong blinked out the afterimage of the explosion and climbed to his feet, trying to figure out what had happened. Suko had been running toward him with the axe, he remembered.

And he'd hit the crystal. Now it was gone.

To his relief, he spotted Suko rising from the rubble behind him. But the Skar King was there too. The Red Ape jerked himself up, grabbed Suko by the throat and held him up in the air.

He was about to kill the little ape.

Kong jumped forward and punched the Skar King in the face. He followed the Red Ape to the ground, grabbed *him* by the throat and hurled him at Godzilla. The Titan swung his massive tail and knocked the Skar King back to Kong. Kong caught him and lifted him over his head.

Godzilla's roar shook the city. Shimo paused, glancing at Godzilla. Godzilla glowed brighter and roared back at the ice

Titan. Shimo paused—then turned her gaze on the Skar King, struggling in Kong's grip.

Her white beam leaped out toward Kong, but not *at* him. Instead it hit the Skar King as Kong lifted the Red Ape higher. Kong felt the Skar King struggle, stiffen, grow cold in his grip.

Very cold.

Kong stared into the Skar King's eyes. His body had become as hard and stiff as stone, but his eyes still stared out at him, still full of malice—but maybe also fear.

Kong roared, heaved the Skar King as high as he could with both arms, and then dashed him to the ground, where he shattered into more pieces that Kong could count on his hands and feet. Then he pounded the remains with his fists, until he was satisfied the Skar King would never move again. He roared in triumph.

Satisfied, he went to retrieve his axe.

"Wow," Hampton said.

"Yeah," Lautier replied. "But the weather pattern the... uh... dragon made..."

"Monster H."

"Right. Monster H's weather pattern. It's still gathering force."

"Maybe not for long," Hampton said as Godzilla turned his gaze up to the thick snow clouds. His jaws swung open, and his energy beam leaped toward space, cutting through the mist, burning it away. The sky churned, the storm broke, and the sun shone through. Monster H watched its handiwork vanish without objection. With the death of Red, the fighting seemed to be over.

"Godzilla protects the planet," Hampton said.

Malenka
Hollow Earth

Ilene climbed out of the H.E.A.V, followed closely by the Iwi queen and the others. They were resting on a shelf high above the Iwi village, an island of upland jungle.

Mothra settled not far away, shedding her soothing light over everything.

Jia dismounted from the Titan and ran toward them.

Ilene had never been so glad to see anyone in her whole life. Once more she had difficulty holding back tears. For a moment, Jia looked like a queen, holding herself in power and dignity. It was as if Ilene's eyes had somehow pierced the curtain of years and was seeing the girl not as she was, but as she would be.

Then Jia broke into a girlish grin and reached for an embrace. Ilene took her daughter in her arms, felt her fit there as she always had. Almost. But she knew it was different now. It had to be.

But for the moment she cherished the hug for what it was.

When they finally broke, Ilene tried to pull it together. Nearby, Mothra beat her wings and made her otherworldly *chukking* sound. She and Jia both looked at the Titan.

"Thank you," she told Mothra, signing it as well. She had no way of knowing for sure if the Titan understood her, but it *felt* like she did. Mothra stretched her wings fully and took to the air. Jia's gaze trailed after her. Bernie, standing next to Trapper, threw the flying Titan a salute.

Ilene turned her attention back to Jia.

I'm so proud of you, she said. Jia smiled and acknowledged that with a nod.

"Look, I..." she was signing with her spoken words, but Jia had turned away and couldn't see what she was saying. She walked over to the Iwi queen. The two met gazes, no doubt speaking in their silent language.

Yeah, Ilene thought. She stepped closer to them. She had to do this now, while she still could.

"Hey," Ilene said. "Can I just…"

The Iwi queen nodded at her. Jia turned around, a question in her gaze.

Ilene cleared her throat. She spoke aloud as she signed. Not for Jia, for herself. She had to hear the words.

"I know this place, you feel like is home. And I… I want you to know that whatever you decide… I'll support."

What are you talking about? Jia asked.

"What am I talking—I assumed you wanted to stay?"

Jia looked at Ilene as if she thought she'd lost her mind.

Wherever we go, whatever we do—we do it together, the girl replied.

This place could be your home. I…

You. Are. My. Home, Jia said.

"You—" Ilene's words failed her. She took Jia back in her arms, tears streaming down her face.

Just like a teenager, she thought. *Throwing my own words back at me.*

But if they were the *right* words, that was okay. More than okay.

She wasn't done crying when something came streaking out of one of the vortices. They followed the Iwi queen to the edge and watched the impacts.

There was Kong, and the little ape…

And Shimo.

"That can't be good," Bernie said. He looked at her. "That's not good, is it?" He searched the hollow skies. "Where'd Mothra go?"

Jia and the Iwi queen were both staring intently at the Titans. Jia shrugged and then turned back to Ilene.

I think it's okay, she said. *The queen says… she says Shimo is quiet, now. That she is no longer in pain.*

What does that mean? She joined her daughter and looked down.

The three Titans weren't fighting. The little ape seemed excited, jumping about, swinging from crag to crag. But Kong and Shimo stood facing each other. The World Ender dwarfed Kong. But he didn't seem threatened. As she watched, the Great Ape reached his hand out, slowly, tentatively, as he did when he reached for Jia. As if he were afraid of his strength, worried he might break something.

Shimo drew her head back, but only a little. Then slowly, very slowly, she stretched it back out, until Kong was touching her on the side of the head.

The two Titans stood like that for what seemed like a long time.

Across the valley, Mothra flew up to the veil the Skar King had torn and began to repair it with her webs.

Monarch Control
Barbados

"Director Hampton?"

Hampton's eyes snapped open. "I'm awake. Just resting my eyes. What is it?"

"The disruption in the membrane has subsided," Laurier said. "We've got a fix on the position of the H.E.A.V."

"And? Are Doctor Andrews and the others okay?"

"We're still waiting," she said. "The H.E.A.V systems are down—something to do with the gravity drive—but the techs think they can reboot it from here."

"And the second Hollow Earth Team?"

"Ready to go. On standby."

"Right," Hampton said. "How long until the reboot is done?"

"They think another fifteen minutes."

"We might as well wait, then," she said. "Whatever was going on down there seems to be over. Hopefully everyone is okay."

"I'll alert you when we have communications."

"Good." She turned wearily back to the report she had started drafting and the various streams of data informing it, reflecting on what the Senate Oversight Committee needed to know and what they maybe didn't. Of course, she didn't have all the facts yet, but it gave her something to do while she waited to find out the fate of the crew of the H.E.A.V.

As far as the Titans were concerned, things seemed to have returned to a state of... if not normalcy, at least guarded peace. Once Red was dead, they stopped fighting. Godzilla had waded into the ocean and was currently cruising through the Atlantic on a northeastern track. Kong, the littler ape, and Monster H had returned to the vortex. There was no sign any other vortex had opened, so they were presumably all back in Hollow Earth. What that meant, of course, she didn't know. All she knew was that the next days and weeks weren't going to be much fun. The Project Powerhouse issue would certainly be raised. But that might be nothing compared to the fallout from Monster H. What had happened in Rio, including the weather event, was impossible to hide. Even if she wanted to obfuscate and keep what Monarch now knew for certain about the last Ice Age, climate scientists outside of Monarch would work it out pretty quickly. If the politicians and pundits and bloviators thought Godzilla was a threat, what would they think about a *real* World Ender?

It could be all the special interests needed to call for a takeover of Hollow Earth.

"Director," Laurier said. "We've made contact with the H.E.A.V."

"Thank God. Put it on."

For a second, Hampton thought she was going to cry, she was so relieved. Instead, she just closed her eyes for a second.

"Well," she said. "Doctor Andrews. I'm happy to see you."

"That's mutual," Andrews said.

"I guess there's been something going on down there?"

"A little bit."

"So, up here Kong and Godzilla trashed Cairo, and then they brought a few friends along and sort of… laid waste to Rio de Janeiro. How are things where you are?"

"Oh," Andrews said. "I guess we have a few things to talk about."

"You reckon?" Hampton said. "You go first. Start with your status. Everyone okay?"

Andrew's face fell. "Not everyone," she said. "Mikael didn't make it. And the crew at the Kong Observation Post were all killed, too."

"Shit. That's awful." She was wide awake now. Her people. On her watch. They had all deserved better.

But she pushed that down too.

"Tell me," she said. "I'm listening."

And she did. In the end she had a lot of questions, but only one that she thought was worth pursuing at that moment.

"And Monster H?"

"Monster H?"

"Shimo, I guess. The one who started an Ice Age or two? What will she do?"

Andrews looked thoughtful for a moment. "You said after she killed the Skar King, she and Godzilla stopped fighting."

"Yes," Hampton replied. "Our working theory is that he had control over her with that crystal—maybe one of her own spines. She started freezing things after he pointed it at her. But after Mini-Kong destroyed it, she started playing nice."

"And she still is," Andrews said. "Her and Kong seem to have bonded. I think—we've been thinking the worst of her, right, because of what she did. Can do. But I don't think she's like Ghidorah. I don't think she had any interest in destroying the world. She didn't before. She may have created an Ice Age, but Earth has cycles like that. Our planet has been completely ice free at times, frozen from pole to pole at others. Life always persisted, even sometimes thrived in the Ice Ages. Life was pushed to adapt, evolve. Maybe Shimo is more like Godzilla. She's here to keep things in balance. Maybe she also protects the planet, or at least steps in when she needs to adjust it. There's so much about all of this we still don't know. What I do know is this. Right now she isn't on the rampage. We know where she is. We can keep an eye on her, study her. If you let them come down here and mess with her—that really could cause a world-ending event. We need to convince them to leave her alone. At least for now. Until we know more. A lot more."

"Yeah," Hampton said. "I agree. So when are you coming up to help me with that?"

"So," Andrews said. "About that."

* * *

Malenka
Hollow Earth

The Iwi on Skull Island—to the outsider, anyway—had been a pretty reserved people. Their relatives down here had proven similar, until now. The emergence of Mothra and the defeat of the Skar King seemed to have opened up something in them, and the next two days were filled with games, food, and abundant goodwill. As Trapper prepared the H.E.A.V to go, they ran up to him by the dozens, festooning his neck with colorful ribbon-scarves, some braided, some not, tokens of their thanks and affection. Trapper appeared almost overcome as he made his way toward the vehicle.

"Oh, wow! Is that for me? That's great! Thank you!" he said. "Just look at that. Aw, you guys are great. Look at that. Look at these."

He stopped talking when the Iwi queen herself appeared in his path and put another strand on him. She bowed her head slightly. So did he. Then he turned to Jia, who stood near the queen.

"Look at you," he said. "Little one." He held his hand up for a high five, but Jia stepped toward him and gave him a hug. He returned it, smiling. Then he went on the H.E.A.V.

Ilene followed him to the ramp, where he turned around and flashed her an uncertain-looking smile.

"Right," he said. "Well. I guess you're gonna stick around here for a bit."

"Yeah," she said. "For a while, anyway. I mean—there's a lot to learn. For both of us."

"Yeah," he said. "No. I mean, I'll probably pop down here, now and then. Just to check on Kong, mainly. Just the... tooth." He shrugged.

"Sure," she said. "Yeah."

"You think the, uh, Iwi would be cool with me crashing here?"

"Yeah," she said. "I'm sure that the... Iwi... would be happy to have you."

He nodded. "That is good to know," he said. "I'll see you around." He glanced over at Bernie, who was receiving his own neckful of ribbons and braids.

"All right, Bernie," he called. "Time to go."

"You know what, Trapper?" Bernie said. "Actually—actually, I think that I'm going to stay down here. Yeah."

"Really?"

"Really. Things got pretty messed up down here. It's only right that we make it right."

Ilene didn't miss the pride in Trapper's look as he patted Bernie affectionately on the head.

"I'm gonna miss you guys," Trapper said. "Come here. Bring it in."

He grabbed her and Bernie both. Tightly.

"I love you guys," he said. He went back to the ramp of the H.E.A.V and raised both arms. "See you, everyone!"

Then he went in. A few moments later, the engines lit up and the H.E.A.V soared away toward one of the vortices above.

The Living Caves
Hollow Earth

The Living Caves still smelled like burnt rock and too many apes.

Kong sat atop the ridge, watching them for a minute. They were still doing what they had been doing when he first saw them. Working in the dim heat. Moving rocks. As if the Skar King were still there, watching them. Coercing them with his whip and awful gaze.

When he had returned to the World Below from the fight on the surface, he'd found a few of the apes dead. One-Eye was among them. But he had followed the trail of the rest of them back here, to the place where they had been trapped for so long. He thought it strange that they would return here. But then he remembered that they did not know the Skar King was dead.

He nudged Shimo with his knees. She carried him further into the cavern.

Now some of them saw him. They began to call, and in moments they were all looking up at Kong, riding on the back of Shimo, with Suko perched on his shoulder.

Suko chattered, loudly.

Kong dismounted Shimo, stroked her head, and chucked her under the chin. She replied by nuzzling him as the assembled apes stared up at the head, up at them, and back. Kong waited for a few heartbeats, to make sure they all understood. Suko came and stood next to him. Kong took the smaller ape's arm and lifted it. In his other hand, he lifted the axe, and roared.

At first, the assembled apes didn't know how to respond. But then one ape raised his arms, and then another, and soon, all of them.

Looking at them, he knew they seemed uneasy. They did not know if he would be like the Skar King. Some of them were going to cause trouble, and he would have to settle it.

But he was ready. He hardly knew any of them, but he knew they had suffered. He knew they wanted something more than they had.

Like Jia, like Suko—these apes were his family. Family could be trouble. But it would be worth it.

Monarch Crew Residence
Barbados

At midnight, Hampton gave up trying to go back to sleep, dragged herself out of bed and made herself a cup of tea. She knew coffee would do the job of waking her up better, but she just couldn't deal with it.

The crisis was over. Why couldn't she get a decent night's sleep?

She stirred in some cream and went to place the spoon on the counter but dropped it instead. She sighed, too tired to curse, and bent to pick it up. As she put her fingers on it, a small motion caught her attention.

Something was looking at her, its pale lavender head cocked so that she could see both beady little eyes. Its body was a deep green, its ribs showing prominently beneath its finely scaled skin.

For a moment she froze, not sure what she was looking at. But then even her sleep-muddled brain recognized that it was just a little lizard: a Barbados anole.

"What are you doing, fella?" she whispered. "You don't look so great."

She knew for a fact that anoles didn't do well inside of houses. They got their water by lapping up dewdrops, and the ones that got accidentally trapped indoors had a tendency to dehydrate and turn into grotesque little mummies. She had found a couple since moving here. This one looked well on its way to that fate.

"Come here," she said.

Terrified, it tried to run, but it was too weak to escape her, and she caught it easily. Carrying it gently in her fingers, she took it out onto her balcony. The night air felt dense and wet. There should be plenty for him to drink.

She reached over her balcony railing and placed him on a leaf. For a moment he stayed still, just watching her, his gaze locked onto hers. In that small moment, she remembered a much bigger one. Godzilla looking down at her.

"Oh," she said. "Huh."

Then the anole slowly crawled into the cover of the vegetation.

Hampton didn't drink her tea. Instead she lay back down, and was asleep within minutes.

Hours later, Hampton woke from the best sleep she'd had in—she had no idea how long. She made another cup of tea and sat outside, watching birds flit about in the trees. Wondering where her little friend was and if he was okay. She had done what she could. The rest was up to him. That was how it was, wasn't it?

A few minutes later, she noticed a pair of male anoles. They both looked too healthy to be the one she had rescued. They were stalking one another. The bigger one was defending his territory. The smaller one was trying to horn in on it. They did push-ups on the branches, inching nearer to one another, inflating their throat sacks.

Territory. That was the name of the game for these lizards, and they were only a few inches long.

Godzilla's territory was the surface of the planet, and it was his again. He had crossed the Atlantic, returned to Rome, and was once again having a nap inside the Colosseum. No one knew why. She had seen pictures of his old haunt; the one Serizawa had nuked. The buildings there had some points of similarity with Roman architecture. Sure, the big fella was the guardian of the planet, but it seemed he had at least a little soft spot for people, too.

She put her cup down and sighed. Time for a shower, and then work.

But she never quite got up from her chair. It was a beautiful morning, and the birds had never sounded more lovely.

Hey, she was the boss, wasn't she? She could take a day off.

She went for another cup of tea.

Malenka
Hollow Earth

Bernie looked through his viewfinder as, a few feet away, Dr. Andrews peered through a pair of high-tech binoculars at her daughter across the small valley. There, Jia stood on a ledge that came up even with Suko's face.

Suko. Bernie still preferred Mini-Kong, but whatever. Apparently, the little guy—who was actually not very little at all, at a human scale—already had a name. Go figure.

He realized he was humming a tune under his breath, an old favorite of Sarah's.

Looking out from my lonely room, day after day...

It had just snuck up on him, and though it made him a little melancholy, he wasn't actually sad. In fact, he felt better than he had, well, since before she had died. He had believed that version of him was gone forever, and maybe it was. But this version, the guy he felt like today—he was doing okay. He was a pretty good guy. The last years of his life felt like a blur of hurt, need, pain, and obsession. He still had those things in him, but he also had light. Purpose focused by hope and even joy. And as weird as it might be, as little as he still understood the Iwi, for the first time in forever he felt like he really belonged somewhere.

Jia was trying to teach Suko to sign. The ape stared at her intently as she shaped motions with her hands, arms, and face.

"That means 'family', right?" Bernie asked Andrews.

"Very good," she said.

Suko hesitated. He raised his arms up near his face. Then he made circles with his thumb and index fingers and put them around his eyes like goggles.

Sort of, Jia signed. Then she turned in their direction and waved.

The earth shook as something heavy thudded to the ground. Bernie jumped and yelped from pure reflex, as did Andrews. What now?

But then he saw it was just Kong. Kong gestured at Suko. It wasn't ASL, but Bernie thought he understood it anyway.

Ready for another adventure, Mini-Kong—uh, Suko?

Suko nodded and gave an excited cry, and together the two apes set off for parts unknown.

ACKNOWLEDGEMENTS

Thanks to the team at Titan – Daquan Cadogan, the editor, Laura Price who commissioned the book, George Sandison, managing editor, and Kevin Eddy, copyeditor.

Thanks to Legendary Entertainment for such a great movie to adapt, directed by Adam Wingard, story by Adam Wingard, Terry Rossio & Simon Barrett, screenplay by Terry Rossio, Simon Barrett, and Jeremy Slater. Thanks to Robert Napton and Nikita Kannekanti of Legendary Comics for being my go-to people for most everything. Thanks also to Mary Parent, Alex Garcia, Zak Kline, Barnaby Legg, Nikita Kannekanti, Jay Ashenfelter, Brooke Hansohn, Abby Gutowski and Brian Hoffman.

ABOUT THE AUTHOR

Born in Meridian, Mississippi, Greg Keyes has published more than thirty books, including *The Basilisk Throne, The Wind that Sweeps the Stars*, The Age of Unreason series, and The Kingdoms of Thorn and Bone series, also writing books for *Babylon 5*, Star Wars, Planet of the Apes, The Avengers, and *Pacific Rim*, and novelizing *Interstellar* and *Godzilla: King of the Monsters*. He lives, writes, fences and cooks in Savannah, Georgia. He is found on Facebook at facebook.com/greg.keyes1 and on Instagram @gregkeyes1.

For more fantastic fiction, author events,
exclusive excerpts, competitions, limited editions and more

VISIT OUR WEBSITE
titanbooks.com

LIKE US ON FACEBOOK
facebook.com/titanbooks

FOLLOW US ON TWITTER AND INSTAGRAM
@TitanBooks

EMAIL US
readerfeedback@titanemail.com